MAVHAD

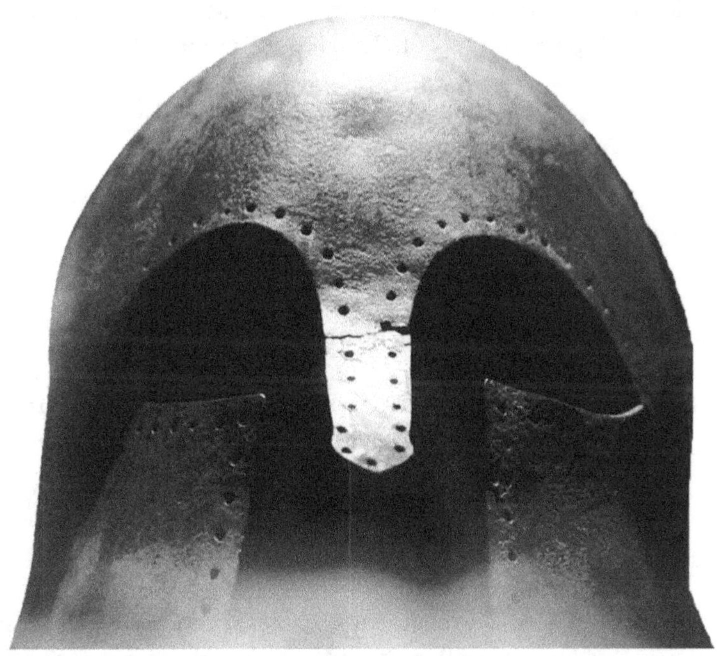

M. L. Hollinger

The Javik series Book One

TotalRecall Publications, Inc.
1103 Middlecreek
Friendswood, Texas 77546
281-992-3131   281-482-5390 Fax
www.totalrecallpress.com

ISBN: 978-1-59095-270-2
UPC: 6-43977-62707-0

Library of Congress Control Number: 2014955307

Printed in the United States of America with simultaneous printings in Australia, Canada, and United Kingdom.

FIRST EDITION
1   2   3   4   5   6   7   8   9   10

To all of my old Boy Scout troop pals.

Acknowledgement

I gratefully acknowledge the support of my wife and family in this project. They provided many helpful suggestions and a good deal of editing support.

Preface

I owe much of what I am today to two organizations; the Boy Scouts of America and Pi Kappa Alpha fraternity. The Boy Scouts transformed me from a shy, wimpy kid to a fit, capable, self-confident young man. The fraternity smoothed off the rough edges and matured a school boy into a man. Of the two, I feel I owe the most to the Boy Scouts. Scouting combined with my faith to provide the foundation for my life. I wrote this book to provide a role model for today's adolescent boys.

Javik, the hero of my story, faces all of the problems boys face today and overcomes them through hard work and a determination to succeed. He has some help along the way, but all boys need someone to show them the right path. For most of us it's our fathers, but when there is no father, someone else must step in to provide the guidance so desperately needed. When that guidance is absent, sinister forces take over. Gangs often provide a warped set of values that lead to either prison or death. I sincerely hope Javik will provide a role model for those boys lacking a man's beneficial influence.

I also hope that the men who aid Javik along the way will inspire modern men to work with boys who lack the firm hand of a mature male in their lives. There are many fine programs available for that purpose; Scouting and the Big Brother program are only two. If you want to change the world for the better, get involved in the process of guiding our youth toward the path of success in life.

To the young men who read this story I say, "Javik is not a superhero." Any boy can do what he does, but it takes education, hard work and someone to guide you along the way. The men in Javik's life give him good advice. If there's no man to do that for you, learn from Goldar, Tao Shan, Browdat and Javik.

Introduction

Javik lives in a country surrounded by mountains and covered in old growth forest. His ambition is to become a warrior like his father, Tolda, but he must pass Mauhad before he can realize that ambition. When his father is killed saving the others in his raiding party, Javik despairs of ever reaching that goal without his father's training. Goldar, who led the raid when Tolda was killed, convinces the King to allow Javik to train with Tao Shan, the finest mentor in the kingdom. Javik finds himself among the sons of the wealthy and must adjust to the situation quickly. While in training he encounters a girl in the forest. She is Allana an escaped slave, but Javik falls in love with her.

The time for Mauhad arrives. Javik must go off to war. Allana vows to wait for him, but when he returns she is gone.

A List of Characters

Javik:	A boy learning to be a warrior in a cruel, medieval world.
Tolda:	Javik's father and mentor who is killed in battle before he can complete Javik's training.
Dana:	Javik's mother.
Goldar:	A 'war leader' in Javik's village.
Browdat:	A wealthy 'war leader'. Javik and his mother are assigned to his house as wards of the king.
Grazhda:	An old witch who lives near Javik's village.
Grucheaux:	Allana's previous owner and the Sentii war leader who killed Javik's father.
Tao Shan:	The best mentor in the kingdom. Javik is assigned to him by the King as a reward for Tolda's sacrifice which saved many of his fellow warriors.
Sigurd:	One of Tao Shan's students. He is from a wealthy family and bullies Javik.
Noka:	Javik's room mate.
Allana:	An escaped slave girl Javik encounters in the forest and falls in love with.
Margan:	A wandering minstrel.
Zuban:	One of Browdat's sons.
Hella:	Browdat's neice.

Chapter 1

Javik admired the brooding mountains surrounding Berglaundia, his homeland. They stood like ranks of white-haired giants standing shoulder to shoulder to protect the woods and vales below. The green fir trees climbed their slopes in a vain attempt to overwhelm their masters, and the dark forbidding forests of oak, beech, maple and elm spread out over the land like a protective blanket. Farmland was scarce and purchased at the price of back-breaking labor to clear the forest away.

He was thankful he was not a farmer. The cool, misty glades of tall trees called to him like a siren. It was fall, and the forest had exploded into an array of color not even rivaled by the wool dyers in his village. The woods teemed with life, and he was a hunter—a hunter learning to be a warrior. He'd lived fifteen winters, and next year he would go on Mauhad, the manhood test of his people, but now he was concentrating on finding game.

He stopped short as he spotted a slight movement in the clearing ahead. He crouched low and approached silently. A quick test showed he was down-wind of whatever made the movement. He found cover just short of the spot and saw a doe standing in the clearing before him.

It stood deathly still while its long, broad ears scanned the dank brush for some sound of danger. Her wet, black nose twitched to extract any scent of trouble from the crisp fall air. Javik pulled the arrow slowly to full draw and raised the point to the spot where it would find his quarry's heart. He began to relax his fingers just as the fawn rose behind its mother. A smile spread across his face as he watched the deer's child search for a teat under the doe's belly, and that moment of hesitation was just enough to allow the clamber of the village alarm bell to send the pair bounding off into the brush.

"The men are back from the raid," he almost shouted as he un-noched the arrow and returned it to his quiver. The boy sped off toward his village, anticipating the celebration following a successful raid on the Sentii villages beyond the mountains.

As he entered the stockade gate, his elation quickly turned to foreboding. Everywhere he looked women wept on their mothers' shoulders, and the wails of mourning told him many houses would be without their men tonight. He made straight for the common house where the raiders would gather, but he was not prepared for the sight greeting him there.

Wounded men lay everywhere. Their women attended to them, unwinding bloody bandages and replacing them with new dressings. In the center near the hearth fire Goldar, the raid leader, sat in a chair with two healers hovering over him. He was bare from the waist up, and Javik could see the scars of many wounds suffered in previous raids marring his muscular torso. A fresh wound gaped on his left shoulder, and this was the subject of the healers' attentions.

"Ahhh! Confound it, man! Quit probing and put an iron to it!" the war leader shouted, sending the healers scurrying for the brazier of hot coals holding the cauterizing irons.

Javik looked around for his father but didn't see him. He was about to leave for his own hearth when Goldar called to him. "Javik, come here, lad."

Javik knelt before the war leader, showing him the respect due from a lad not yet mature. "Yes, sir."

"I've sad news for you." He paused trying to find some way to deliver his terrible story more gently. In the end, he could find no better words. "Your father's dead."

Javik looked up at the sad face of the great man and fought back his tears. A boy who aspires to warrior status must not break down and cry even at such horrible news.

"How did he die, sir?"

At that moment the healer applied the cauterizing iron. Goldar flinched but did not cry out. The smell of scorched flesh almost made Javik sick, but he fought the urge to vomit with what was left of his resolve. Goldar recovered quickly.

"He was leading the advance guard through the high pass when the Sentii ambushed us. They let his party through before they attacked, and Tolda could have saved himself, but he led his group back and cut an escape route through the Sentii lines for us. His action saved many lives but it cost his own. A Sentii arrow struck him down, and the last thing I saw was their war chief holding his severed head high for all to see. We had no hope of recovering his body. I'm sorry, Javik, but your father died as he would have wished to die."

The implications of Goldar's words began to dawn in Javik's mind. "What'll I do now, sir? My mother and I have no other family. We'll be assigned to some house as wards of the king, and I'll have no mentor. How will I be able to complete Mauhad?"

Goldar placed one hand on Javik's shoulder. "I'll speak to the king. I'm sure he'll recognize your father's bravery. I remember something about a blood price in our ancient laws, but it hasn't been invoked in many years. Don't worry. Everything will turn out well. Now, go to Dana. Your mother needs your strength."

Javik rose and bowed to the warrior his father respected above all other men and went directly to his mother's hearth. He found Dana staring into the embers with her hands folded in her lap. Swollen red eyes and the tracks of many tears clouded her beauty and she looked suddenly old.

"Mother," Javik sobbed, losing all control of his emotions. He fell into her arms and let the tears flow freely.

She looked at the boy, and her eyes brightened. "My son, my lovely son," she murmured as she embraced him. Her boy was almost a man, but he was still her baby. He'd seen fifteen winters, and his beard was showing a golden color a little darker than his hair. At 18 hands he was as tall as his father and every bit as muscular. With his deep green eyes and a chiseled face, every girl in the village wished he would woo her only, but he was too deep in training to notice them now. Next year he would go on Mauhad, the manhood test of his people, and join the warriors going off to raid as his father did before him. After that, he'd have time to notice their obvious signals.

"He's gone, Javik," she whispered. "We can't change that. He died the warrior's death he always hoped for, saving the lives of his comrades. Now's the time for mourning, but we must also prepare ourselves to face the future. Think of the great husband, father and warrior he was, but think also of what he'd want us to do. We have to go on with our lives in spite of our loss."

"I'll kill fifty Sentii swine to avenge his death," Javik boasted, breaking free of her embrace. In spite of his bravado, the tears ran down his face.

"I'm sure you'll kill many Sentii, my son, but you must grow much stronger before you can challenge such mighty warriors. Besides, you haven't yet completed Mauhad. Stay with me for a while. There's plenty of time left for killing."

"I know, but if we're assigned to another house as wards of the King, it may be a bleak future."

"I know, I only pray it will be someone who'll honor your father's memory."

Javik was well aware of the customs of his people. Widows and orphans must be cared for, and their own families usually took them in. If they had no family, like Javik and his mother, they were assigned to one by the King. No one wanted another mouth to feed, but if the sons were strong and the women healthy, they could carry their own weight well enough. The very young and very old fared the worst.

Sometimes the wards of the King were treated no better than slaves. Javik knew he would have no status in any family they were assigned to, and his mother would be given the hardest and dirtiest work. Their prospects were not bright.

"Why can't we just stay as we are, Mother?"

"You're not yet a man, Javik. You're strong and an excellent hunter, but you must complete Mauhad before our people recognize you as a man, and allow you your own hearth. With your father dead, you have no mentor. Who will train you?" Once more the tears welled in his mother's eyes.

"Tao Shan serves as mentor for many boys my age. I could join him."

His mother smiled, "We don't have the gold Tao Shan requires for his services. Only the most wealthy families can afford him."

"But, Father was a great warrior. He must have kept some gold from his raids, surely the game he brought to the longhouses was worth something?"

"What gold we have must last us the rest of our lives. We'll receive little enough from the family we are assigned to. I know what my lot will be, but I may be able to bribe the head of our new family into adopting you as a son. That's the only way to insure you'll be treated fairly."

"I'll speak with the King myself. He must allow us to stay together as a family. Many of the men know my skills; they'll vouch for me, and I can complete Mauhad without a mentor. Others have done it."

"Javik, why would the King speak with a boy not yet through Mauhad? Know your place, my son. We must accept the customs of our people."

"Father wouldn't want me to sit idly by while you're made little more than a slave."

"You're very brash, Javik. The ways of our people are wise, and we'll do whatever the King commands."

Chapter 2

Buran, the village law keeper, arrived at Javik's longhouse two days later to inform them the King's audience was set for of the next day. Javik questioned him about the blood price.

"Young Javik, the blood price is an old custom long abandoned by our kings. I'm not sure King Olgar is even aware of its existence. Don't pin your hopes on that piece of tradition."

Dana spoke. "Good Buran, we've no horses now that my husband's mounts are lost to the Sentii. Will you help us travel to the capital?"

"Oh yes, I have some errands there myself. I'll take a cart, and you're welcome to ride along, but I leave early."

"We'll be ready with the sun," Dana assured him.

The next day Dana woke Javik early. "Get up, son. It will be dawn soon, and we must be ready for Buran.

Javik pulled the furs over his head and moaned, "I need more sleep. I'll be ready when it's time to go. Leave me alone."

"Nonsense. Get up now and you can have some breakfast before we go. We may not get another meal until late today. Get up." She pulled the furs off her son and threw them aside.

Javik grudgingly rose to a sitting position on the edge of the sleeping platform and rubbed his eyes. Sleep would have been welcome, but the thought of a day without food was all the motivation he needed to rise and shine.

They were both ready and dressed in their finest clothes when Buran arrived.

"Good morning lady," he greeted her. "My aren't we lovely today."

"Thank you, Buran, but we need to make a good impression on the King," she said.

Buran smiled and held back his laughter. Even the finest clothes in their small village were rags in comparison to the finery of the court.

"I'm sure you'll do that," he said. "Climb aboard."

The journey to the King's castle was not long, and the fall scenery along the way was breathtaking. The trees and grass sparkled in the early dawn from the hard frost of the night before. Javik dressed in his best clothes, and he thought his mother never looked more beautiful.

When they reached the castle, Javik was awe-struck by its size. "Look, Mother! It's larger than our whole village, and there are more longhouses here than I ever dreamed existed."

"Your father should have taken you to our capital long before now, my son," she said. "It is really just a very big village."

Javik did not agree. People swarmed everywhere, and the marketplace boasted many amazing things. They passed a man eating fire and belching flames like a dragon. Another man juggled daggers. Four boys leaped about and tumbled through the air to land on the shoulders of huge men in crimson clothes. A minstrel sang and played his lute while the crowd threw copper coins in his hat. Several stalls featured freshly cooked food, and the aromas assaulted Javik's nose like a besieging army, reminding him there would be no meal until after the audience with the King.

The guards at the castle gate were bigger than his father or Goldar, they each leaned on swords nearly reaching to their chins. Their helmets shone brightly in the morning sun, and a fine, plate armor cuirass covered their chests. King Olgar was a mighty king, indeed.

Javik was even more impressed with the interior of the castle. Fireplaces ringed the great hall, and a fire burned in each one. Minute tiles arranged in intricate patterns covered the floor. Weapons captured from enemy warriors hung on the walls alongside the heads of fierce looking animals. Windows high in the walls admitted sunlight in golden shafts illuminating massive paintings of epic battles on the far wall. Torches blazed where the light from the windows or the fireplaces did not reach. Men and women dressed in clothes Javik never imagined could be so fine stood in groups around the King. The men were groomed to perfection, and the women were so beautiful Javik thought they must not be real. He looked down at his homespun attire and felt very poor.

The King sat on a gold, jewel-encrusted throne at the north end of the room. Four men stood around the throne, two on either side of the King; but the only one Javik recognized was Goldar. The first man on the King's left was an elderly fellow in a bright blue tunic and buff-colored pants. His boots were soft brown leather, and a large, gold medallion hung from a heavy chain around his neck. Next to him stood a fierce looking man in black garb embroidered with silver thread depicting the symbol of his family. Goldar was on the King's immediate right dressed in his battle clothes. The man next to Goldar was one of the priests of Zhou. Javik could tell this by his modest clothes and the wreath of holly on his head.

An older man, whom Buran identified as the Royal Seneschal, greeted Javik and his mother. He said they would be the first item the King would decide that day. They must be patient and only speak when spoken to. Javik thought King Olgar must be a very lazy man. By this time of day he'd finished all of his exercises, run his snare lines, cut several day's supply of wood and practiced archery and fencing with the other boys. The King had not yet decided one case.

The hall began to fill with people. Some wore fine clothes and some were dressed in rags. Some held animals or led them with ropes. The smells of perfume mixed with the aroma of animal dung teasing his nose then evoking revulsion. The room buzzed with conversation in spite of the warnings of the Royal Seneschal. Javik had never seen so many people in one spot before. The Royal Seneschal moved to the front of the room, pounded his staff on the floor to gain silence then spoke in a voice resembling summer thunder.

"Hear me! Hear me! Hear me! All who have business with the Royal Court are urged to draw near and present their petitions to our most gracious King."

He stepped back and the old man on the King's left stepped forward. The Royal Seneschal handed him a scroll.

"That's Nungore, the King's chief counselor," Buran whispered.

Nungore unrolled the scroll and called for Dana and Javik.

Javik felt his knees wobble as he walked to the throne. He was relieved when he knelt before the King.

"The Lady Dana and Javik, Son of Tolda, are here to accept your assignment, my lord," Nungore intoned.

"Rise Lady Dana and Son of Tolda," The King's voice was soft, and he took Javik's mother's hand to help her up. "No warrior in my kingdom could compare to Tolda. We all feel his loss."

The King moved to Javik and extended his hand palm down.

Javik did not know what to do, but an unfamiliar and heavily accented voice from somewhere behind him whispered, "Kiss his ring."

Javik took the King's hand and pressed his lips to the large stone. The King grasped his hands and pulled the lad to his feet.

"Goldar tells me you're worried about passing Mauhad."

"Yes, Sire. I fear we will be assigned to a family where I will have no status, and no one will mentor me or recommend me for the test."

The King studied the boy for a moment while the assembled crowd regained its composure after so brash an outburst by a mere boy. "Our law is clear in this matter. I have no choice."

"But, you do, Sire," Javik blurted out. The crowd gasped in astonishment. A boy not yet through Mauhad dared to remind the King of his duty. He could be whipped for such an insult. One of the King's guards moved toward Javik, but the King held up a hand to stop him.

"You have your father's audacity, young Javik. Your father often tried to remind me of my duty, but he was a valiant warrior and not a green lad. I will pardon your outburst for his sake, but I'll not warn you again to hold your tongue. I am aware I could invoke the Blood Price. Certainly, your father's bravery would warrant it; but that is an old custom last used by my grandfather. When the Kings were poor they needed the Blood Price to give rewards for bravery they could not give themselves. That is not so today."

The King continued, "No, Javik, I will assign you and your mother to Browdat's house. He is of your village and has asked that you be assigned to him. I believe he is sincere in wanting the best for both of you."

Javik's heart fell. Now they would be little more than slaves.

Browdat's son, Zuban, a young man recently through Mauhad, had a reputation for cruelty. He would have to live under Zuban's thumb until he could complete Mauhad and set up a hearth of his own. That could take years – years of suffering the abuse of a cowardly bully. He fought back tears as the King continued.

"As a reward for Tolda's service, I grant his lady twenty gold crowns."

The crowd gasped again. It was a very large sum even for one as brave as Tolda.

"To his son I give this sword and armor."

A servant appeared carrying a fine set of chain mail, a beautifully decorated helmet and a sword with a large purple stone in the pommel. All of this lay on a round, wooden shield.

"These were my brother's, Javik. He was also killed by the Sentii. Wear them with pride when you avenge him and your father."

Javik stared at the expensive tokens of the King's gratitude for a moment, then turned to the King. "May I speak now, Sire?"

"Yes, you may."

"I thank you, Sire; but I despair of ever completing Mauhad now. Your assignment has sealed my fate to be a servant the rest of my life."

The crowd drew in its breath at the reckless audacity of a green youth. The King only smiled as he raised his hand to silence the growing murmur.

"Nonsense, boy, I have never known one of Tao Shan's pupils to fail Mauhad."

Javik was struck dumb. He felt a hand on his shoulder and turned to see the old mentor standing behind him. It was he who told him to kiss the King's ring. He must have slipped in as they were walking up to the throne. Now he could not hold back his tears. He fell on his face in front of the King.

"My Lord, I will serve you ten times better than my father for your kindness today," Javik blurted between sobs.

"A rash promise, young Javik. I will hold you to it as a warning to weigh carefully what you promise in the future. Rise now, and go with my blessing."

Tao Shan helped Javik to his feet, and Dana swept her son into her arms.

"Oh, Javik, it's everything we could have wanted," she said.

As they walked back through the room to the applause of the court, Javik asked his mother, "What about you, Mother? I'll live with Tao Shan until I complete Mauhad, but you must live in Browdat's longhouse. Will you be all right?"

"It is for a short time, Javik. When you complete Mauhad, you may set up your own hearth. I can come live with you then if you wish. Until then, Browdat is a good man; and your father's memory is honored at his hearth. Not even Zuban would dare mistreat me. The King has judged well today."

As the happy pair left the audience room, the King turned to Goldar with a stern countenance. "Does that satisfy you, Goldar?"

"Your Majesty is more than generous," Goldar said as he dropped to one knee before his sovereign.

"Rise, Goldar," the King laughed merrily as he spoke. "It is small reward for the service of Tolda. The boy is just as rash as his father, but he has the makings of a fine warrior; don't you agree?"

"Yes, Lord. He is truly his father's son in many ways."

Chapter 3

Tao Shan's solitary longhouse sat deep in the forest over three kilometers from the village. The tall trees surrounded it like a hostile army of shadowy giants, and even at noon on the brightest day the pathway was dark. Javik passed it many times while hunting, but he avoided getting close to the foreboding structure. He never dreamed he would one day be living there. The large, wooden door looked capable of withstanding the stoutest battering ram, and there was no knocker or bell. Javik raised his fist to strike the formidable entry; but before he could bring it down, it opened, and a slightly built boy who looked to be a year or two younger than himself greeted him. He had short, curly, red hair, and his face was a mass of freckles.

"You must be Javik!" the lad's voice dripped with optimism. "The Master told us you were coming today. My name is Noka."

Noka wore the uniform identifying him as one of Tao Shan's students. The dark green tunic and pants were designed to blend in with the forest while heavy, black leather boots provided the protection needed for the rough mountain trails.

"I'm Javik, son of Tolda." Javik extended his arm to Noka palm up in the Berglauni formal greeting gesture. The boy responded by placing Javik's hand between his hands.

"Welcome, Javik. The name of Tolda is well known in every village. We were saddened to hear of his death."

"Thank you, Noka. He was a fine mentor, and I'm fortunate the King sent me to Tao Shan's house for training."

Noka looked around instinctively to see if anyone overheard the conversation, then whispered to Javik, "You must never use his name here, Javik. You must learn to refer to him as 'Master.' Calling him anything else will get you a caning."

"Thanks for the warning. I have much to learn about the house of Tao... I mean, the Master."

"He asked me to see that you're settled in. Come, I'll show you where to put your things."

Javik followed Noka to a row of small cells on each side of the longhouse's central aisle. The stark efficiency of the place jumped out at once. Spartan would have been a flattering description. There were eight cells on each side with two hearths to serve them. The floor was immaculate and the cells were neatly arranged, all in the same manner. Noka pointed to an open door on the left side of the aisle.

"This'll be your room, Javik. It was Barda's and mine until he went on Mauhad. You and I will share it now."

"I hope the Master will think I am ready for Mauhad next fall," Javik said. He'd felt confident about Mauhad until he entered this house. Here, he was a bit awed by the strict discipline seeming to exude from the very walls.

"How do you like being here, Noka?" While they talked, Javik stowed his meager possessions in accordance with Noka's directions. Each item had its unique place and must always be there when not in use.

"It was very hard, at first; but I got used to it. My backside was raw from caning for a month until I decided disobedience wasn't worth the cost in skin. Now I'm a model student." The boys laughed together at the thought of Noka's discomfort.

"Do you go on Mauhad next fall?" Javik asked.

"I hope to, but the Master won't select Mauhad candidates until a week before the actual trial date. He likes to keep us guessing."

"Where are you from?" Javik asked.

"My village is a full day's journey to the North. It's called Timann. You're lucky to live here in Holliga so close to the Master's house."

"What does your father do in Timann?" Javik asked.

Noka lowered his chin and spoke softly. "He is the Village master there." Even a man as important as his father could not compare to a warrior like Tolda.

"An important position. I'm sure he's respected by the people of your village." Javik tried to sound impressed hoping to bolster Noka's self esteem a bit.

Noka smiled in recognition of Javik's tone of respect, even if he did sense it was a bit forced. "He's a good father, but knows nothing of mentoring. Luckily, he could afford to send me to the Master's house."

"Where are the others?"

"They're on an endurance run, the Master's favorite torture for us. I was excused only to see that you get settled. He'll make me run twice as far next time."

"I don't want to make trouble for you, Noka."

Noka laughed. It was a knowing laugh that made Javik feel uncomfortable. "That's small trouble indeed around here, my friend. You'll see. Let me show you the rest of the house."

Noka led Javik into the central part of the huge building. It was an open, square area as long as the house was wide. The floor was firmly packed sand neatly raked into a swirling pattern, and Javik hesitated.

"It's okay, Javik. It only has to be this neat for final inspection at night. Each of us takes his turn at raking the floor.

This is where we hold our practice duels. We also train here on the days we can't go outside; but those are few and far between. The Master will only keep us in on the coldest days."

They walked across the sand floor to a wooden gate inscribed with symbols Javik had never seen before. Noka noticed him staring at the writing.

"That's the Master's native language. Isn't it strange?"

"What does it say?" Javik asked.

"I don't know. Only the boys going on Mauhad are told what it says, and they're sworn to secrecy. The Master says that it is the secret of life."

The gate opened into a small area filled with weapons of every description. Javik had never seen some of them before. He recognized bows and some of the spears and swords; but many of the clubs were strange to him. Tao Shan even had a hand cannon. These new weapons were rare and expensive. He stared at it in awe. He'd heard such weapons existed in a kingdom far to the East, but he'd never seen one.

"Go ahead, pick it up," Noka encouraged him.

Javik picked up the long, shining weapon. It was surprisingly heavy, but it balanced nicely just behind the metal casing holding the firing works.

"It would take a man to handle one of these," Javik commented.

"Wait 'til you fire it. It has the kick of a war-horse, but it is lethal beyond three arrow shots. The Master says someday we'll all have such weapons, but my father says he's crazy and they're only toys. Look at this, Javik."

Noka picked up a flat wooden stick as wide as Javik's wrist. It curved in the middle forming a "V" shape.

"The Master says fierce black-skinned men in a far-away land use these to hunt fantastic birds that run like horses. When you throw it correctly, it'll come back to you if you miss your target. It's my favorite. I'll show you how to use it when the time comes."

The far end of the longhouse was reserved for Tao Shan. The boys did not go there unless invited. If you wished to speak to the Master, you must make an appointment in advance. Noka told him of the exotic things inside Tao Shan's rooms and how he used some of them as object lessons for the boys. The wonder of the place made Javik's head swim, and he was cowed by his own ignorance of the world. He truly had much to learn.

The tour ended as Tao Shan returned with the other boys. The great door burst open and thirteen sweating, panting boys collapsed on the sand floor. There was no banter or joking only the sound of labored breathing as they tried to regain their wind. Right behind them came Tao Shan holding a hickory branch as thick as his thumb and as long as a man's leg.

"I suppose you all think that just because you've completed a long run no punishments will be given. Well, you're wrong, as usual. Up, and bare your backsides," he shouted.

At his command, all of the boys stood and dropped their pants, then bent over to expose their behinds. Tao Shan walked down the line of buttocks administering at least one blow to each student. Two boys were given much more attention.

"Harld, I saw you take a shortcut in the woods. You should know that even when I'm not in view I see all." He administered three blows with the branch.

"Verd, you drank from the stream in spite of my orders not to take any water." Two blows were the price of the stolen refreshment.

"Now, all of you, go clean up. Supper will be served in one hour."

The boys dispersed in silence. None of them even winced at Tao Shan's blows, and Javik was amazed since he flinched at the mere sight of the caning, and the swooshing sound of the wand as it descended sent chills up his spine.

Tao Shan turned to Javik and Noka. "Welcome to the house of Tao Shan, Javik."

Javik dropped to one knee out of respect for the teacher. "I am honored to be here, Master."

"I see Noka's taught you some of our rules already. Rise Javik and join the other boys. Your training begins at supper. See to him, Noka."

"Yes, Master," Noka bowed as the teacher turned and entered his own quarters leaving the boys alone.

"Come, Javik. You must meet the others."

They entered the living area where thirteen naked boys were scrambling to heat water for baths and washing out sweat soaked clothes. Their bodies were hard and lean with the hint of muscles developing into manhood. Javik was impressed by the results of Tao Shan's training program. He doubted he could best any of them in a wrestling match.

"Here's the fresh meat," one of them called as he spotted Javik and Noka.

"I'll bet he even has a clean butt," another chided.

Javik smiled and said, "I am honored to be among such fine men. I hope I prove worthy of the Master's training."

A chorus of laughter rang from the boys and drowned out Javik's enthusiasm.

A tall boy with hair the color of charcoal approached Javik and looked him over in detail.

"I don't know you, boy. What house are you from?"

"I am of no house," Javik replied. "I am the son of Tolda, the Hammer of Zhou."

"I thought I smelled the stink of the longhouse hearths on you," the boy sneered. "How is it you can afford to have our Master as your mentor?"

"The King granted it because of my father's bravery in battle." Javik was trying to be as humble as possible, but he felt his bile rising and a rush of adrenaline began to cloud his thinking.

"Hear me, boy. I'm Sigurd of the House of Odum. The Master won't let us use our titles and wealth in this place, but know that after we finish here the difference between us will be restored. Never forget that I'm as far above you as the sky above the Earth. Don't think me a friend, for I abhor the sight of you. Speak to me only when I have spoken to you, and never touch me. If I give you an order, I expect you to carry it out. Do you understand me, boy?"

Javik felt the blood boil in his neck, and the pressure on his brain was unbearable. His instinct told him to strike the arrogant snob, but he remembered his father's first lesson of combat; a cool head is as valuable as a sharp sword. He thought the throbbing in his temples must be almost visible. He chose his words carefully.

"When we leave this place, Sigurd of Odum, I will render you the respect due your rank among the warriors. While we are here I will obey the Master's rules. If he bids me follow your orders I will gladly do so."

Sigurd's face went red. He drew back a hand to strike Javik, but a large, redheaded boy grasped his arm before it could deliver the blow. "Enough, Sigurd, you know the punishment for striking another student without the Master's permission. Leave the boy alone."

Sigurd gave in to the redhead's logic, but sneered as he turned back to his bathing, "Remember, boy."

The redhead extended his hand, "I am Bogard called 'The Red.'"

"Thanks for your help," Javik took his hand.

"It was to save you both a caning," Bogard said. "Be warned, though. Sigurd means what he says. He can be a dangerous enemy. Watch your step around him. The other boys have equally impressive heritage, but only Sigurd seems to want to make something out of it. You'll find the rest of us good comrades in our mutual suffering. He picks on every new student, particularly those he feels superior to. Come now, wash and dress for dinner."

Javik met the other boys. He knew none of them as they were from a social strata far above the longhouses. They all smiled and welcomed him, however; and he felt much more at home. Several of them also warned him about Sigurd and told of receiving the same threats from the snobbish bully.

Dinner was served in a long room mostly filled by a large, wooden table. The chair at the head was slightly raised above the rest of the seats, and Javik guessed it was Tao Shan's. Noka briefed the newcomer on the proper ritual for meals, and Javik stood behind the last chair on the side of the table to Tao Shan's left, the proper place for the newest student.

The food on the table was beautiful, if one could describe food that way. There were some dishes he knew, but many he was not aware existed. The aromas floated up to his nose and made the saliva flow in his mouth. He swallowed hard and was embarrassed a bit, but no one seemed to have noticed. All of the boys were standing at stiff attention awaiting the arrival of Tao Shan through a large door behind his chair.

It seemed to Javik they stood there for hours before Tao Shan entered and took his seat. Three waiters came in behind him and took places along the wall away from Javik.

"Seats," Tao Shan commanded.

The boys slid their chairs out noiselessly and sat down, still at attention. Javik pulled out his chair without thinking about what he was doing, and it made a scraping noise as the wood rasped across the stone floor.

"Javik," Tao Shan shouted. "I do not like music with my dinner. Please put your chair back in place and pull it out silently."

Javik slid the chair back with another scruntching noise.

"No, Javik, I want no noise either coming or going. Try again. Pull it out and put it back without scraping," Tao Shan said.

Again, Javik pulled out the chair. This time he lifted it up so the legs would not touch the floor. The chair was very heavy, and it was all he could do to accomplish a noiseless movement. The problem came when he set the chair down with a soft clunk.

The boys snickered, but Tao Shan gave a stern glance to silence them.

"I desire neither woodwinds nor percussion, Javik. Try again."

Javik thought about the problem, but could see no way out. If he slid the chair it would scrape, and if he lifted it up it would clunk when he put it down.

"Master, you've given me an impossible task," Javik protested.

"Did the other boys make a noise when they sat down?" Tao Shan asked.

"No, Master, they did not," Javik admitted.

"Then they must know something you do not. In any case, the food is getting cold, and we cannot wait on you to master moving your chair. You will leave the table until you can move your chair without noise. Take your chair with you as you go. You may practice elsewhere."

Javik gazed longingly at the food. He hadn't eaten since early that morning, and his stomach writhed in anticipation of the meal laid out before him. It took all of his will power to pick up his chair and leave the dinning room as ordered.

Back in the sleeping quarters, he tried every trick he knew to move the chair without noise. He even tried setting it on his own toes to muffle the clunk, but he could only account for two of the four legs that way. He closed his eyes and re-created the scene at the table. The other boys clearly slid their chairs out and back because Javik was careful to imitate them. What was the difference?

"Of course," Javik shouted almost loud enough to be heard in the dining room. "What a fool I am. They've placed something at the end of the chair's legs that allows it to be slid without noise."

He turned the chair upside down and studied the large, square legs. He mused over different materials to use for padding. Leather might work, but it would have to be greased; and Tao Shan would not like the grease marks on the floor. Metal of any kind would be worse than the wood at making noise. Then it came to him.

He ran to the kitchen where the cooks were busy cleaning up and eating their own meals. A tall, thin wisp of a man accosted Javik.

"Here now, you're not allowed in here young man."

"Please sir," Javik turned on his most obsequious manner. "I would like to look in the garbage pit. Could you show me where it is?"

"I hope you're not that hungry, boy." He laughed, and the other cooks laughed with him. "I guess there's no harm in that," he shrugged. "Come along."

He took Javik through a heavy door and led him down a narrow, but well-traveled path to the garbage pit. As they approached, the wind shifted and Javik recoiled at the assault on his nose. He'd dumped his mother's garbage many times, but he could not remember it having such a foul odor. The skinny cook laughed at Javik's reaction.

"You boys are a stinking lot indeed. Good to see you get some of your own back."

Javik ignored the comment and held his nose while he stirred the debris with a fallen branch. What he wanted was not to be found.

"Where are the bones?" he asked.

"You'll find no bones here, lad. Bones is used in soup and boiled down for stock. When we gets finished with them there's not much left, even for the Master's dogs."

"I was hoping you'd have one for me to use on my chair legs to make them quiet," Javik said.

"Oh, you're the new lad, aren't you? I'll show you what you need, boy. Come over here."

He led Javik to a pile of antlers, which constituted all that remained of the dozen or so deer served in Tao Shan's house over the last winter.

"What you do, boy, is cut the ends off these antlers. Then you makes a hole in the end of the chair legs and stick in the antler so the pointed end sticks out a bit. Make sure you set the antler in the hole good and solid so as it don't vibrate. That'll make your chair quiet."

Javik took one of the antlers and thanked the cook for his help. It took him all evening to modify the chair legs, but when he finished, it slid across the floor without so much as a whisper of noise. He practiced until it was time for lights out.

At breakfast the next morning, the ritual repeated. Javik's chair was as quiet as the rest. Tao Shan spoke, "I see Javik has learned to seat himself at the table in the proper manner. Now we must see if he knows anything about eating."

Steam rose from the large bowls of food along the center of the long table. Most of the dishes were familiar to Javik; several were things he had heard of but never tasted. He watched carefully as the bowls were passed down the line of chairs. Each boy took a portion on his charger and passed the dish to his left. This was simple enough to emulate, and Javik took his serving from the first bowl to come to him just as the others had done.

"Stop!" Tao Shan shouted. "Javik, are you not the newest of the boys?"

"Yes, Master," Javik answered from his seat.

"Stand when you are addressed, boy," Tao Shan bellowed.

Javik jumped to his feet knocking over the heavy wooden chair in the process and eliciting a snicker from the others.

"Silence," Tao Shan ordered and the room grew quiet as a tomb. "Pick up your chair, Javik."

"Yes, Master," Javik replied from a face as red as Tao Shan's jacket.

"Now, Javik. You must know that as the newest boy you are not allowed to take from a bowl until all others at this table have had a chance. You will pass each bowl along without taking any from it until it reaches you a second time. Then, you may take all you want. Is that clear?"

"Yes, Master," Javik whispered.

"Did you say something?" Tao Shan asked.

Sweat poured from Javik's forehead, and he could feel his armpits growing damp. "I said, 'Yes Master.'"

"Did all of you hear Javik?" Tao Shan asked.

"No!!" the boys replied in chorus.

"I am a little hard of hearing, Javik. You must speak loudly and very clearly when you address me. Try again." Tao Shan commanded.

"Yes, Master," Javik shouted as the other boys cupped their hands over their ears in a mocking gesture.

A red fog of rage began to fill Javik's brain. Had he worked so hard to secure a place in Tao Shan's school only to be humiliated? His hand moved instinctively to his belt, but there was no dagger. Noka took his knife when he showed him how to arrange the items in his chest, assuring Javik a new one would be issued in due time. Javik scanned the table for a carving knife, but this was breakfast, and there were none. Tao Shan's voice cleared his mind a bit.

"I am not that deaf yet. Try it again a bit softer."

"Yes, Master," Javik moderated his voice a bit. The rage was gone now, and his good sense regained control.

"Very well, you may sit now," Tao Shan commanded.

Javik sat down and passed each bowl to the next boy on his left. The smell of the food nearly drove him mad with hunger. He had eaten nothing since leaving his mother's hearth the day before. His eyes followed the first bowl around the table until it reached him again. Only small traces of its contents remained. He scraped them on his plate and waited for the next one. It too, was nearly empty, as were all of the others except for the basket of bread, which held one small loaf. He used the bread to soak up the liquid on his plate and wolfed down the small portions from the other dishes. Each one was delicious, and he longed for the day when he could command an equal share.

After the meal, Tao Shan rose and addressed the group. "Today we are going to take a little walk. Get your gear together and assemble outside immediately. The last one on line will be caned three strokes."

Javik pushed back his chair and ran for his room, but a shout from Tao Shan stopped him dead in his tracks. "Javik, you have not been excused. Come back here instantly!"

It was only then Javik noticed the other boys standing at attention behind their chairs. He assumed the same posture.

"Dismissed!" Tao Shan bellowed. "Except for Javik," he added hastily.

The boys ran for the sleeping area while Javik stood almost shaking in fear of Tao Shan's wrath. The mentor walked slowly up behind him and spoke softly. "You have much to learn, young Javik. I trust you will make this learning process as painless as possible for yourself. Dismissed."

Javik ran to his room and changed into marching clothes. He shouldered his backpack and strapped on his sword and canteen. The other boys were gone, and he knew he would be the last in line and subject to a caning; but there was no helping it this time. He ran to the assembly point, a large, cleared area just outside the longhouse.

Tao Shan glared at him as he took his place at the end of the rank. "I see Javik will be providing the entertainment tonight. One of you advise him on the correct procedure since, it seems, he never cares to ask what might be proper in my house."

He pointed to two servants who were standing nearby. "Now draw your rations and load your packs. I will lead and you will follow at my pace. Anyone who does not keep up will join Javik at the caning ceremony tonight."

Tao Shan trotted off down the path with an ease belying his reputed age as the boys lined up in front of the servants. Javik observed the first one placing several rocks in each pack. He smiled in the knowledge he could easily carry such a load. When it was his turn the weight in his pack seemed hardly noticeable. It was the servant passing out rations that surprised him.

"Is this all we get?" Javik reacted to the small sack of grain handed to him.

"Quiet, Javik. You've got enough stripes coming as it is," Noka whispered.

"But, how can we run all day on no more than this?" he held up the bag for Noka to see.

"It's the Master's special blend of grains. Eat it only when he tells you and only with as much water as he allows. You'll be surprised how far it'll take you," Noka nudged Javik forward. "Hurry up. We're already far behind."

Javik trotted off with Noka close behind. He could not see the next boy ahead of him and wondered if he was on the right path. Noka spoke again, "Speed up, Javik. We don't want to lose them."

Javik quickened his pace and soon spotted the shape of one of the boys ahead of him. He fell in behind him, but Noka scolded again, "That's Mingor. He's always last. Pass him."

Javik passed as ordered and found no one ahead of Mingor. Once more he picked up his cadence until he managed to fall in behind Sigurd and his friends. So far, the course was relatively easy. He was beginning to breathe a bit faster, and he noticed the boys ahead of him were barely breaking a sweat. Javik felt he was in good shape; but these boys were, obviously, in better condition.

The run left the path and veered into the forest. Sigurd looked behind him and saw Javik. "I thought I smelled you, longhouse boy," he sneered. The others turned to smirk at Javik and went back to their running.

Javik felt relieved that Sigurd only cast insults until a large branch slapped him across the face sending him sprawling backwards into Noka. The chorus of laughter ahead told him who was responsible. A large, red welt began to grow where the branch met his face.

"Get up, Javik," Noka pushed Javik off his lap. "Watch for those kind of tricks in the future. Sigurd's a horse's ass, but he's a rich horse's ass. There's nothing you can do about it."

"I'll find some way to get even," Javik muttered as he regained his feet and sped up to overtake Sigurd and his group once again.

"Now your face will match your ass tonight," Sigurd smirked and was applauded with laughter from his cronies. "Not that it didn't already." More laughter in response to Sigurd's slur made the blood rush to Javik's temples. He put his hand on his sword, but Noka stopped him.

"Don't Javik. It will only get you more stripes, and you're no match for Sigurd. He's the finest swordsman among us," Noka whispered through gritted teeth.

There were no paths now. The only clue to the route was the trampled brush where the boys ahead broke trail. Tree roots made traps for the unwary foot, and low branches caused Javik to run half crouched most of the time. At times the trail dropped into a gully, and it was all Javik could do to stay on his feet during the steep descent; but instead of following the gully, the path always led directly up the other side in a gut-wrenching climb with unsure footing.

The smells of the forest, once perfume to his nose, were now stifling. The turpentine aroma of the pine trees seemed to saturate the air, robbing Javik of his breath. A skunk had sprayed the forest near one point making the passage almost unbearable. The tall trees filtered the sunlight into small shafts giving little light to the leaf-covered ground, but the chill of the autumn morning could not penetrate the barrage of heat radiating from the boy's body.

He thought Tao Shan must surely rest soon, but by the time the command to halt came, Javik was near collapse. In spite of the cold air, Javik had lost a lot of water to sweat. He fell against a large tree and reached for his canteen.

"Don't Javik!" Noka whispered. "We can't drink until the Master gives permission."

The Master walked down the line of panting, sweating boys clucking his disapproval. "If this were a forced retreat you would all be entertaining our enemies by exposing your guts. I suppose I must let you drink even though you haven't earned it. Water is authorized."

The boys gulped at their canteens as soon as the word was given, but Javik took only a swallow or two.

"Drink all you need, Javik," Noka advised him. "The Master says you must drink water freely while you have it to keep your body at its best performance as long as possible."

"I see you've never been thirsty," Javik responded. "My father said a warrior should never drink as much water as he wants so he will always have some in reserve."

"I'm sure your father was a wise man, but Tao Shan wouldn't approve of such advice. He can tell if you're rationing water, and he'll cane you for it," Noka said.

"I respect our Master in all things; but in this case, I think he's wrong," Javik insisted as he placed the cork back in the neck of his canteen.

"You children have rested long enough," Tao Shan bellowed. "Up and onward!"

The boys groaned as they regained their feet and fell in behind the old man who seemed to have more energy than any three of them put together. Javik decided his place near the middle of the chain of runners was the best choice since the ones ahead of him trampled the ground flat, making his going a bit easier.

It was a long time before the next stop, and Javik thought he was going to collapse before Tao Shan called another halt. Knowing the routine now, he waited for the Master to give the order to drink.

"Drink and food!" Tao Shan commanded.

Javik looked at the small sack of grain and wondered how he would manage to survive on such meager fare. He noticed the other boys were devouring their rations eagerly and followed suit.

The dry grain made him even thirstier than he already was, and he nearly drained his canteen washing it down. Strangely, he felt his hunger satisfied after only a handful of the stuff. His grain bag was still over half full, yet he wanted no more.

At the next stop, Javik's canteen was empty after only a few swallows. *My father would not be proud of me,* he thought. *I used too much water flushing down that grain; and now, I must go without. Surely, we must be near the end of the run.* His legs were beginning to feel rubbery, and a familiar pain in his sides signaled the need to stop. Tao Shan dashed his hopes.

"Get up you lazy slobs! We're only half way there, and we have to get back home before sunset. I don't intend to sleep in the woods tonight." He prodded the protesting forms from their resting places and, once more, led off down the path at a brisk pace.

It did not take long for Javik to feel the loss of water. His legs began to cramp a bit, and he remembered a trick his father taught him about the Spanga plant. He began to watch for its bright green leaves along the path as they ran.

A turn back into the woods brought Javik what he was seeking; a small stream to fill his canteen and a stand of Spanga.

He dropped out of the line and squatted to fill the canteen.

Noka stopped beside him. "Javik!" he shouted. "Come on! You must keep up."

"I will catch up to you in a moment," Javik protested. "My canteen's empty, and I need these Spanga leaves. I'm starting to cramp."

"Run it off, Javik," Noka insisted. "The Master'll be very angry if he knows you stopped."

"Go on, Noka," Javik waved him away. "I'll be back behind you in a moment."

Noka frowned but resumed his pace as the last of the stragglers passed.

Javik chewed on the Spanga leaves and waited as his canteen gurgled away under the surface of the stream. He savored the rest and quiet of the forest, while congratulating himself on making a sound decision. He never heard Tao Shan.

"You are a dead boy," Tao Shan whispered as Javik felt the edge of a knife burning against his throat. The voice was not like any Javik ever heard the man use before. It was almost as if he relished the idea of slitting Javik's throat.

Javik started to turn, but the knife bit ever so slightly into his skin stopping him cold. He did not think Tao Shan would actually injure him, but he was not going to take the risk. Javik was never so close to death before. He visualized an enemy holding the knife and knew he would be dead by now if that were the case. A cold hand grasped his heart. He knew real fear for the first time in his life. Tao Shan spoke again, this time in a more normal tone.

"This unauthorized stop will cost you even more stripes tonight. Now, get up and get going."

Javik grabbed a few more Spanga leaves and pulled his canteen from the water without corking it. He never looked behind him to see if Tao Shan was there. He ran with every ounce of his energy until he came upon the rest of the boys lying about in a clearing. Noka looked at him with a mixture of fear and sympathy.

"He found me, Noka," Javik sputtered as he fell next to the young boy, exhausted from the extra effort it had taken to catch up.

"He always does," Noka panted in response.

To Javik's amazement, Tao Shan entered the clearing from the other side as fresh as when they'd started that morning. "We have two lessons to learn today courtesy of young Javik, here," he prodded Javik with his stick. "Javik decided he needed more leisure time than I gave the rest of you; so, he stopped by himself. Tell us what happened to you, Javik."

Javik stood and lowered his head in shame. "I was captured by the enemy," he whispered.

"Did you hear him?" Tao Shan asked holding one hand to his ear.

"No!" the other boys responded loudly.

"I was captured by the enemy!" Javik shouted.

"That's better," Tao Shan smiled a diabolical smile. "Now, what happens to captives?" he asked.

"They're tortured!" the boys shouted gleefully.

"That's correct," Tao Shan congratulated them. "Now, Javik, you are in the enemy's camp, a captive. Do you know what awaits you?"

"No, Master!" Javik responded, truly unaware of what an enemy might do to him.

"First they have some fun with you," Tao Shan's smile was still devilish. "You, Sigurd; and you, Noka. Come here and bring your ropes."

The two boys responded as ordered.

"Sigurd, throw your rope over that tree limb there," Tao Shan pointed out the branch he wanted on a large tree at the edge of the clearing. Sigurd responded eagerly.

Tao Shan took Noka's rope and bound Javik's arms together behind his back so tightly the circulation was cut off. Then, he led him over to the tree where Sigurd's rope hung.

"Now observe this closely," Tao Shan commanded. "I think you will all agree Javik is a healthy boy and strong for his age. His father was a brave warrior for the Berglauni people and taught him well before he was killed." Tao Shan took one end of Sigurd's rope and tied it to the bindings on Javik's arms. "But, no man can withstand this."

Tao Shan hung on the other end of Sigurd's rope and lifted Javik off the ground so that only his toes touched. The grimace of pain on Javik's face gave evidence of the supreme effort he was making to avoid crying out.

"You see, at this point even a boy can hope to remain silent; but not here," Tao Shan lifted Javik a foot off the ground as a scream escaped the boy's lips. He released the rope and lowered Javik to a crumpled heap on the ground. "Untie him," he commanded Noka and Sigurd.

Echoes of the pain reverberated inside Javik's head, but the numbness in his hands began to fade as the boys loosed the ropes binding his arms. His shoulders felt as if horses had pulled his arms off. He decided to lie on the ground for a while to recover. He felt ashamed at having screamed, but the pain overcame even his most concerted efforts to hold it back.

"What you have seen here is merciful compared to what the enemy will do to you if you are captured," Tao Shan continued. "Javik hung but for a moment. They would leave you there for hours. Do not think Javik weak because he screamed. I have seen grown warriors with many kills do worse. Any of you who think you are better may take his place." He looked around for volunteers, but none came forward.

"Now for another lesson. You older boys know this from last year, and I hadn't planned to bring this up until later for you newer students; but Javik provided us with a good example in this case."

Javik sat up at the mention of his name, wary that he might soon be the point of another painful object lesson.

"Notice this plant," Tao Shan pulled a small Spanga bush twig from his pack. "It is a Spanga plant. Your mothers made tea for you from its roots when you were sick, but it has an even more important use for warriors." Tao Shan pulled several leaves from the branch and held them out for inspection. "When you start to cramp up from running, take a few of these leaves in your mouth and chew them slowly. Don't swallow them; just extract the juices and swallow that. It will do two things. It will ease the cramps, and it will give you a boost of energy. Each one of you take some leaves and pass the plant on to the next boy."

The boys did as they were commanded screwing up their faces at the bitter taste of the leaves. Tao Shan continued, "Javik, here, knew of this plant; probably from his father. He made an unauthorized stop to fill his canteen and to gather some leaves. Unfortunately for him, I also saw the plants and doubled back to pick some. Now you know how an old man like me can outrun young boys like you, but you would have learned this eventually anyway. The older students learned this last year, but they knew better than to stop without my permission. You may thank Javik for your early initiation into this knowledge." Tao Shan looked around him for a response and glowered when he received none.

"Ungrateful pups!" he snarled. "Javik has given you

wisdom before your time and paid the penalty for his lapse of discipline, and you will not cheer him?"

"Hurrah, Javik! Hurrah, Javik! Hurrah, Javik!" the chorus grew louder with each one.

Javik rose to his feet rubbing his arms to remove the welts from the ropes and bowed to his peers. Even if it was forced, he was pleased to be acknowledged in some way after all of the humiliation he'd suffered so far. His father's training paid off in at least one area.

"Now," Tao Shan barked. "We return home along the path we came unless someone knows a shorter way."

Their path had been very contorted since leaving Tao Shan's house. None of the boys had any idea where they were in this part of the forest; so, they lined up facing back along the way they came waiting for Tao Shan to lead them off. Only Javik held back.

In spite of the pains in his arms, he managed to pull himself up to the first branch of the large tree he'd hung from. Once there, he climbed easily up the trunk.

The others looked after Javik astonished, then to Tao Shan. The Master had not moved to lead them out but followed Javik's movements with a small grin on his face.

Javik reached the crown of the tree and searched around him for some sign of civilization. Wisps of smoke rising above the trees in the East told him the village must be in that direction. It was only a little over a kilometer away. They'd traveled in a huge circle since morning, and their home was only a few minutes away now if they went on, but a long run back if they retraced their steps.

"Master," he called. "I see the village."

"Which direction, Javik," Tao Shan questioned.

"To the East, Master. Less than a mile."

"Come down, Javik, and lead us there," Tao Shan called back.

Javik almost raced back to the ground remembering the direction they needed to go from the sun angle. He pushed off through the brush at a fast pace induced by the Spanga leaves and his need to rest.

Chapter 4

Javik collapsed in the common room of the student quarters along with the others. He slipped his pack off his shoulders and removed his sword and canteen after draining it into his parched mouth. The other boys recovered and began to wash up for dinner, but Sigurd swaggered over to Javik striking a defiant pose.

"So, you think you're some kind of hero, do you?" he taunted.

"Sigurd, I'm no hero. I just thought of climbing the tree before you did. You've been here much longer than I, and I'm sure you would have done the same thing." Javik tried to be diplomatic. He wanted no fight with Sigurd. The boy was much larger and more muscular than Javik, and Tao Shan's penalty for fighting was sure to be severe, adding more pain to the thrashing he would undoubtedly receive at Sigurd's hands.

"Don't mock me, swine," Sigurd shot back. "Just remember who is head of the boys in this school and wait for me to act the next time. This is my last warning. The next time you'll feel my wrath the first moment the Master isn't looking."

"I'm sorry, Sigurd. It won't happen again." The words nearly choked Javik, but he knew that they must be said.

As soon as the boys cleaned up, they assembled in the large central area of the longhouse to receive the daily punishment meted out by their mentor. Javik knew he would get the lion's share of Tao Shan's attention.

"Now it is time for you whelps to pay for your poor performance today," Tao Shan said in an even tone, belying the menace of the bamboo cane he held in his right hand and beat into the palm of his left. The smack of the rod brought involuntary jerks from the boys who knew their fate.

"First is Javik. He owes us penance for being the last on line this morning and for making an unauthorized stop. Come forward, Javik!" he commanded.

Javik received his strokes as did several other boys, but all were surprised when Tao Shan called for Sigurd.

"Sigurd, you failed to warn one of your fellows about a branch you released today. I believe the phrase you used was something like, 'Your face will match your ass tonight.' Come forward and feel my judgment for your actions."

Sigurd came forward with a perplexed look on his face. Tao Shan never caned anyone for such behavior before. Why should he start now? He was even more surprised when Tao Shan applied the rod to his face. He held back the scream of pain and fought back the tears. He would not allow the other boys to enjoy his reaction to the Master's unusual punishment.

"Now assume the usual position so that your ass will also match your face," Tao Shan commanded in a voice more bitter than Sigurd ever heard before.

With the daily punishment ritual completed, the boys were glad to sit down to dinner, even if it was somewhat gingerly for many of them. When the meal was finished, Tao Shan rose to speak. "You are probably wondering why I singled out Sigurd for some unusual punishment this evening. Let me tell you my reasons. It is time you all learned to use your brains as well as your brawn. You must think like a warrior as well as act like one. When we are on the march into battle we must look out for each other. A branch let free to hit the man behind you could be the cause of your own death. He might be the one set to protect your back when the fighting starts, but if he has an eye swollen shut, he may not be able to do so. Remember, the kindness you give comes back to you many times over. Never do to another what you would not want done to you. You are dismissed."

The boys went silently to their rooms and thought about Tao Shan's words. Noka was in bed quickly but turned on one elbow to speak with Javik. "Javik, you've made a powerful enemy in Sigurd. He'll never forget tonight."

"I know. He'll do everything in his power to destroy me if I can't find some way to turn him around."

"Just be careful. He'll kill you if he can find a safe way to do it."

"I will, Noka. Good night."

"Good night, Javik."

Javik did not go to sleep immediately, though he was bone tired. Twinges of pain from his caning were just enough to keep him from falling into slumber. Had it been a mistake to accept Tao Shan as his mentor? Since coming to the longhouse, he'd only managed to make a bitter enemy and be embarrassed by the one man he felt could help him pass Mauhad now that his father was dead. No, he had to admit he needed Tao Shan's help whatever the cost to his pride, and he thought he saw a slight gleam of admiration in the old man's eyes in spite of the caning and humiliation. He knew if it came down to life or death, Tao Shan would be at his side.

Sigurd was another matter. The boy was a snob, and his enmity was only to be expected. Javik even felt flattered that the bully would pick on him. He must feel the challenge to his leadership Javik presented, and knowing Sigurd felt challenged created a sense of pride.

As the pain in his backside eased, Javik slipped off to sleep confident in the knowledge he could endure any amount of humiliation Tao Shan could heap upon him, and he could hold his own against Sigurd if it came to a fight.

Chapter 5

The next morning, the boys awakened in the usual manner—a servant walking through the sleeping quarters pounding a gong. Sigurd was the first one out to check the morning weather.

"We've got over three inches of snow this morning, comrades. What torture do you think the Master has in store for us today?"

Tao Shan provided the answer. No one saw him enter or noticed he was bare-chested. "Today you will each get a chance to kill me," he announced.

The boys were struck dumb by that remark and turned their full attention on the rippling muscles and the yellowish skin bearing many battle scars.

"Assemble in the central arena dressed as I am. Immediately!" he shouted.

The boys wondered if breakfast would be served this day, but quickly obeyed. They found Tao Shan pacing the sand floor in front of an array of weapons. He was holding a small, wooden shield in his left hand.

"Today you will learn some of the finer points of hand-to-hand fighting. We will begin by giving each of you a choice of these weapons and one pass at me. You will do your best to kill me or you will be punished. Is that clear?"

"Yes, Master," the boys responded in chorus. Each one

wondered if their Master was mad. Surely, several of the larger boys could easily wound him with any of the weapons arrayed before them. There were pikes, halberds, glaives and throwing spears, all honed to razor sharpness and gleaming boldly in the flickering torchlight. They wanted to shout out their objections to such an unfair test, but all knew enough to keep silent.

"Good. Sigurd, you're first. Select your weapon."

Sigurd rose and strode to the rack of weapons where he picked out a straight pike. The boy outweighed his mentor by a good fifty pounds, and the pike was all of twelve feet long with a sharp, double-edged metal blade on its tip adding another foot. He hefted the pole to find the correct balance. Obviously, he had some training in its use. Javik saw no way Tao Shan could avoid being seriously injured in this confrontation.

"Good choice, considering your lack of experience," Tao Shan complimented as he assumed a semi-squatting position holding the small shield in front of him. "Now, Sigurd, try to kill me."

Sigurd's face betrayed his hesitancy. He could not kill his mentor; yet he was ordered to do just that. He knew if he attacked with anything but full force there would be hell to pay that evening at punishment time. Perhaps he could make it look good without actually threatening the Master's life? He charged toward the small man planning to deflect the point of the pike at the last minute.

Javik could see Sigurd's attack was half-hearted. Tao Shan deflected the point of the pike downward with his shield and grasped the wooden pole with his right hand. Using Sigurd's own momentum, he flung the lad sprawling on the sand floor while he wrenched the weapon from his grasp. An amazingly quick motion of Tao Shan's right hand brought the pike into fighting position with the point pressed against Sigurd's chest.

A collective gasp escaped the lips of the other boys. Javik was amazed at the old man's agility and impressed by his strength considering the Master's smaller stature.

"You see that a half-hearted attack is easily defended," Tao Shan lectured keeping the pike aimed at Sigurd's heart. "Sigurd has some experience with a pike, but he didn't use it well. He knew I would try to deflect the point with my shield yet he let me do it. I don't think he would have done that in an actual battle. If he did, he would now be feeling cold steel between his ribs. Get up, Sigurd, and try again."

Sigurd rose from the sand and Tao Shan threw the pike back to him. He assumed the fighting position once more and studied the eyes of his mentor. There was no hint of play now in the depths of the cold, black pupils, only the intense stare of one who's seen this situation many times before. This time Sigurd's charge was furious.

Once more Tao Shan moved the shield to intercept the point of the pike, but Sigurd dropped the tip at the last minute circling it upward and to his left around the wooden obstacle. Tao Shan smiled as he sidestepped the steel point and brought the shield crashing down on Sigurd's shoulder. With a scream of pain the boy dropped the pike and reached instinctively for the injured joint. Again, Tao Shan retrieved the pike and held the point against the boy's chest.

"Much better. That one saved you a caning, but you see there is still much to learn about the pike. Sit down," Tao Shan ordered.

Sigurd resumed his position but flexed his arm to help relieve the ache in his shoulder.

"Noka, you're next," the Master commanded.

Noka selected a broad sword and grasped the long handle with both hands as he assumed a fighting stance. Tao Shan nodded he was ready.

With the speed of a snake striking, Noka whirled the long blade in a wide arc at his mentor. Tao Shan ducked the blade and dove for the boy planting the edge of the shield firmly in his mid-section. A rush of breath flew from Noka's mouth as he collapsed backward in a heap leaving the sword to fall where it willed. Tao Shan soon had the blade pointed directly at Noka's throat.

"A good attack, but not the way to take on a single opponent," Tao Shan lectured the other boys. "The broad sword is an excellent weapon against groups of men or to stop horses. A good man with a broad sword can break a horse's legs with a single blow, but a nimble foe can easily duck under a high stroke. Remember to keep the swings low to avoid Noka's fate.

The other boys took their turns being embarrassed by their mentor. Finally, it was Javik's turn. He stood surveying the weapons before him. His best weapon was the bow, but none were present. Only the short sword was familiar to him, as his father was just getting around to instructions on pole weapons before his death. He pulled the blade from its scabbard and approached the formidable Tao Shan. He remembered the mentor's tactics with the other boys and played them back in his mind looking for a weakness somewhere. There was none. The mentor countered every trick with ease, but the attacks were all head on. Perhaps a trick his father taught him might work.

Javik circled his mentor and watched him move to keep his opponent directly in front of him. No matter which direction Javik moved, Tao Shan responded with equal alacrity, though he seemed to be a bit slower moving to his left. Javik lunged as his father coached him, and Tao Shan raised the shield to counter. Javik smiled at the startled look on his mentor's face as he deftly shifted the sword to his left hand and pivoted on his left foot bringing the edge of the blade to within a hair's breadth of Tao Shan's left ankle. It took a moment for the older man to regain his composure.

"Excellent! Who taught you that trick?" Tao Shan asked in a voice barely betraying his astonishment.

"My father, sir. He insisted I be equally good with both hands when using a short sword."

"Tolda taught you well. I was not expecting such an expert move from one so young, but it has earned you a stripe for not wounding me. Sit down."

Javik returned the sword to the weapons rack and sat down amazed that what he considered superior skill would be met with punishment. Sigurd bent close to him and whispered in his ear, "Never embarrass the Master. It's not worth it." He, obviously, spoke from experience.

There was no breakfast.

Training continued in the use of weapons until lunch. The famished boys eagerly wolfed down the venison anticipating another indoor session due to the snow. To their surprise, Tao Shan ordered everyone outside.

The snow was several inches deep by now, and drifts piled deeper against the side of the longhouse. The wind shook sharp crystals from the trees and drove them into the boy's faces. Javik was wearing every piece of warm clothing he had, but he still felt the white cold sucking precious heat from his body.

"Snow provides both a challenge and an aid for the warrior," Tao Shan shouted above the wind noise. "The challenge is to survive the cold and prevent your enemy from using your footprints to track you down. The aid is that you can easily track your enemy if he is not wise. Snow also provides a source of water when the streams are frozen over, but you must not put the snow in your mouth directly. You must melt it first. Snow can provide shelter from the storm, but it can also be your grave if you are not careful. During the heat of summer, perspiration is your friend. It cools you off; but in the winter, it is your worst enemy. You must stay as dry as possible or the water will sap precious heat from your body. Follow me, and I will show you some of snow's secrets."

Tao Shan led the boys down a forest path they'd traveled many times before, but the deep snow made it a new experience by covering up many familiar landmarks. The teacher stopped from time to time to point out the tracks of animals and places that would make good shelters from the storms. The silence was almost tomb-like. Only the sound of the wind in the treetops and the crunch of the boys' feet packing down the pathway told them the world had not died during the night.

The wind was not so strong among the trees, and the snow filtered down through the bare branches like a fine ash. Javik's feet were beginning to go numb, and he remembered his father's warning about such messages from his body. He must find heat soon, and it was a long way back to Tao Shan's house. As if he was reading Javik's mind, Tao Shan stopped the group in a small clearing with several large fallen trees.

"Each of you pick a partner and find a spot sheltered by one of these fallen trees. Clear the snow from the ground before you sit down. Do not sit in the snow unless there is no other choice. Once you have seated yourselves take turns warming your feet against the other person's stomach. Do not try to use your hands. All you will accomplish is making your hands cold. The blood in your stomach will soon replace the warmth the cold feet sap from you."

The boys busied themselves clearing resting places, and the air was soon full of the shrieks prompted by icy toes against warm flesh. Javik and Noka paired off, and Javik gave the other boy the first turn at warming his nearly frozen extremities. The shock of the frigid appendages was almost too much to bear, but he was surprised at how quickly both his stomach and Noka's feet returned to normal. He felt badly when it was his turn since his feet were much bigger than Noka's, but a few moments more and his feet would have been frozen.

Tao Shan walked among the boys checking for frostbite. Javik noted he was using no one's stomach and made it a point to study his boots. They were not the leather kind the boys wore but a soft, furry type with a lining of sheep's wool.

"Master, what kind of boots are those?" Javik asked pointing at the strange footwear.

"There are people who live in this kind of weather all their lives, Javik. These are the boots they fashion for themselves. One of my servants learned how to make them when he lived among those people many years ago."

"Will we learn to make them?" Noka asked.

"No, but if you can afford the price you may buy a pair from him. I'm afraid they are very expensive and they take a long time to make. The material is called felt, and he makes it from the hair of animals. Time to move on now." Tao Shan roused the boys and led them back to the longhouse and a larger-than-usual fire.

Chapter 6

As the winter days grew more bitter, Tao Shan's outside lessons became fewer. They spent more time studying the subjects Javik hated. Mathematics was his worst enemy, and he felt it was easier to master the long bow than find the answers to the intricate problems posed at each math lesson by Brindle, the strange looking servant with the humped back and high, creaking voice.

Tao Shan would tolerate no laughter over the man's appearance or voice. Any boy who mocked the funny looking foreigner did so at the expense of severe pain in his backside. The Master made sure each boy knew he would not be recommended for Mauhad without a thorough knowledge of Brindle's subject.

It seemed the entire winter would be devoted to the most boring subjects imaginable until one evening after supper when Tao Shan brought out a large mat featuring 64 black and white squares. He laid it on the sand floor of the common room and motioned for the boys to stand around its edges.

"This mat is a battlefield," he began as the servants brought out 16 wooden carvings in dark wood and another set just like them in light colored wood. "And these are the warriors," he pointed to the carvings.

Javik saw each piece was carved to resemble a different type of warrior. Each set contained eight pike men, two crossbowmen, two horsemen, two archers, one chieftain and one female figure. Tao Shan explained the way the pieces were positioned on the mat and how each piece was allowed to move.

"The pike men move forward two squares on the first move only; thereafter, only one square at a time. They kill by thrusting to either side. The crossbowmen may move any distance forward or backward or side-to-side as long as no other piece blocks their way. They kill the same way they move. The archers may move any distance along the diagonals where no other piece intervenes. They also kill the same way they move. The horsemen move in combinations of two squares and one square, and they are the only pieces that may jump over other pieces. They kill as they move. The chieftain is very limited in that he may only move one square in any direction. The object of the game is to capture your opponent's chieftain. Which piece do you suppose is the most powerful?" he asked the boys.

Sigurd broke the long silence. "The horseman, of course. He has the advantage of his horse's power to aid him."

"A logical answer, but incorrect," Tao Shan smiled. "This piece is the most powerful," he said as he picked up the female figure and held it high. "This is the chieftain's mate. She may move as far as she can in any direction and kills the same as she moves."

"Why should a mere woman be given such power in a battle?" Sigurd protested.

"You are all young and full of fire for battle, but you have not yet learned of the power women wield in the affairs of men. Who of you here would not die for your mother?"

A murmur of understanding ran through the students.

"None of you has known a woman intimately yet, but after Mauhad you will be free to couple with the young girls who make your pants uncomfortable."

This remark was met with nervous laughter.

"Once you taste that fruit you will understand why the female figure is the most powerful. Now, which of you is willing to try to beat me at this game?" he asked.

The boys held back knowing their Master was probably an expert and not wishing to be embarrassed. Noka finally stood up. "I think I understand the game, Master. I'll try."

"Good, Noka. Come here and take the light pieces. They get the first move."

The boys watched intently as Noka moved one of his pike men forward and Tao Shan responded in kind. Javik noticed one of the servants writing down each move and wondered why. After only a few turns Tao Shan moved his female next to Noka's chieftain and said, "Your chief is dead."

Noka was surprised. He hadn't noticed the female positioning herself for the move, and now there was no way to defend against her.

"You're right, Master. I have no way of killing her and there is no piece I can move to protect my chief."

"Your chief could run away if he had somewhere to run, Noka; but, as you see, he's hemmed in by his own men."

Noka marveled at the speed of his defeat. The mentor quickly moved to soothe his feelings. "You did well, Noka. This game requires much study and practice, and I've played it many years while you're just beginning." He turned to the students, "You, Javik; and you, Sigurd. You're next. Sigurd will take the light pieces."

The two boys moved to take up their positions as a servant placed the pieces in their original locations.

A confident smirk twisted Sigurd's face into a grotesque mask. "Are you ready for your beating?" he asked.

"Just do your best, Sigurd; and I'll try to give you a good fight," Javik answered.

Sigurd moved the pike man in front of his left-hand crossbowman out two spaces. This was going to be easy. He, Sigurd, had seen actual battles, and he doubted Javik had that experience. Besides, he felt Javik was not bold enough to win at games like this one.

Javik studied the board for a while and decided it would be best if he kept his pike men in a solid rank as far as possible. He remembered his father describing battles where a good line of pike men was essential to the safety of the forces behind them, but only his horsemen could move past the pike men. He would need to free the movement of his other pieces in order to attack. He quickly deduced the two center pike men would free both of his archers and his female leaving only the crossbowmen out of the action. Again, Javik remembered his father telling him crossbowmen were good for nothing but defense anyway. Their bolts, though powerful, were not accurate at long range. He moved one of the center pike men.

Sigurd smiled as he moved the next pike man in line two places. He had seen how the side that gained ground won the battle. He would keep advancing until Javik was hemmed in. Then, his horsemen would attack showing no mercy.

Javik moved one of his archers out to protect the central part of the board and free him for action.

Sigurd moved his next pike man up to challenge Javik's pike man, and that is when Javik saw the perfect move. Sigurd would not be able to resist the opportunity to kill one of Javik's men, and if Javik moved his woman to the right space he would be able to attack Sigurd's chieftain as soon as Sigurd killed his pike man. He made the move.

Tao Shan tried his best to hold a neutral expression, but

Noka thought he saw the Master's mouth melt into a slight smile at Javik's move. The old fox had set this match deliberately to create a lesson for both Sigurd and Javik.

"Javik you're a fool," Sigurd laughed. "You've failed to protect your pike man, and his life is mine." Sigurd chuckled with glee as he removed Javik's man from the mat and replaced it with his pike man.

"No, Sigurd, you're the fool," Javik smiled as he moved his woman to the space next to the chieftain.

"Javik, Javik. You will never learn," Sigurd taunted as he moved his chieftain to kill Javik's woman.

"No, Sigurd, you may not do that," Tao Shan reprimanded him.

"And why not? A woman is certainly no match for a chieftain," Sigurd protested.

"No, but the chieftain is no match for an archer," Tao Shan pointed out the fact that Javik's woman was covered by the archer he'd moved out earlier in the game.

"That's not fair," Sigurd pouted. "Javik failed to warn me of that archer."

"It is not his job to warn an opponent of his clever moves or to caution you about foolish ones," Tao Shan replied. "Javik is the winner."

Sigurd slammed his chieftain to the ground and strode back to his seat. Javik began to reset the pieces.

"The servant will do that, Javik. Go back to your seat," Tao Shan commanded.

As Javik resumed his seat Tao Shan asked, "Can anyone tell me what mistake Sigurd made?"

Noka raised his hand.

"Yes, Noka."

"He did not see the danger in Javik's archer?" Noka offered.

"Correct, but before that he moved his pike men too rashly. You should keep your pike men in line as long as possible only moving those that must be moved in order to free the other pieces for movement. This is only a game, but what you learn here may be valuable to you in a real battle."

"First, never underestimate an opponent. The mouse is small, but the cat is hard pressed to catch him. Second, think well ahead to see the consequences of your moves. You may be falling into a trap as Sigurd did here. Third, remember your objective. Sigurd concentrated on killing Javik's men instead of capturing his chieftain. Javik kept his eye on the goal. You will be given smaller versions of this game to use in your spare hours. Play it often among yourselves. You will learn much. Dismissed."

The boys moved back to their quarters chattering about the new game. Sigurd blocked Javik's path and shouted to Tao Shan.

"Javik embarrassed me in front of the entire school," Sigurd snarled. "I will have my satisfaction, sir."

"It was only a game, Sigurd. Javik defeated you fairly. All of you are new to the game. There is no embarrassment in losing a mere game, even less since you are both novices. Go to bed," Tao Shan scolded.

"Master, by your own rules you must grant my request for satisfaction," Sigurd reminded him.

"You are making something out of nothing, Sigurd. Do not press me on this," Tao Shan retorted.

"I demand my rights," Sigurd insisted.

Tao Shan turned to Javik. "Do you know what he asks of me?"

"No, Master," Javik replied.

"Sigurd demands that you face him in a personal fight. I do not feel his complaint is warranted, but the rules of my longhouse are clear in this matter. Any boy may demand satisfaction of any other at any time with the outcome to be settled by personal combat. In this case, no shame will fall on you if you refuse him. I do not judge his challenge to be a matter of honor."

Javik looked at Sigurd. The boy had a good ten kilos on him, but Javik doubted Sigurd was any stronger. Certainly, Javik was as skilled a wrestler as any boy in the school. If Sigurd wanted to fight perhaps it was time the matter was settled.

"I accept his challenge," Javik said with as calm a voice as he could muster, considering he was sure acceptance would be painful.

"Very well," Tao Shan turned to his servants. "Prepare the ring," he commanded.

The rest of the boys took up seats in one end of the central, sand floor area while the servants carefully marked out a large circle using a stake and a section of rope attached to a funnel shaped device. One servant drove the stake into the sand, then another servant stretched the rope taut and moved around the stake letting red dye escape from the funnel as he walked. The result was a red circle approximately three meters in diameter. Tao Shan stepped into the center of the circle and motioned for the two boys to join him.

"Remove your tunics and your boots," Tao Shan commanded. As the boys complied, he gave the instructions. "This fight is for honor only. There is to be no blood. If any is drawn, the one who draws it will lose and receive a caning on top of the loss. Do you both understand that?"

The boys nodded as they stood facing each other with Tao Shan between them.

"Good. The winner of this match will be the one who

manages to throw his opponent outside the circle. Any holds are allowed, and either of you may concede at any time. Is that clear?"

Again, both boys nodded. Tao Shan stepped from the circle as he shouted, "Begin!"

Javik lunged and was surprised by Sigurd's agility in moving away from the charge. He was barely able to stop short of the red line. He felt Sigurd's arms wrap around him pinning his own arms against his sides as the older boy lifted him up to throw him outside the circle.

Javik threw his legs upward and back taking advantage of Sigurd's momentum. Both boys toppled backwards onto the sand with Javik on top of Sigurd and still in his grasp.

The impact with the ground temporary relaxed Sigurd's grasp, and Javik slid down Sigurd's chest to free himself. Javik rolled to his left and lunged from his knees to pin Sigurd to the sand, but the boy was too quick and rolled out of the way while scrambling to his feet. Javik sprawled on the sand where his target should have been, but he had the sense to somersault back to his feet and turn to face Sigurd again.

The boys circled each other while Javik searched his memory for some part of his father's teaching that might help him. Sigurd was an experienced fighter – that was certain. He probably knew every trick Javik knew and a few more besides. Perhaps the best plan would be to wait for Sigurd to make his move and counter it.

"Take him, Sigurd," one of his cronies yelled.

"He's no match for you," another added.

Only Noka cheered for Javik. "Watch him closely, Javik. He's tricky."

The rest of the boy's shouts blended into a ragged chorus of noise. Only Tao Shan stood silent, studying the two boys' moves. The skill they both displayed made him proud.

Javik waited while Sigurd stared at him and circled to his left.

Sigurd is right handed, Javik thought. *If he's circling to his left it must mean he intends to feint with his left hand and attack with his right. I must be ready for that right hand.*

As he thought it, Sigurd did it. A quick left almost forced Javik to parry with his right hand, but he sidestepped the fist and used his left hand to block the uppercut aimed at his chin. Now Sigurd had to recover, but before he could regain his balance Javik sent his own right hand toward Sigurd's jaw.

In a move whose quickness surprised Javik, Sigurd's head bobbed down below the thrust. Javik was now over extended, and Sigurd took advantage of his unbalance. He grasped Javik's arm and, turning his back to Javik, used the momentum of the blow to throw him out of the red circle.

Javik landed flat on his back, and it took a brief moment for him to realize what happened. He looked back to find he was over a meter beyond the line. A smirking Sigurd stood in the middle of the ring, reveling in the cheers of his companions. Only Noka stood with his head down.

"I declare Sigurd the winner," Tao Shan shouted as Sigurd's friends lifted him to their shoulders and carried him off.

Javik sat for a moment, not believing he was beaten so quickly. He regained his feet to find Tao Shan smiling at him.

"You have had your first encounter with the fighting techniques of my people," he said. "Sigurd has been an excellent pupil, but you have not started your instruction yet. We will begin tomorrow." The old man turned and walked to his quarters. His back was to Javik, but Javik thought he could hear the Master softly whistling a merry tune.

The next day the boys were divided into two groups. Sigurd

and the older boys comprised one while all the younger boys made up the second. Javik expected Tao Shan would teach both groups, but he was surprised when one of the servants appeared and called his group to order.

"My name is Ling. Everywhere else in this house I am servant Ling, but here I will be addressed as Master Ling. I may be a slave to Tao Shan, but he has granted me the power to discipline any of you during training. Is that clear?"

The boys shouted in unison, "Yes, Master Ling."

"Good. This is your first lesson in the art of Fung Dai. Fung Dai is an ancient form of combat developed by my people many generations in the past. I will teach you to use your enemy's strength against him. I will teach you how to use common items as weapons, and I will teach you how to kill a man with your bare hands. But first, I will teach you how to control your emotions and make your body obey your mind. You must do exactly as I say, even if it makes no sense to your dense, Berglauni brains. Perhaps some of you witnessed Javik's defeat by Sigurd?" A murmur of acknowledgment rippled through the boys. "Sigurd was one of my star pupils last year. Learn well, young pups. What I show you here may save your life in battle one day."

For two weeks, Ling put them through exercises seeming to have no bearing on combat skills. Javik was beginning to think it was more of a dancing class than battle training, but he soon felt his body responding in a way he never experienced before. It seemed he could sense each individual muscle responding to his mental commands, sending back signals containing valuable information on his balance and movements. His father emphasized something like this in his training program, but not at the level he saw here with Master Ling.

Noka was not responding well to Ling's instructions. He

was mechanical and awkward in his moves. Javik could see Noka needed help, and thought it only fair to repay the kindness Noka had shown him since his arrival in Tao Shan's longhouse. One evening, Javik tried to help him.

"Listen to your body, Noka. Don't block out what it's trying to tell you."

"It's telling me it's tired of this dancing routine. When are we going to get into some real battle training?" Noka protested.

"Master Ling knows what he's doing. Don't fight him. Try this move with me." Javik performed one of the delicate movements Ling started them with. "Remember that one?"

"Yeah, yeah." Noka lashed out with one arm as he stomped a foot against the floor.

"Not like that. Feel it here," Javik pointed to his head. "Listen to what your arm is trying to tell you. Do it slowly so you can get the messages. Try it again along with me."

Javik slowed his movements and watched to see if Noka followed him.

"That's more like it. Did you notice any difference?"

"Yeah, it hurt more," Noka responded wearily.

"Noka, that wasn't pain. It was your body telling you what it's doing. Communicate with your arm muscles. Don't let them do things on their own. Give them orders and listen for their acknowledgment. Again!"

Once more Noka moved in unison with Javik.

"Hey, I felt that one," Noka smiled.

"Keep at it. Let's try this one." Javik worked with his friend until Tao Shan called for lights out.

As they pulled the fur covers up over their beds, Noka spoke, "Thanks, Javik. I think I know what Ling wants now."

"That's Master Ling," Javik corrected.

The next day, Noka suffered less of Master Ling's wrath; but he was still a good week behind the rest of the boys in his understanding of Fung Dai. It wasn't until Ling began training with the flails and scythes that the purpose of the initial training hit home.

"Many times you will find yourself without weapons," Ling began. "Armor, shields and swords are hard to come by and not always close at hand; but these things are available in every longhouse and hut." He held up a winnowing flail and a hand scythe. "If you know how to use them you can be a match for any man armed with sword or pike. We will begin with the flail. Come here, Javik."

Javik sprang to the front where Ling handed him a sword and shield. "Take these weapons and attack me," Ling commanded as he picked up a second flail in his free hand.

Javik smiled at the teacher's vulnerable position and lowered the sword point to the sand as he dropped his shield arm to his side. He was rewarded with a blow to his head that sent him sprawling.

"When I say 'attack' I mean attack," Ling barked. "Do it again."

Javik felt a welt rising where the flail crashed against his skull. If Ling wanted to hurt people, Javik was just the one who could make him pay for it. He rose to his feet on full guard and circled Master Ling; shield ready and sword poised to strike. He contemplated how large a wound he should inflict to make his point. After all, the student should not seriously injure his teacher. A small cut across the bare left arm of the Master should do the trick. This time he attacked as if Ling were an enemy.

The sword flew from Javik's hand as the flail came crashing down on his wrist. Only a rapid movement of the shield saved him another blow to the head. He staggered back in reaction to the force of the impact and turned his head to locate his weapon. It was too late. The flail knocked his foot from under him, and Ling was upon him in an instant holding one of the wooden implements across his throat.

"Not bad, Javik. In another month I would not try this with you." Ling whispered as he helped Javik to his feet. "You see how easily I defeated him. Now, humble yourselves and learn to use what is at hand for a weapon."

Over the next week, Ling showed them how to defend themselves with things they could easily find in any village. Javik learned how to reinforce the power in his blows by using the force of his mind as well as his body.

At first, it did not seem logical that thinking about a blow could add force, but as the training progressed, Javik realized combat was as much concentration as it was quickness and muscle. Ling broke stones with his bare hand – stones Javik would have needed a steel hammer to break. Javik's initial attempts only produced a sore hand, but by the end of that phase of the training he could break a piece of limestone easily, providing he set his mind to it.

Before they could start the final phase of Fung Dai, the Spring Festival was upon them. Each year with the first signs of green growth, the Berglauni people celebrated the end of winter by holding sacred rituals in the holy groves. All was not serious worship of the Earth Goddess, however. It was also an occasion for much eating and drinking and courting between boys and girls.

Tao Shan called all of the boys together one morning to announce they would be allowed to visit their families for an entire week to celebrate the holiday. Everyone but Javik greeted the news with cheers.

"Why so glum, Javik?" Noka asked.

"My mother lives in the house of Browdat where Zuban, Browdat's son, is my enemy. I'm sure she is little more than a slave, and Zuban will do everything he can to make my life miserable while I am there. I don't see any reason for going into that longhouse for a week of misery."

"Don't you want to see your mother?"

"More than anything, but I was hoping it'd be after I completed Mauhad. Then, I could take her to our own hearth and free her from bondage."

"I don't think Tao Shan will let either of us go on Mauhad this fall," Noka sighed. "You'd best take advantage of any opportunity you have to see your mother until then."

"I suppose you're right," Javik agreed, "but it'll be a hard week."

"You should be thankful you're so close to home, Javik. It's nearly a day's ride to my home. I will only have five days there while you will have most of the whole week."

"You're right, Noka. Even putting up with Zuban is a small thing next to seeing my mother."

Chapter 7

The next morning Javik packed his few belongings and began the lonely walk to Browdat's longhouse. The green buds of spring were just beginning to show on the trees, and the forest flowers pushed small spear points of green from the earth, testing the air to see if it was safe to emerge. The path was wet but not muddy, and Javik made good time. It was well before noon when he arrived at the village stockade.

As he approached the gates, he saw his mother carrying a load of firewood back from the forest. The wood was in a large skin with long straps tied together to make a kind of harness she wore across her forehead. She was bent low at the waist to carry most of the wood's weight on her lower back using her head only for balance. Javik had seen her do this many times. Carrying wood was a woman's job, but it seemed to him her step was not as lively as he remembered.

"Mother, Mother," he called.

Dana turned at the sound of the voice she had not heard in months, and a smile brightened her face. Javik thought he saw her straighten noticeably under her load. She shifted the wood to the ground and held out her arms to welcome her son. "Javik, how good to see you, Son!"

Javik fell into his mother's arms and almost wept for joy. It was hard for him to hold back the tears, but he felt he must be strong for his mother's sake. "Mother, it's good to see you too."

She pushed him away and surveyed him carefully. "You've put on some muscle under Tao Shan, and it looks like your stomach has suffered for it." She poked his flat stomach.

"We're fed well, but not as well as if you were the cook. I'm afraid Tao Shan runs off most of what we eat as soon as we eat it." Javik used the opening remarks to study his mother. Her face was a bit on the gaunt side, but she'd lost no weight. Her eyes bothered him more than anything else. They were dull, and lacked the dancing light he remembered. She was not completely happy in Browdat's household—that was obvious.

"I do most of the cooking for Browdat. I'll fatten you up a bit before you go back to Tao Shan. How long will you be home?"

"I have the whole week, Mother, and I've been looking forward to some of your cooking." Javik lied, but he felt it was the thing he should say. In truth, he was dreading a week in that house as the poor son of a King's ward.

Another factor making the week even more unpleasant would be the presence of Zuban, Browdat's son. He was only three years older than Javik, but he'd completed Mauhad and was considered a warrior. He would surely do everything he could to make Javik's stay miserable.

Dana stooped to pick up her load again, but Javik stopped her. "Let me carry this for you, Mother."

"Javik! You are almost a man now, and men don't carry wood," she admonished him harshly in spite of her joy at seeing him again. She repositioned the load and stepped off with a new spring in her stride.

"Tell me of your life in Browdat's house," Javik asked.

"I am treated well. I have a good bed, and I get my share of the food. I work hard, but hard work is good for me."

"What of Zuban?" Javik asked.

"Zuban is a boy, though they say he is a man now, and I must treat him as such. Browdat corrects him all the time, but I don't think he pays any attention to his father any more. Fortunately, he's out of the house most of the time on raiding parties. At least, that's what he says he's doing."

"Has he mistreated you in any way?" Javik's voice was stern in a way reminding her of her husband's sober tones.

"He's really only a boy, Javik. I don't take him seriously." Dana did her best to minimize Javik's concern over Zuban. She was genuinely afraid of the wrath boiling up inside the hard, lithe boy beside her who now spoke with the awful threat of a warrior in his voice.

"He'd best watch himself while I'm here," was all Javik said, but his eyes conveyed the rest of the message.

"He's planning to take a wife in the fall," Dana added to defuse the situation.

"Then he'll move from his father's hearth by winter." Javik smiled for the first time since the subject of Zuban came up.

"Yes, he plans to set up his hearth in a new longhouse he and his toadies will build this summer. The other men are also planning on taking wives, and they'll all move in together when it's finished."

"I wish I could help him build it so he could be out all the sooner." He did not like the idea of his mother living under the same roof as Zuban.

They entered the big door of Browdat's longhouse, and Dana dropped her load in the wood bin. "Frieda, Hella, come see who's here," she called.

The familiar face of Frieda, Browdat's wife appeared around the partition. "Javik, Dana said you might be coming home for the festival. Welcome to our house." She embraced the boy, smothering Javik with her ample bosoms. "Hella, come meet

Javik," she called over her shoulder.

A girl two or three years younger than Javik appeared in the doorway. Her long, blonde hair hung in braids on either side of her head. Her dress was the ankle length, loose fitting sheath customary for young girls not yet ready for marriage. She blushed bright red at the sight of the older boy.

"I'm pleased to meet you, Javik," she almost whispered as she looked at the ground and dropped to one knee out of respect for one she perceived to be a man. Javik pulled her to her feet.

"I am pleased to meet you too, Hella, but I am not yet a man to be kneeled to." Javik said as he felt an unfamiliar twinge deep inside his body.

"Hella is Browdat's niece," Dana explained. "Like us, she has no hearth of her own. Her parents were killed by a bear that entered their longhouse this past winter. She only escaped by pretending to be dead. The poor girl had no place to go, and Browdat took her in." Dana moved to embrace Hella as tears welled up in the girl's eyes.

"She is certainly welcome here, as are you, Javik," Frieda smiled. "Come now, you must be hungry after that walk from Tao Shan's house. Your mother has some venison stew on the fire, and I baked fresh bread this morning. Come eat."

The four of them moved into the central part of the longhouse which served as a combination kitchen, dining room and living room. Browdat was rich enough to have a longhouse all to himself. Most longhouses were shared, with four to six families to a building. Javik dove into the savory stew with gusto. He hadn't tasted anything this good in months. For a moment he forgot about Tao Shan, training and Zuban.

"Where is the Lord Browdat?" Javik asked between bites.

"He is at the capital attending the King's council," Frieda

answered. "He's been there for two days now. It seems there's some sort of trouble with the Wallan people. He's very close mouthed about it around here, but maybe he'll open up to you, Javik."

"And Zuban?" Javik added.

"Away on another raid with his friends. They seem to enjoy harassing the Wallandians, but they bring home little booty for their risk. When he's here, he spends most of his time working on the new longhouse for his future bride and getting drunk."

"Who will be the lucky girl?" Javik asked with a degree of sarcasm in his voice that was hard to miss.

"Javik! Frieda and Browdat are our protectors. Don't speak of their son in that manner," his mother scolded.

"I'm sorry, Lady Frieda," Javik apologized.

"Don't bother, Javik. I am his mother, and even I think he's much too arrogant," Frieda said. "As to his wife, he seems to favor Drussia; but I'm not sure she returns his interest. Her family's eager to form a bond with ours, though; and they may force her into it if Zuban's courtship looks like it may fail."

Javik knew Drussia only by sight. She was a lovely girl and from a good family, though a poorer one compared to Browdat's hearth. Javik thought she was pretty, but she was too old for him. Poor Drussia, to be Zuban's bride was truly a curse in Javik's mind.

Javik finished his meal quickly. He was eager to find his friends and tell them of his adventures with Tao Shan.

"Mother, may I be excused now to visit with Karl and Berda?"

"Yes, Javik. We women have much to do to prepare for the festival, and you're best out of our way."

Javik ran off to his friends while his mother helped Frieda and Hella prepare the longhouse for the coming festival. There was mistletoe to hang, laurel boughs to be cut for wreaths, and sacrifices to be made ready for the altar of Verna, the goddess of spring. She must be welcomed back with great celebration and ceremony so she did not turn away to the south again leaving the countryside to withstand several more weeks of winter weather.

The villagers greeted Javik cordially as he roamed the streets seeking Berda and Karl. It was not long before he spotted them returning from a hunt carrying several rabbits on a pole between them.

"Berda, Karl!" he called. "It's me, Javik!"

"Javik!" Berda called back, dropping his end of the pole and running to greet his friend. Karl laid down his end, along with the bows and quivers, and walked to Javik.

"You look good!" Berda complimented as he tested Javik's arm muscles with his hands. "Tao Shan must work you very hard."

"He does, Berda, but you've been working hard too, I notice." Javik pushed the boy's hard stomach muscles. "And Karl," Javik turned to the other boy. "I've missed both of you."

"Oh," Karl scoffed. "You must have many friends at Tao Shan's longhouse. We thought you'd forget all about us lesser folk."

Javik embraced both of his companions at once. "None like you two. I see you have some fine rabbits." He led them back to the pole and inspected the kills.

"The swamps are full of them this year, Javik. It will be a good summer," Berda said.

"Tell us about Tao Shan," Karl said as the boys resumed their burden and marched off to the longhouse their families shared.

"I didn't realize how stupid I was until I entered his

training," Javik admitted. "He's taught me so much I never could have learned elsewhere—not even from my father, if he were still with us. I must show you some of the special fighting tricks one of his servants taught us."

"You're very lucky, Javik," Karl was genuinely happy for his friend. "Our fathers are good teachers, but they only know so much. They say Tao Shan is a magician and very wise because he's lived three lifetimes. They also say he uses special potions to keep himself young."

Javik laughed at his friend's gullibility. "Karl, you don't believe those old wives' tales, do you?"

"No one's ever seen him sick, and he seems not to age, though many say he's an old man," Berda added.

"The Master says his people do not show their age the same way our people do," Javik said. "He once told us he has no idea how old he is himself."

"Very mysterious," Berda cooed and then broke out in a fit of laughter.

They reached the boys' house where their mothers welcomed Javik warmly. The rabbits were properly hung up to be dressed and cooked for that night's meal, and the boys found a quiet corner of the house to renew their acquaintance.

"What news of the village?" Javik asked.

"There is a new girl at Browdat's house. Very lovely she is too," Berda smiled.

"I met her. Her name's Hella. She's Browdat's niece," Javik told the boys her story.

"Karl hasn't had the courage to ask her name yet," Berda teased as the other boy punched him on the shoulder.

"I was planning to do that at festival time," Karl retorted.

"What of Zuban?" Javik continued.

"Oh, that's another story," Karl grew very somber. "He says

he's raiding our enemies, but some of the booty he brings back looks strangely like things from allied villages. There've been no complaints, but my father says it's only because he's probably disguising himself as a Sentii when he raids."

"Do Yarl and Guyam still run with him?" Javik asked.

"Yes, they are inseparable," Karl said. "They even plan to live in the same longhouse when Zuban establishes his own hearth."

"Pity me," Javik said. "My mother and I must live in the same longhouse with him until then. The sooner he's out of there, the better."

The three boys spent the rest of the day catching up on their adventures since Javik left for schooling with Tao Shan. Berda and Karl were particularly interested in the training routines, and Javik swelled with just a bit of pride as he told them of the hardships he faced as one of Tao Shan's students.

At suppertime, they parted to attend the preparations for the festival processions at their respective longhouses. To honor the return of spring, each longhouse formed its own parade. The residents dressed in their finest clothes, and the men wore a diadem of holly leaves while the women plaited a band of ivy for their hair. Everyone carried some sort of sacrifice to appease Verna. The processions wound through the streets of the village so each longhouse could show off its finery and ended at the sacred grove dedicated to Verna.

Javik returned to Browdat's house and found the women laying out their gifts for the goddess. Hella had made a gown of hay and wild flowers to adorn the goddess's statue. Frieda baked sweet cakes laced with honey and topped with the seeds of the Lico plant giving them a delicate, tangy flavor. His mother fashioned a lovely necklace made from carved deer antlers to compliment Hella's dress as part of Verna's spring apparel.

"What will you give Verna?" Hella asked Javik.

"Me?" Javik had given the matter no thought at all. The women usually did gifts to Verna, but men sometimes brought wild game to the altar. "I don't have anything. I could hunt some game, I suppose."

Hella giggled and blushed. "Lord Browdat ordered his servants to bring a stag. I don't think there'll be any need for more game."

"Why don't you give her a staff?" Frieda suggested.

"Yes, a staff'd be good," his mother agreed.

"Maybe yours'll grow," Hella smiled shyly.

Some men made staffs for the goddess, and the priestess stuck them into the ground next to her statue. It was considered a mark of good fortune if the staff sprouted green growth before the summer was over.

"I'll go look for one now," Javik laughed as he rose from the table and moved to an ax hanging on one wall. "I'll be back before dinner."

He left the longhouse and trotted deep into the forest. He scanned the small trees to find a suitable candidate, but none seemed to be the right size. He was surprised by a creaky voice calling to him.

"Over here, Javik."

He turned to see an old hag standing next to an Elm sapling. He'd never seen her before, but he knew who she was by reputation. This was the "Old Woman of the Fountain," Grazhda.

No one knew how old Grazhda was. Some said she'd lived over a hundred winters and would never die. Everyone agreed she'd formed alliances with all the demons of the forest and could cast spells of fantastic power. She wore a black shawl drawn around her head and a long, gray dress that drug the ground. The wide leather belt around her waist held a fearsome knife; and a soft, skin bag, bulging with things best not asked about. The skull of a bird hung by her side on a thong passed through the vacant eye sockets. The old crone's face was wrinkled beyond belief, and her lips were a thin, red line; but alarmingly bright blue eyes gleamed from the dark caves of her eyes transfixing Javik.

"How do you know me?" he asked.

"Grazhda knows all, haven't you heard?" she cackled. "Take this tree, young warrior. It will do what you wish it to do."

"And how do you know what that is?" Javik blustered.

Grazhda only laughed shrilly. "Does Tao Shan take on ignorant pupils these days? You know well who I am, son of Tolda; and I know well what you want. You long to have your own hearth so your mother may cease being a servant in the longhouse of Browdat. Am I not right?"

"Yes, you are, but I can't do that until I'm truly a warrior. You called me by a false name just now, for I'm not yet past Mauhad."

"A trifling matter!" Grazhda shrugged off Javik's protestation. "Only a matter of time, and a short time at that. Shorter than you know, young Javik." The old crone cackled merrily at her secret knowledge.

"But, why would you help me?"

"Your father once saved my life, and now I return the favor. Cut this sapling for Verna's staff, and you'll know what it means to have Grazhda's gratitude."

A rustle of leaves behind Javik made him turn, but nothing was there. When he turned back Grazhda was gone. He walked to the sapling she indicated and looked it over. There was nothing to recommend it above any of the others as far as he could see, but he cut it anyway. He was not superstitious, but who could afford to anger the "Old Woman of the Fountain?"

It was well known she could curse as well as bless, and anyone who treated her poorly or took her advice lightly always suffered ill fortune. Many said she could make cows go dry or cause hens to stop laying. Javik's father never told him of his encounter with Grazhda, and he wondered what happened. Perhaps his mother would know.

As he entered Browdat's longhouse, he sensed a new aura in the building. When he saw Zuban sitting at a table in the common room, he knew what it was. The warm feeling he encountered that morning was replaced by a cold dread. The servants moved silently and warily as Zuban shouted slurred commands to them. A large drinking cup sat on the table before him, and Javik was sure his enemy had downed several measures of dark beer from it already. He looked up as Javik came in.

"Well, it's Tolda's whelp back from school for the holiday." Zuban emptied the cup spilling a good deal of it down the front of his dirty tunic before slamming it back on the table.

"More beer! And bring my *friend* Javik a cup also," he commanded.

A servant scurried to do his bidding, but he stopped him with a kick. "Not you. Get that bitch Dana to do it. It's for her spawn, after all."

Javik felt his blood grow warm and his mouth go dry. He was ready to leap over the table and beat the drunken face to a pulp when the lessons of Ling came flooding into his head. *Calm and cool will defeat rage in any battle*, the Master's words echoed through his mind. Javik forced his brain clear of the red haze clouding his judgment. "Greetings Zuban. How was your luck on the raid?" he asked as calmly as he could.

"Oh, you should have been there, Javik. We killed three Wallans and captured six horses. The wretched piss ants had very little gold on them, though. This will be my gift to Verna at the festival tomorrow." Zuban pivoted his chair and kicked a large bag leaning against the near wall. The bottom was stained with a dark substance Javik calculated was blood, and from the shape of the bag, it surely contained the heads of the three unfortunate Wallans.

"A worthy gift, Zuban," Javik praised him. Heads of enemies were always a prestigious gift to the gods. At that moment, his mother entered the room carrying a pitcher of beer. She moved to Zuban and filled his cup then turned to leave.

"No, woman! Pour your son a drink also. He's our guest." Zuban slapped Dana across her rump and laughed out loud as she poured the beer into Javik's mug. She saw the rage smoldering in her son's eyes, but fixed her gaze on Javik and shook her head firmly. Javik nodded in response.

Zuban lifted his cup. "A toast, Javik. A toast to spring, love, marriage and a good planting."

It was a reasonable toast, and Javik rose to join it. "To spring," he responded.

Zuban downed a large draught from his cup as did Javik. As Javik sat down, Zuban added, "I'm going to get married this summer, Javik. Did you know that?"

"Lady Frieda told me of your plans. Congratulations, Zuban."

"Yes, with all of these raids I've been going on, I haven't had much time to sharpen my skills with the ladies. My bride will expect me to be an experienced lover, so I must practice with someone. What do you think of the lady Dana as a practice partner?" Zuban broke into maniacal laughter.

Javik drew his knife and was about to make his move when

Browdat entered followed by several armed servants.

"By Zhou, if you ever touch a hair on that woman's head, I'll skin you alive myself," Browdat raged.

Zuban was suddenly quite sober. "Javik and I were just having a drink together, sir. It was only a jest, I assure you," he groveled.

"I don't think Javik found it funny," Browdat said through clenched teeth. He turned to his servants. "Take this piece of drunken baggage to his room. He can sleep it off until the festival tomorrow morning."

Two husky servants lifted Zuban from the chair and carried him out of the room. As he left, he called over his shoulder, "Father, you spoil all my jokes. You shouldn't be so serious at festival time."

Browdat sat down opposite Javik as a servant placed a mug in front of him and filled it with beer. "It's good to see you, Javik. Pay no attention to Zuban. Your mother is respected at my hearth. You have my word no one has mistreated her in the past and no one will do so in the future. How goes it with Tao Shan?"

"It goes well, Lord Browdat. He's a hard Master, but I've learned much in only a short time."

"Good! Will you go on Mauhad in the fall?"

"Tao Shan won't tell us until just before the test. I want to go as soon as I can, but I fear I've much more to absorb before he'd deem me ready."

"He's the best mentor in the kingdom. His previous pupils now command many in times of war, and we may not be far from war now."

"With the Sentii?"

"No, with the Wallans. The Sentii are a thorn in our side. We raid them and they raid us, but they dare not come against us in force."

Browdat's words sent a chill through Javik. War—he'd only heard the stories of the men around the hearths, but he knew what it could mean. Too many hearths would be without a man, and too many widows and orphans would mourn long into each night. This time, he could be one of the warriors in the thick of the battle. This was what he was hoping for since he was old enough to wield a wooden sword, but now it was real, not play, and he felt the grip of fear on his insides.

"Let's hope it won't be." Javik's voice was more solemn than Browdat expected.

"You're wise beyond your years, Javik. There's no glory in war, though some would have you believe it's the only fit occupation for a man. Consider this, a farmer can grow enough food to feed a village, but the only mouth war feeds is the insatiable maw of death. Don't get me wrong. I won't shrink from battle, but I'll do all in my power to avert a war."

"Our people are fortunate to have you counseling the King," Javik paid the man a sincere compliment.

Frieda rushed into the room out of breath followed closely by Hella. "We were picking wildflowers in the woods when your servant found us. Welcome home." Frieda threw her arms around her husband's wide neck and fell into his lap."

"It's good to be home again, woman; but what's for dinner? I'm starved."

"You'll be lucky to get cold chicken with that attitude," Frieda mocked him as she rose to attend her cooking pots.

Browdat smacked her on the behind playfully. "Know that I'm starved for other things, too," he bellowed as Hella blushed beet red.

* * * * *

Zuban was quiet during dinner that evening, largely due to the effects of too much beer. The whole household went to bed early since the ceremonies of the spring festival would begin with offerings on the altar of Verna at sunrise.

Chapter 8

Breakfast was quick and cold in the darkness before sunrise. Javik dressed in his finest tunic and trousers and pulled on the boots he'd spent so much time polishing the previous night. Hella was radiant in her festival gown, and he thought he'd never seen his mother look so beautiful before. Even Frieda managed to make the most of her ample frame in a brightly patterned dress and silver headpiece. Browdat wore his best armor and carried his family's ceremonial sword, while Zuban had to make do with tarnished chain mail because he was too drunk the day before to polish it.

When all was ready, the family formed its procession with Browdat at the head followed by two servants carrying his sacrifices of wild game. Zuban followed bearing his grizzly bag of battle trophies. The women came last with Javik among them since he was not yet counted a man.

All over the village families formed outside the longhouses dressed in their most colorful clothes and carrying treasures to appease Verna, inviting the continuation of warm weather. Several members of each gathering carried small torches to light the way.

In the village square, vendors were busy setting up the fair booths, and the aromas from the food vendors' cooking fires made Javik's mouth water. Perhaps his mother would allow him some money to buy a treat after the ceremonies.

The order of the procession to Verna's sacred grove was fixed according to the status of each family. Goldar was first since he was the highest-ranking war leader, but Browdat followed immediately behind him. Each family knew its place and fell in as Goldar led the parade past the longhouses in the correct order. When the last family was in place, the procession turned toward the sacred grove. The long line of flickering torches made it seem the very stars of the heavens were moving to pay tribute to the goddess.

It was still dark when they reached the edge of the forest, but each family extinguished their torches in pails of water as they entered. From this point on, torches lighted earlier by the priestesses of Verna illuminated the path. Javik had been part of this ritual many times, he always felt a sense of awe, walking through the dimly lit natural arbor.

The sky was just beginning to lighten as they entered the sacred grove. The wide, circular clearing was easily large enough to hold the entire village. At the center, a larger than life statue of Verna looked sinister in the gray of false dawn. Deep shadows formed in every crease of her gown, and her face was gaunt and hollow-eyed, but soon the rising sun would burn away the shadows and transform her into a thing of beauty.

A great stone altar stood before the statue—a single rock, uncut and pristine. It was said every man in the village was needed to move it from the nearby mountains to Verna's grove, and that it was only possible with help from the goddess herself.

The priestesses chanted hymns and waved smoking censures over the altar. The sweet/sour scent assaulted Javik's poorly fed stomach, but he held back the urge to empty it of its meager contents. The people joined in at the appropriate time. Everyone knew the ritual by heart. Only the smallest children were unable to respond with the usual words.

The chanting rose to a crescendo as the sun climbed above the horizon and bathed the statue in a pink glow.

The high priestess spoke in the ancient tongue only she and the other priestesses knew, but the assembled villagers understood it as the signal to recite the spring prayer.

The priestess began, "Oh blessed Verna, look down upon your people and have mercy. We bring you the fruits of our labor, and we pledge our lives to the land you have given us. We sing praise for your wisdom and thank you for the bounty you have bestowed upon us. Have mercy blessed Verna. Have mercy upon your people. Forbid the harsh winter god to dwell longer among us. We praise you."

The people responded, "Blessed be Verna."

Once more the priestess chanted, "We praise you."

Again, the people responded, "Blessed be Verna."

For a third time the priestess intoned, "We praise you."

The people responded, "Blessed be Verna."

When the prayer was finished the statue stood in full daylight. The high priestess moved behind the altar and called out her invitation.

"Let the people bring forth their offerings to Verna," she said.

Each house of the village joined the procession to place their gifts on the altar in the same order they observed in the march to the grove.

Browdat's game was welcomed with a coo of appreciation from the people, since they knew it would be part of the feast later in the day. Frieda's cakes were also appreciated, but a gasp of horror arose as Zuban dumped his bloody heads on the altar. Zuban's mouth twisted into a cruel smile as he arranged them so the dead eyes stared back at the assembled crowd.

Javik was sure he saw the priestess turn away in revulsion for a moment.

Javik waited his turn and walked to the area on the south side of the statue, designated for staffs. The ground was dug-up in anticipation of the gifts, and the priestess on duty had no trouble planting the sapling deeply into the black earth. Hella draped her gown over the statue, and his mother's necklace gleamed in the sunlight around its neck. Javik re-joined Browdat's group at their appointed place and waited as the rest of the houses made their presentations. Four more staffs joined Javik's in the special plot, and food piled high upon the altar. The feast this year would be very bountiful indeed.

Karl's house brought baskets of newly sprouted mushrooms, while Berda's hearth offered casks of beer. Even Tao Shan was represented. He led his household servants, and those boys who could not return to their own villages, up to the altar and placed a fine pair of felt boots on the stone. Javik noticed they were very small and delicately embroidered to suit the feet of the high priestess. She smiled broadly when she saw the gift. Tao Shan said he did not believe in Verna, but he knew how to hedge his bets. When the altar was nearly hidden by the mound of gifts, the high priestess spoke again.

"Oh goddess of life, may our gifts find favor in your eyes. Look upon your people with compassion and bless our plantings. Let the animals of the forest bring forth many offspring, and let the rivers run with a bounty of fish. We beseech thee great Verna to help us. Accept the gifts we bring to you out of the bounty of our hearts. We have planted five staffs this year. Show us through them that you look favorably upon us. The heads of our enemies lie before you. These were evil men who did not know you—men who trusted to their own skills instead of praying to you. Bless Zuban, the instrument of your justice who has brought them low."

The priestess turned to face the crowd and raised her arms high above her head in supplication. "Blessed Verna, do not withhold your rain. Let our harvest be bountiful. We stand before you as your humble servants."

As if in answer to the priestess's prayers, a sudden wind rustled the trees bordering the altar clearing and the smell of impending rain permeated the air. Many looked to the sky in anticipation, but the clouds withheld their bounty for the present.

The sun shone brightly now, and the villagers broke the regimentation of the procession to return to the village in smaller groups. Many left the altar of Verna to see what excitement had been gathering in the village square while they worshipped. Gaily painted wagons surrounded the main village well with signs boasting all sorts of mysteries and delights. Javik was drawn to one sign reading, "Come in and learn what fate awaits you! Madam Zagra sees all."

The fortuneteller's wagon was painted in shades of gray with black trim. Only the red letters on the sign showed any color. A woman Javik guessed to be in her thirties sat on the steps leading to the interior of the vehicle. She had olive skin and jet black hair held off her face by a golden head piece that would be worth a fortune if it were real, which he doubted it was. A faded green tunic fit her loosely, hiding any trace of her figure. She sat with her knees spread wide apart and a long, dark brown skirt sagging between them. Only the toes of handsomely embroidered slippers showed under the hem. Her deep black eyes fixed Javik in a penetrating gaze, making him very uncomfortable. He wanted to move on, but he felt his feet glued to the spot in front of her sign.

"Come into my wagon, young man; and I will tell you all the

gods have planned for you." Her voice was soft and sultry, with an almost masculine quality.

"I have little money, Madam Zagra." He guessed she was the one the sign advertised.

"Show me a coin," the woman commanded.

Javik reached into his purse and fingered the contents. There were three coins and his salla, the signaling whistle of his people. One coin was a gold piece his father gave him years ago after a successful raid. The second was the silver piece Tao Shan gave each of the boys to buy a treat at the festival. The last was a copper penny he found by the roadside on his way home. He suspected the woman would probably keep whatever coin he gave her. Part of Tao Shan's schooling included exposure to various frauds commonly found in the world, and remembering that soothsaying was one of them, he decided on the copper penny.

The woman sniffed haughtily as he placed it in her palm. She studied it carefully then fixed her eyes on Javik's for what seemed an eternity. "You chose well, young warrior," she was solemn.

"I'm not a warrior, Madam Zagra," he corrected her. "I've not yet been on Mauhad."

She nodded knowingly. "But you'll go soon, and you'll be successful." She turned the coin over and over in her hands.

"Fate has given you this coin. Do you know the image on it?"

"No, I think it's a Wallan coin; but I don't know who the face belongs to."

"This is Umbric, the king who ruled Wallandia a hundred winters ago. Since you don't know him, you probably don't know the legend about him either. Do you?"

"No, ma'am."

"Umbric died a horrible death after killing his wife and raping his own daughter. The high priest of their god Murgaan condemned Umbric for his sins, and it is said demons invaded his body and ate him up from the inside out. The priest prophesied the kingdom of Wallandia would be cursed from that day onward and that the curse could not be lifted until a stranger was crowned king."

"An interesting story, but what has that to do with me?" Javik asked.

"Perhaps nothing," she shrugged as she tossed the coin in the air, catching it in her mouth. Javik was very surprised to see her swallow it without blinking. As if he never existed, she turned her stare back to the dirt of the village square.

Javik moved on glad he'd only given her the penny. Tao Shan was right. Fortunetellers were hopeless charlatans. Wallandia bordered the Berglauni lands to the North across the great river called Callistra by the Berglauni and Walla by the Wallandians. Browdat feared there might soon be war with Wallandia, and there was no love lost between the two peoples. The idea that he might one day be king of Wallandia was absurd. Javik moved on to the wrestling exhibition.

One corner of the square was roped off into a small ring. Inside the ring a small, old man touted the prowess of his wrestler and challenged anyone to fight him.

"Wager one silver coin my good fellows, and if you pin my man I'll repay you with twenty of the same kind." He held up a leather bag full of coins and jingled it loudly. "Who's brave among you?"

The wrestler looked formidable indeed. He stood head and shoulders taller than Javik and weighed at least half again more. Firm muscles rippled under light brown skin, oiled until it glistened like gold in the sunlight. He had no beard, and his head was shaved clean. Only a large, bushy mustache showed the black color his hair would have been. He glared at the crowd with gray eyes that reminded Javik of a well-polished sword. No one was taking the bet.

"Come now, you brave warriors of the Berglauni. Is there no champion among you willing to risk his coin? I heard you were fierce fighters. Did I hear wrong?"

"You heard right, old man," one wag shouted. "Give me a sword and I will try him out."

The rest of the crowd laughed, and even the wrestler let a smile soften his glare for a moment. Javik noticed Zuban eyeing the scene as he sipped at a mug of beer. Zuban would be no match for this giant even if he was completely sober, and Javik guessed this was not his first mug of the day. He was beginning to wonder if anyone in the village would take on this hulk of a man. Suddenly, Goldar stepped from the crowd .

Yes, if anyone could challenge it would be Goldar, war leader of the Berglauni. Javik remembered Goldar was severely wounded in the battle that took his father's life, but there seemed to be no trace of the injury now.

"I'll try your champion," the war leader announced as he handed a silver coin to the old man.

The crowd whistled and cheered wildly. There was no warrior in the village as fierce as Goldar. He was a raid leader and wise beyond his years. If he could not defeat this foreign champion, no one could.

"Goldar will kill him!" one shouted.

"Be kind to him, Goldar," another pleaded in a mocking tone.

The big warrior passed the belt carrying his weapons and purse to one of his servants and stripped off his tunic. He was as well muscled as the giant, and the scars of many battles marred his skin in sharp contrast to the smooth shine of his opponent. Javik watched the giant's eyes as Goldar took off his tunic, and saw him flinch as the scars were revealed. One scar on Goldar's left arm was fairly new, but it had healed well.

"The fight is to be bloodless," the old man shouted, and Goldar nodded his agreement.

"You must pin my man for a count of three to win," he cautioned; and, again, Goldar nodded.

"And if you leave the ring or beg for mercy, you forfeit." Another nod confirmed Goldar's understanding.

The two men circled warily sizing each other up. Goldar was probably just as powerful, but he gave away almost a head in height and several kilos in weight. The giant was solemn, but Goldar smiled confidently. A quick charge by Goldar landed a shoulder in the giant's stomach as he wrapped his arms around the thick waist. This time the giant smiled.

The blow would have knocked another man senseless, but the giant only stepped back two paces in reaction to the force of the impact. Raising both of his hands above his head, he joined them together and crashed the double fist down upon Goldar's back just below his neck. Goldar collapsed as if he were made of rags.

The giant did not press his advantage. He circled around behind Goldar as the warrior raised himself on his hands and knees shaking the cobwebs from his brain. The giant's eyes glowed with pleasure as he bent to grab his opponent by the hair, but his gloating turned to terror as Goldar rolled on his back and grasped the approaching wrist in a vise-like grip. The move was faster than anything Javik had ever seen in Ling's lessons, and it caught the giant completely by surprise. He screamed in pain as Goldar twisted his wrist into an awkward position and used the leverage to force the giant to the ground.

Releasing his grip, Goldar jumped to his feet next to the writhing body. Lifting one knee to waist level, Goldar dropped his whole body, planting the knee squarely in the giant's stomach. A rush of air from the grimacing mouth was followed by a glazed expression on the formerly terrible face. The giant gasped for air with both hands on his mid-section. Goldar moved his body over the wrestler's chest and held him down as the crowd counted, "One, two, three!"

Goldar rose and acknowledged the cheers of the men around the ring by holding one arm high in the air. He turned to the old man who was busy trying to revive his champion.

"You owe me twenty silver coins, old man," Goldar chuckled.

"Here, take them," he tossed his bag to the warrior who counted out the proper sum and dropped the bag on the giant's chest.

With a sweep of his arm, Goldar flung the coins into the crowd. As the people scattered to pick up the booty, he dressed and began to leave the ring. Noticing Javik, he turned to speak to him. "Javik! You look well. Tao Shan's training's agreeing with you."

"Thank you, Lord Goldar. I'm a fortunate boy to be in his house. Almost as fortunate as you in defeating that hulk there." Javik indicated the giant who was just now recovering from Goldar's blow. In contrast, Goldar seemed to have recovered completely from the giant's attack and showed almost no signs of fatigue.

"There was no fortune to it, Javik. I've seen men like him at many festivals. Did you notice he had no battle scars?"

"I did, sir."

"That gave him away. He's used to farmers who trust in their strength alone and warriors who are more boast than experience. You must let one like that think you are defeated, then, he'll drop his guard because he wants to make a spectacle out of you. That's when you strike and strike hard. You'll not have a second chance. If he'd been able to grasp me in one of his holds, I'd be lying on the ground now instead of him."

"I've learned a valuable lesson today, sir. It seems you've given me much, and it must be repaid at some point. This, as well as your good words with the King which made me a student of Tao Shan."

Goldar smiled and placed a brawny arm around Javik's shoulder. "Your father was my friend. He saved my life so many times I lost count. I owed him much more than you've received from my hands so far. How does your mother fare at Browdat's house?"

"She is well, sir. Browdat has nothing but respect for her, but I fear Zuban may try to harm her when he's drunk. He obeys his father when he's sober, but the beer gives him false courage."

"It does that to all men, Javik. Learn to use it in moderation. There are times it's better than water, but it can make a fool of any man. Don't fear for your mother. Browdat will let no harm come to her."

"She works very hard, sir."

"As she must to earn her keep, but she's still a good looking woman, Javik. Yes indeed, a good looking woman." Goldar smiled broadly as he contemplated Dana. His own wife was very sick these days; and, though he prayed with all his might she would recover, he knew who he would woo if he were suddenly left a widower.

Goldar rejoined his servants, leaving Javik to wander among the booths and wagons of the festival. Javik contemplated having Goldar as a father, and was very pleased with the thought. A soft voice broke his concentration.

"I hope your staff gains life, Javik." It was Hella. Her blonde hair was tied back in a brightly decorated leather band, and her soft skin was radiant in the noonday sun.

"Thank you, Hella. Your gown was the most beautiful one there."

The young girl blushed and turned slightly away. "The feast this evening will be very fine," she changed the subject.

"Yes, there were many food offerings." With that remark, Javik exhausted his store of subjects for conversation with Hella.

"Look, Javik," she smiled. "It's an amber seller."

Hella pointed to a booth where a middle-aged man dressed in odd looking clothes was setting out his wares on a rough, wooden table. His hair was as blonde as Hella's, and he wore no beard or mustache. Javik's father told him of the peoples to the far North where the precious stones were found. They were wanderers who carried their goods on their own backs in large knapsacks they called "Jillas." They seemed to appear out of nowhere wherever there was a fair or market and vanished just as mysteriously when the celebrations ended. They spoke a guttural language, making them hard to understand even when they spoke Berglauni.

"Let's go look." Hella shouted as she dragged Javik with her to see the precious items.

Necklaces and bracelets made from the honey-colored beads glistened in the sunlight. The man was just taking some rings from his bag as they arrived.

"Good festival to you," he greeted the boy and girl.

"And to you," Javik responded.

"You have some fine wares," Hella complimented.

"The finest amber in the realm. It comes from a land far away to the North across many rivers. See how it glows." He held a necklace so the sunlight filtered through it revealing the warm interior of the hardened sap. "Such a lovely lady should always have amber at her throat to protect her from evil spirits."

"What nonsense," Javik sniffed.

"It's true, Javik. Frieda says a woman wearing amber will never be bothered by curses or the evil eye," Hella corrected him.

"Aye, I've known many who thanked me for telling them about the magic qualities of the stones," the peddler reinforced Hella's comment.

"They won't protect you from Zuban," Javik said.

"Lord Browdat's my protection from Zuban," Hella smiled. "He'll see that no harm comes to me in that regard."

"Lord Browdat isn't home all the time to control his son," Javik added.

"Then you must be my protector, Javik."

Hella's words struck Javik with a sudden warmth that almost made him blush. He fought back the sensation, but he thought he saw both Hella and the peddler smile at him.

"How do you like this one?" Hella held up a leather thong with a single stone dangling in its middle.

Javik took the pendant from Hella and held it up to the light. "There's a fly in it," he snorted.

"Oh, that makes it even more powerful. The spirit of the fly's imprisoned within the stone and now belongs to whomever owns it," the peddler assured them.

"I think I'll buy this one. How much is it?" Hella asked.

"For a lovely lady only ten coppers," the man smiled.

Hella took her purse from her belt and counted out eight pennies. "Oh my, I don't have enough. Will you take eight?"

"Lady, I make no profit at ten. It's only because I like you that I offer it at such a low price."

Javik saw Hella's face fall in disappointment. If he was to be her protector, he must not let her down at a time like this. Besides, another of Tao Shan's lessons was that a man should always have a lovely woman in his debt. He reached into his own purse for the silver coin Tao Shan gave him and handed it to the peddler. "Here, take it out of this," he said as he scooped up Hella's coins and deposited them in her hand.

"Oh, thank you, Javik," Hella cooed as she tied the pendant around her neck.

The peddler handed Javik ten pennies in change. "You're a true warrior, sir," he complimented. "Treasure is never wasted on a lady," he added with a sly wink.

Javik studied the coins in his hand and realized half of his money was gone. Was Tao Shan right, or had he wasted his treasure on a trinket around a girl's neck? There was barely enough left for the sweet cake his mouth watered for, but a savage voice in the dark recesses of his skull told him it was a good investment.

The boy and girl walked on marveling at the jugglers and fire breathers. They avoided the food stalls for now since the feast would be ready soon, but a minstrel sitting on a barrel strumming a gourd-like instrument captured Javik's attention.

He was not much older than Javik himself, though he gave off the aura of someone wise in the ways of the world. He had a handsome face but something about his body didn't look quite right. The lad's hat lay on the ground in front of him half full of copper coins, and several people sat around him to hear his song. Javik thought he heard his father's name and stopped to listen more closely.

"And Tolda died at the head of his men,
Never to lead the Berglauni again."
The minstrel finished with a flurry of strummed chords as the small audience applauded his efforts.

"Will you sing that song again, good minstrel?" Javik asked.

"Well, sir, my throat is very dry after such an arduous song. Perhaps if you could spare a few coppers for some beer?" he pointed to his hat.

Javik dropped two coins into the hat as the minstrel watched.

"Beer costs three coppers," the minstrel slyly smiled.

Javik added another coin, and the minstrel strummed an opening chord as his previous audience began to disperse. They'd just heard this one.

The tenor voice of the minstrel rang out with the story of Javik's father. He told of his prowess in battle and the many maidens he de-flowered. Javik was glad his mother was not around to hear that part. The song cursed the Sentii and proclaimed the righteousness of the Berglauni cause. It described the evil treachery that trapped the main party under Goldar and ended telling how many Sentii Tolda slew that day. It painted a vivid picture of Tolda holding back the Sentii to make an escape route for the rest of the party then mourned the death of the brave man. Javik was in tears as the last note died on the evening breeze.

"My song's moved you greatly, young man," the minstrel said as he noticed Javik's tears.

"The man you sing of was my father," Javik composed himself as he dried his eyes with the back of his hand. He hadn't noticed it before, but Hella's hand was resting on his shoulder - her gaze fixed on his face.

"I'm honored to meet the son of Tolda," the minstrel jumped from the barrel and bowed before Javik. Now he saw why the minstrel's body looked odd; his back was terribly humped. The singer's posture on the barrel and his motions playing the instrument almost hid the deformity.

"Don't bow to me, minstrel. I'm just a boy not yet through Mauhad. You pay my father great honor with your song, and that's enough."

"Everywhere I go people want to hear of Tolda," the minstrel said. "I am Margan. What is the name of Tolda's son?"

"I am Javik, and this is Hella," Javik responded.

"Your sister?" he asked.

"No, a cousin of the lord Browdat and no relation to me. My mother lives in the house of Browdat," Javik explained.

"And her name is?" the minstrel coaxed.

"Dana, the lady Dana," Hella offered.

"Are you two betrothed?" he asked.

Hella giggled and Javik blushed.

"No, I'm only here for the festival and must return to the house of Tao Shan to finish my training for Mauhad. I just met Hella yesterday."

"You must excuse my questions. A minstrel is expected to know everything, and I'd be a poor craftsman indeed if I didn't find out all there was to know. You've given me another song to sing, good Javik and lovely Hella. I'll tell of the love between Javik, son of Tolda, and the beautiful Hella. Let me see, shall you die in each other's arms or shall you marry? If you marry, Javik must be killed in battle so you may mourn him all your life, fair Hella. No, those endings are both too sad to suit the smiles on your faces. I'll have you live happily ever after with a dozen children around your hearth."

The three of them laughed heartily at the minstrel's humor. The sound of the great gong signaling the start of the feast interrupted their merriment.

"Won't you join us?" Hella asked Margan.

"Mistress, would I be welcome?" Margan nodded toward his hump.

"Sing of my father, and you'll be made a member of the family," Javik laughed.

The feast was every bit as tasty as Javik anticipated. He ate to excess, but he knew a few days of Tao Shan's routine would take off any weight he might add. The beer was new and had a kick. Javik remembered Goldar's warning about it.

Margan was a hit with Browdat. The huge man listened to his first song about an ancient Berglauni king and roared his approval. He dumped his purse on the ground in front of the minstrel and commanded, "You will sing here all night. I want to hear every song you know, young Margan." When Margan sang of Tolda, the fierce old warrior cried openly.

Hella stayed busy serving and clearing tables through most of the feast, but after the work was finished she sat down next to Javik at one of the large, wooden tables set up in Verna's sacred grove. She wiped the perspiration from her brow with her apron, and Javik noticed the fatigue in her face.

"You've worked hard this night," he said.

"It's pleasant work, but tiring," she sighed.

"Did you get anything to eat?"

"We ate as we served. It's a woman's lot." She turned to Javik and smiled weakly.

A dozen couples were performing the ceremonial dance of spring in the middle of the grove to the music of drums and flutes. Javik and Hella watched for a while until Hella said, "Let's go for a walk, Javik. I'm tired of the festival." She rose and looked at him invitingly, extending a hand reddened by the strong soap used to wash the dishes.

Javik downed the last of his beer and rose taking her hand. He led her to a path he knew would end at the river. They were silent as they walked through the dark forest. The moonlight bathed the nearly naked trees in a silver glow casting grotesque shadows on the carpet of dead leaves beneath their feet. Hella's hand pressed into Javik's and sent a strange warmth coursing through his veins. He wanted to stop and kiss her right there, but he decided it would be too brash an assumption since he had known her less than two days. They walked to a fallen tree offering a convenient bench overlooking the rippling river.

They sat next to each other with Hella's warm body meeting his at the thigh. He felt himself becoming aroused and fought back his lust.

"Look at the moon in the river, Javik," Hella pointed to the distorted image. "It's all wrinkled, like an old man."

"Some say a god lives in the moon, and gods are very old."

Hella fingered her pendant. "I love my amber, Javik. Thank you for buying it for me."

"It was nothing. I saw how much you wanted it."

"Do you see how much I want something else?" She turned to face Javik, and her eyes told him all he needed to know. He was about to give in to his desires when his head filled with an explosion of stars. The last thing he remembered was Hella's scream.

Chapter 9

Javik came-to in a ring of torchlight. Browdat was standing over him glaring like a wounded bear.

"The culprit's waking up," Javik heard Goldar say as he shook his head trying to regain his senses. He only felt severe pain for the effort, and his hand moved to the large throbbing bump on the back of his head.

"What happened?" Javik asked.

"Not that you don't know," Browdat growled as he grabbed Javik by the throat and lifted him to his feet. "How shall we deal with this living pile of dung, Goldar?"

"He's yours to kill, Lord Browdat. You're the one offended, and the evidence is clear," Goldar replied.

"What are you talking about?" Javik pleaded.

"Her blow caused him to forget his sins." Goldar spat.

"Whose blow?" Javik was beginning to panic. Something was wrong, and he had no idea what it could be.

"Hella's last attempt to save herself, vermin. Look!" Browdat's grip tightened on Javik's throat as he turned his captive slightly. The ring of torches widened to show Hella sprawled on the ground with her dress above her waist and Javik's knife in her bosom.

"Hella!" Javik called as the tears began to stream down his face.

"Tears are no good now, murderer and rapist," Browdat

barked. "I claim the right to take this boy's life by the death of a hundred cuts."

The ring of torchlight shouted its approval as some of the flickering shadows moved to bind Javik's arms.

"I didn't touch her. I swear it on my father's spirit," Javik shouted over the snarls of the mob. His voice broke at the effort, and he fought hard to keep from crying.

"Now he profanes the spirit of a great warrior on top of his crimes," Goldar shouted, and the crowd went wild with outrage.

Javik was shoved and kicked to the village square where two posts were set up. Javik was stripped naked and tied between them.

"Lord Browdat, you must believe me. I did not harm Hella," Javik called.

At that point Javik's mother ran into the square and threw herself at Browdat's feet sobbing.

"He's a good boy, my lord. He could not have harmed Hella. Take my life instead of his."

"Silence, woman. This is man's work, and I'd advise you to leave now before this execution begins."

"No, no, my lord. You must not kill my son. He's all I have left. I beg you for mercy."

"Get her out of here," Browdat turned to his servants who lifted Dana by the arms and carried her away crying and screaming for mercy for her son.

Browdat took the knife from his belt and walked toward Javik. "Now you will suffer as my niece suffered." His eyes shone with a red rage and spittle dribbled from his mouth as he moved to make the first cut.

"Wait!" a tenor voice called from the crowd. "Javik's innocent. I know. I saw it all happen."

Browdat turned to the new voice and lowered his knife. "Who speaks?"

"I'm Margan the minstrel, Lord. You know me. You listened to my songs tonight."

"Step into the light where I can see you," Browdat commanded.

Margan moved to face the huge man and knelt at his feet. "I saw it all, Lord. Javik did not rape and murder your niece."

"Speak your piece, minstrel. If you saw it happen, tell us why you were there and what you saw."

"I followed Javik and Hella into the forest with my lute. I knew she liked him, and I was going to serenade them when the proper moment came. I was hiding in some brush just up the path. Javik and Hella were sitting on the log by the river when another man came up behind Javik and hit him with a stone. He grabbed Hella and began to wrestle with her. I didn't know what to do. She screamed, but he shoved something into her mouth to keep her quiet. It was only then I realized what was happening. I ran through the forest to get away. I was afraid the man would kill me, too, if he knew I'd seen him." Margan turned to Javik shaking with horror and fear. "I'm sorry Javik. I was afraid. I just ran as fast as I could then I heard them calling for your blood and ran back here."

"Miserable wretch!" Browdat moaned. "Why didn't you save my niece?" The big man's arm swung back ready to strike Margan.

"Remember his back, Lord Browdat," Goldar called.

Goldar moved his torch to illuminate the minstrel, and Browdat's arm fell limply to his side.

"You would have done little good against any real man," he sighed. "Release Javik."

Hands moved to untie Javik, and someone handed him his

clothes. Javik's strength deserted him, and he collapsed in a heap on the ground as soon as he was free. He had come so near dying he could still feel the cold breath of death on his neck. He was shaking in spite of all his efforts to control himself.

"What did this man look like?" Goldar demanded of Margan.

"I did not see his face clearly, lord. He was about Javik's height, but heavier. I can tell you little else about him, I fear. The moon went behind a cloud just before he struck. Perhaps he was waiting for that moment to attack."

Browdat turned to the men around him. "Get horses. He cannot have gone far. Goldar, you take four men to the West. Ganda, take another four through the woods. Riggen, you and Harl check the other side of the river. He can't have come back toward the festival, or we'd have seen him. A hundred gold coins to whoever finds him and brings him here to me."

The men scattered to do Browdat's bidding as Javik tried to recover. His hands shook as he tied his tunic, and it took all of his effort to pull on his boots. Browdat turned back to him.

"I'm sorry, Javik; but what was I to think? She was with you, and your knife was in her." Browdat's vast bulk sagged under the weight of his loss and the heavy sorrow in his heart.

"I'll recover, lord. Thank Zhou for Margan. Where did he go? I want to thank him."

"I'm here, Javik," the minstrel answered stepping to Javik's side. "I'm just glad I was in time."

The wailing of the women as they carried Hella's body into the square stopped the conversation. Javik stood on his wobbly legs and moved toward the sound.

"I must see her again," he moaned.

Browdat held him back. "Death is not a pretty sight, Javik."

He shook off the big man's hand. "I only knew her for a short time, Lord Browdat; but she captured my heart. I must see her one last time."

Leaning on Margan for support, Javik moved to the table where Hella was laid out. Frieda and his mother were sobbing over the still, white form. Javik moved to his mother's side.

"Thank Zhou for Margan," she sobbed. "I thought you were going to be killed for something you didn't do."

"It's all right, Mother. That's over now. We must find the swine who did this," he said as he swept a hand toward Hella's body. It was then he noticed her amber pendant was missing.

"Mother, her necklace is gone. The murderer must have torn it from her neck in the struggle. I have to go find it." He took a torch from a servant and started for the forest.

"Be careful, Javik," his mother called. "Whoever did this may still be out there."

"I'll be careful, Mother," he called back over his shoulder. Javik was on a mission. He must find the necklace Hella loved so much so it could be buried with her. He ran back down the path to the scene of the crime and searched carefully for the missing pendant, but had no success. Perhaps the criminal threw it into the river? Javik surveyed the muddy waters swollen well above the normal level by the spring run-off. There was no hope of finding it there. The tears flowed freely from his eyes as he headed back to the village square. He was not sure what feeling Hella aroused in him, but he suspected it may have been what others called love. She was a sweet girl with simple desires, what kind of animal would rape and murder such an innocent?

Javik entered the square to find Hella's body had been moved so the women could prepare her for burial. Nearly all of the men were scattered about the countryside searching for the murderer, but he noticed one figure slouched over a table, apparently asleep. The light of his torch revealed a soaking wet Zuban grasping a mug of beer. He stirred as Javik approached.

"What's all the commotion about, Javik?" he slurred.

"Where have you been, Zuban? You're soaking wet."

"I fell into the river and was washed downstream by the current before I could swim to the bank. I was hoping I could find a blanket and a fire here, but everyone has gone home. Get me a blanket, Javik," he commanded.

"You're drunk, Zuban. Come, I'll help you get to bed."

"You still haven't told me what all the shouting's about," Zuban insisted as Javik hoisted the drunken burden to his feet.

"Hella has been raped and murdered, and the men are searching for her killer; but you're in no condition to help with that right now. Come along, I'll get you to the house."

"I have to help find the dog who would do such a rotten thing," Zuban shrugged off Javik's support and staggered a few paces toward the forest before he fell in a heap.

"Not tonight, Zuban," Javik said as he hoisted the drunk to his shoulder and headed for Browdat's house.

All the way back to the house, Javik could hear the wailing and weeping of the women and the shouts of the men in the forest. He would join them as soon as he got Zuban settled.

The house was empty except for Sasha, the old man in charge of the servants. He met Javik in the common room and reached out for Zuban.

"I will take care of him now, master Javik," he said. "I'm used to doing this."

Javik shifted his load into Sasha's arms, and the old man staggered a bit under the extra weight of the wet clothes.

"Let me take him, Sasha. He's too heavy for you," Javik said as he resumed his burden. Sasha led the way to Zuban's room, lighting the way with a small candle. Once there, Javik dumped the unconscious Zuban on his straw mat and began to undress him.

"We must get these wet clothes off of him," Javik advised.

"Yes, master Javik. I can handle it from here if you like."

"I'll stay and help you in case you have to lift him," Javik said.

The old man pulled off the heavy boots and unwrapped Zuban's feet. The foul smell of the unwashed wool was almost more than Javik could stand, but the old man seemed to take it all in stride. Next he unlaced the leather breeches and slipped them down over Zuban's limp legs. He stopped abruptly as the trousers exposed Zuban's undergarment.

"Look, master Javik," he pointed to a faded bloodstain on the dingy white linen drawers.

"Did he cut himself, Sasha?" Javik asked.

In response Sasha began to search for a wound on Zuban's stomach. Finding none there, he inspected Zuban's hands; but they were un-marked.

"I see nothing that might have caused this," Sasha replied.

"Strange," was all that Javik could manage as Sasha unlaced Zuban's tunic and unbuckled the wide belt holding his purse and knife. As he pulled the belt from under the snoring man, the knife fell from its sheath. Javik picked it up and surveyed it in the candlelight. It was clean.

"Would you please help me with him while I remove his tunic?" Sasha asked.

"Yes, certainly," Javik replied as he lifted Zuban's upper body.

Sasha pulled the tunic up over Zuban's head and off his arms. As the old man folded the garment to carry it away something fell out and hit the hard packed dirt floor. Javik moved the candle to illuminate the spot, and the soft, brown glow of amber revealed the identity of Hella's murderer. She must have shoved the pendant into Zuban's tunic hoping he was too drunk to notice. Now he knew where the blood on Zuban's undergarment came from.

"Sasha, go find your master," Javik whispered between clenched teeth.

The urgency in Javik's tone made Sasha turn toward him. The combination of horror and rage in Javik's face caused the old man to hesitate a moment. He knew there was no love lost between these two, but the sight of the amber pendant on the floor seemed to be the source of Javik's concern.

"What is that?" Sasha said pointing to the pendant.

"I bought that for Hella at the festival today. It means that Zuban's her killer."

"I can't believe Zuban would do such a wicked thing," Sasha said as he moved to pick up the trinket.

Javik snatched it from his hand and shouted at Sasha, "Quickly, man, before this scum revives enough to make a run for it."

The servant nodded and ran from the room as Javik moved the candle to light Zuban's face. How could this wretch sleep so soundly? How could his mouth form that half smile Javik knew so well as a sign of his haughty attitude and affected bravado. The knife at his belt screamed at him to be used in vengeance as his fingers curled around the handle. It took all of his will to leave it sheathed. *Zuban, you waste of Zhou's sacred breath, why didn't you just court Hella? The simple girl would probably have been in awe of you as the scion of Browdat. You could have easily seduced her and had your way without this, but no, that is not your way; is it? You know only to take what you want and damn the consequences.* Javik turned the amber stone in his hand and thought, *"Now you will pay for all of your past follies with your life."*

Browdat burst into the room followed by two warriors. "What is it, Javik? Sasha is about to wet his pants."

"Lord Browdat, I found this in Zuban's tunic." He handed the amber to Browdat.

"So? Zuban bought some amber."

"No, sir. I bought this piece of amber for Hella at the bazaar today. I know it because of the fly."

"What fly?"

"Hold the stone up to the light, sir; and you will see the insect imbedded in it."

"I see," the lord drew out the phrase to emphasize his understanding.

"His undergarment was also bloody," Javik held up the item, "though there are no wounds on his body."

"Wake him!" Browdat ordered the men behind him. They pulled the nude Zuban from his bed and held him while Sasha brought a pitcher of cold water. Browdat threw the water into his son's face.

Zuban uttered a cry of astonishment as his eyes popped open. It took a moment of sputtering before he could focus on the situation.

"Father, what's going on?" he managed.

"How drunk are you?" Browdat asked.

"Your cold bath has driven out all the beer," Zuban shivered. "May I have a blanket, please?"

Sasha pulled a blanket from the pile near the hay pallet and draped it across Zuban's shoulders.

"Thank you, Sasha. Now, Father, will you tell me why I have been treated so rudely?"

"Explain this," Browdat held out the pendant.

A look of surprise flashed across Zuban's face, but he

recovered quickly.

"I bought that today at the bazaar. I thought I would give it to Mother."

"I see," Browdat mused. "How about these?" He held up the bloody underwear.

"There is one less virgin in the village," Zuban laughed.

"Her name," Browdat demanded.

"Father, please. You would not ask me to betray a woman's trust; would you?"

"I will have her name," Browdat thundered.

"If you must know, it was Gunna, Kamar's niece from the next village."

"Let him go," Browdat ordered his men. "You, Harl, find Kamar and tell him about this. See if he can verify what my son says."

"Yes, lord." The warrior left immediately.

"Mikka, find the amber peddler and bring him here. Take some men with you if you like."

"I can handle it on my own, lord," Mikka answered as he too left the room.

"Sasha, find the minstrel and bring him here. Where are the clothes Zuban was wearing?"

"Here, my lord; but they are all wet," Sasha protested.

Browdat picked up the clothes and threw them at his son.

"Put these on."

"They're wet and cold, Father. Must I?"

"Do as I say." Zuban dropped the blanket and donned the soggy clothes, shivering as he did so. "Tell me more about this necklace. How much did it cost you?"

"The amber merchant drives a hard bargain, sir. I paid a silver piece for it."

"He lies," Javik thundered. "I only paid ten coppers."

"Alas, Javik is closer to the peddler's social level and probably speaks the wretch's language better than I," Zuban said using his haughtiest tone. "Either that or he bought one that was much inferior to this perfect specimen."

Browdat's eyebrows rose in response to Zuban's last sentence. "Perhaps that is the case? Did you inspect the amber thoroughly before you paid the man?"

"Oh, yes. It was a flawless piece of the highest quality, Father. You taught me well how to gauge value," Zuban fawned.

As Zuban spoke, Sasha entered the room followed by one of the village men dragging Margan. "He did not want to come, lord, but I insisted." Sasha brandished a rather large piece of firewood.

Margan was visibly shaking in the presence of Browdat and Zuban. Javik thought he might collapse at any moment.

"Tell me, minstrel! Is this the man you saw attack Hella?" Browdat demanded.

"I'm not sure, lord. It was dark, and I was far away," Margan hedged.

"Look closely, man. You saw it happen. Tell me!" Foam from Browdat's mouth flecked his black beard, and the fire in his eyes made Margan's knees wobble.

"Move the candle to the other side of the room, please," Margan asked.

Javik moved behind Browdat and cupped the candle flame with his hand so that Zuban was in the shadows. Margan studied the scene carefully.

"I can't be sure, lord. It looks like him. He's the same height and build. The clothes were dark like his, but I can't be sure."

"Wretch," Browdat bellowed as he raised his hand to strike the minstrel.

"Father, patience," Zuban urged as he stayed the great paw from smashing the singer's face. "The cripple is obviously not a worthy witness. We all know that a physical deformity also affects the mind. He is a simple singer with no wit or intellect. He doesn't even know what he saw."

The insult seemed to trigger something inside Margan. He straightened his back as best he could and jutted out his jaw.

"Yes, it was him. I'll swear to it," Margan's voice was firm now.

"You will have to prove your testimony by trial," Browdat cautioned.

"I am ready," Margan stated with a confidence that Javik had not given him credit for.

"Very well. We will summon the village judges and try this matter now. Sasha, send servants to the judges and have Goldar call off the manhunt. Put on your boots, Zuban, and compose your thoughts if you are able. I want to believe you are innocent, but many things weigh on the scales against you. I will see that you have a fair hearing, but you must stand trial."

"What about Javik?" Zuban pleaded. "He was with her tonight, too."

"Javik will also stand trial at the same time. We will have the truth before the sun rises." Browdat took his son by the arm and shoved him out the door motioning for Javik to follow.

Torches were set up around several tables in the square while the judges assembled. Goldar returned with the men from the search to take his place. Harl would sit in for Browdat since Browdat's son was a defendant. The third judge was old Tahsla, the wisest man in the village and once a respected warrior. Buran, the Law Keeper, sat directly behind the judges ready to provide them with assistance if needed.

Word of the trial soon spread through the village, and Frieda ran to the square, followed closely by Dana. Frieda screamed at the sight of her son in the chair reserved for the one on trial. Javik was seated next to him, which made Dana's heart rise in her throat. Dana approached Browdat.

"My lord, I thought Javik was cleared of this matter by Margan's testimony. Why is he here?"

"He has accused Zuban of the murder, and if Zuban is found innocent, Javik must also be cleared of the crime by this tribunal."

"What about our son?" Frieda wailed clutching her husband's arm.

"He must stand trial against Margan's accusation." Browdat dropped his official pose and led his wife outside of the turmoil where they could speak more privately.

"It doesn't look good for our son, Frieda. Javik found a necklace he bought Hella in Zuban's clothes, and there was blood on Zuban's underwear."

"Javik could have planted that necklace on our son. He hates him." Frieda was grasping for any shred of hope that her son was innocent, though she feared he was not.

"Sasha was with him when Javik found it. He saw it fall from Zuban's clothes. Zuban claimed he bought the necklace, but he said it was flawless while Javik knew there was a fly in the amber. I fear our son may be guilty." Browdat spoke the words with a hoarse voice that almost broke under the realization that his own flesh could commit such a heinous act.

Frieda stared at her husband in disbelief. "You must defend him. You must not let my son be killed," she pleaded.

"He is my son, too, woman," Browdat spoke with the old air of authority in his voice again. "I will do my best to save him, but if he is guilty, I will not beg to have him spared."

"All I ask is that you do your best." Frieda's head dropped

to her chest in resignation. She knew her husband too well to think he would disgrace himself in any matter of honor.

"We still have hope, woman. Javik is a boy, and has no standing at the trial. His evidence will not be heard. The minstrel must withstand the test of the hot blade for his testimony to be believed, and I doubt he can do that. Zuban claims he was with Kamar's daughter all evening, and I have sent for her. If she says she was with him, Zuban may be cleared. I doubt we will be able to find the amber peddler, and I'll suggest he might have been the killer. Have faith in your husband's wisdom, woman."

Chapter 10

Browdat and his servants, along with Zuban, returned to the square, which was now well lit and full of people. The rest of the village crowded around the periphery eager to see the spectacle. Browdat began the trial.

"Respected judges, my niece was cruelly raped and murdered this night. She was seen leaving the festival with Javik, here. Many can attest to that." Several shouts of confirmation from the crowd affirmed his statement, and the judges nodded approval. "When the hour grew late and she did not return, I went with Goldar and some other men to find her, thinking she and Javik may have met with a she bear just out of hibernation. What we found was Hella lying dead, her clothes above her waist and Javik's dagger in her chest." A murmur of concern ran through the crowd.

"Silence," Tahsla called and waited for the noise to abate. "Go on, Browdat."

"In her hand, was a large stone. Javik lay beside her with a swollen knot on the back of his head. It appeared she felled him with her last breath. To me, it was obvious Javik was the killer. I claimed his life and was about to execute him when this minstrel intervened. Tell the judges what you saw, minstrel."

"Come forward, lad," Tahsla called. "Don't be afraid. If you tell the truth, you have nothing to fear."

"Yes, Lord," Margan mumbled.

"Speak up, boy! I don't hear as well as I used to."

"Yes, lord," Margan repeated in a louder tone. "I followed Javik and Hella into the forest thinking to serenade them. I saw the way they looked at each other during the feast, and I knew what they were about." A titter of understanding rippled through the spectators.

"Silence," Tahsla called again.

"I saw someone attack Javik with a large rock. Then, I saw this same person attack Hella."

"Go on, boy," Tahsla prompted.

"I saw no more, sir. I was frightened. I feared the attacker would turn on me next. I ran into the woods to hide, determined to leave as quickly as possible so that I would not be involved. When I heard the crowd screaming for Javik's blood, I knew he was innocent. So, I came back to save his life."

"Who did you see attack the girl?" Tahsla asked.

"It was that man," Margan pointed to Zuban as the crowd sucked in its collective breath.

"He lies, lord," Zuban shouted. "I can explain everything, but first, I insist you put his testimony to the test of fire." The crowd mumbled its concern.

In the flickering light of the torches, Javik could see perspiration breaking out on Margan's forehead. The early morning air was chilled, yet Margan did not notice it. Zuban's face was calm, though the arrogant smile was gone.

"Bring a torch," Browdat called, and a warrior stepped forward carrying a burning brand. Browdat unsheathed his knife and held it in the flames, turning it from side to side for what seemed to be an eternity. Great drops of sweat ran from Margan's nose and chin. He knew what was coming. So did Zuban, and the corners of his mouth began to turn up ever so slightly in anticipation of the minstrel's screams when he grasped the hot blade.

Browdat spit on the blade and watched as his saliva sizzled into steam. He thrust the blade back into the flame and called, "Come here, minstrel."

Margan moved to Browdat, and Javik thought his hump seemed to dominate his whole being. His eyes transmitted the fear coursing through his body, and Javik was almost frightened himself. He had seen this ritual before and had never seen a man pass the test.

"When I present you the knife, boy, you must grasp the blade and repeat your story as you just told it. If you release the blade before you finish, we will know that you lie. Do you understand?"

Margan nodded and held his hands in front of him in a clapping position. They were shaking terribly.

Browdat placed the knife between the trembling palms. Margan looked away from the knife as he closed his hands upon the hot blade. Javik could hear the sizzle and smell the sickly sweet odor of burning flesh, but no sound escaped the minstrel's lips. He thought the singer was going to faint, but he blinked back the pain and began to relate his story again in a voice wavering with repressed reaction to the searing pain in his hands. When he finished, he collapsed in a heap at Browdat's feet.

The crowd was silent, and the judges stared open-mouthed at the twisted boy who survived an ordeal many seasoned warriors failed. Zuban's face was ashen white knowing that Margan's testimony sealed his fate. Javik could only wince at the sight of the red imprint of the dagger on the minstrel's palms. Margan made his living with his hands. Would he ever play again? Goldar spoke for the judges.

"It is enough. I am convinced Zuban is guilty."

"He lies, lord. I was with Kamar's daughter, Gunna, the whole evening. She will swear to it."

"Browdat, have you sent for Kamar and his daughter?" Tahsla asked.

"Yes, lord. He should be here before dawn."

"Is there any other evidence to be presented?" Tahsla intoned.

"There is the bloody underwear, lord," Javik inserted.

Goldar frowned terribly and shook his head at Javik.

"Who are you, boy?" the old judge asked.

"I am Javik, son of Tolda."

"He is a boy not yet through Mauhad," Goldar explained.

"You understand you have no standing in this trial boy. Only men may testify here," Tahsla explained.

"I know that, lord. Still, I can say what I saw. There was blood on Zuban's undergarment. Sasha was there, he can verify what I say."

"Is this true, Sasha?" Tahsla asked the servant.

"Aye, lord. The boy speaks the truth. Here they are." Sasha placed the underwear on the table in front of the judges who took turns inspecting them.

"Can you explain this, Zuban?" Tahsla asked.

"My lord, Kamar's daughter is, or I should say was, a virgin. It is her blood on my underwear." The crowd tittered at the revelation of Zuban's conquest.

"We will know that when she arrives," Tahsla said. "Is there nothing else?"

"The necklace, lord," Javik blurted out again. "Lord Browdat has the necklace."

"Do you have it Browdat?" Tahsla asked.

"Yes, lord; but it is nothing. A trinket my son purchased from an amber merchant at the bazaar."

"I would see it," Tahsla said.

Javik was beginning to feel very uncomfortable. Browdat knew the truth yet he seemed to be holding back. The look of surprise on the warrior's face when the minstrel withstood the test should have alerted Javik to the fact that Browdat was now weighing the life of his youngest son against the truth, and his son was winning. Browdat had no intention of bringing up the necklace if Javik had not called attention to it.

"Here it is, lord. As you can see, it amounts to nothing." Browdat held up the necklace for the crowd to see.

"I gave it to Hella. She had it when we left the village," Javik blurted out as he leaped to his feet.

"Silence, boy. I'll not warn you again. We have been very lenient with you for your father's sake, but our limit has been reached. Keep your piece unless you are asked to say something. Do you understand me?" Tahsla's voice was stern.

"Yes, lord," Javik lowered his head and sat down.

"The lord Kamar is here!" a man in the crowd shouted as a rather small man wearing rich clothes moved through the throng leading a young girl by the hand. She came reluctantly, and the tracks of tears could be seen on her face.

"Hail, Lord Kamar," Tahsla greeted him. "Do you know why we meet here in trial this night?"

"I do, Lord Tahsla. Browdat's man told me all that happened. It is true that Zuban was with my daughter most of the evening. The harlot will tell you of it herself." He flung the girl to the ground in front of the judges. "Tell them!"

The girl began to cry and looked first at Zuban, then at her father, then at the judges.

"Lords, I laid with Zuban in the forest after the feast just as he said." She dropped her head and let the tears flow again. Her body shook with sobs.

Tahsla spoke in a calm tone as he held up Zuban's underwear. "Zuban claims that this is your blood on his underwear. Is that true?"

Gunna mopped the tears from her eyes and faced the old judge squarely. "Yes, lord. Zuban was my first lover."

The crowd erupted in gasps of surprise, and Javik began to believe Zuban would get away with his foul deed after all.

A warrior entered the arena of light from the torches and spoke secretly with Browdat.

"My lords," Browdat spoke. "We have not been able to find the amber seller. I'm afraid we will have to proceed without him."

"He is of little importance," Tahsla waved off the news.

"I suggest, Lord Tahsla, that the amber merchant may have been the person this minstrel saw and not Zuban," Browdat said.

No one noticed Margan raising himself to a sitting position. He stared at his palms, now blistering and swelling badly. He was blinking to regain his faculties, but he came fully alert at Tahsla's last speech.

"My lord! May I speak again?" Margan asked.

"Yes, lad. You have proved that your word is good. Speak!" Tahsla commanded.

"Hella showed me her amber necklace. She was very proud of it, and proud it was a gift from Javik. I believe that is her necklace," he pointed to the pendant still dangling from Browdat's hand.

"It is not hers," Zuban shouted. "I bought that pendant for my mother. I paid a handsome price for it too."

"Lord Tahsla, Hella had no necklace when we found her," Browdat advised.

Javik wanted to scream out his protest, but he knew any

further words from him would only result in punishment from the tribunal.

Goldar caught the significance of Zuban's statement. He picked up the necklace and held it up to the light.

"Describe the necklace you purchased," Goldar asks.

Zuban's smirk began to weaken and his forehead beaded with sweat as he searched for words.

"It was a pendant, much like that one, but a fine piece of flawless amber."

Javik could restrain himself no longer. He leaped to his feet. "May I speak more?"

"If you have some evidence to add concerning the necklace, yes," Tahsla nodded.

"That necklace is the one I bought for Hella. If you will look at it closely, you will see a fly imprisoned in the amber. Zuban didn't mention that."

"It's true, Tahsla. Look for yourself." Goldar hands the pendant to Tahsla

Browdat's head sank to his chest while Zuban's eyes danced with fear.

"That's why it cost me so much," Zuban squealed. "The peddler made a special point of the fly's spirit adding power to the thing."

Tahsla held the stone up to the light then passed it to Harl who did the same. Both men turned to Goldar, and the three conversed in low tones.

Zuban was sweating even more profusely now, and Browdat's eyes betrayed his fear for his son's life. Browdat licked his lips, and his hands clenched and unclenched nervously. Tension hung in the air as even the noisy crowd fell silent.

The judges conferred for what seemed, to Javik, an eternity, but at last they nodded in agreement. Tahsla laid the necklace on the table.

"The stone proves nothing," Tahsla said. "Many amber pieces contain insects. This could be one of dozens the peddler sold in the bazaar. We also give great credit to the Lady Gunna's words. She has shamed herself to help Zuban, and we must respect that."

Margan started to interrupt, but Tahsla raised a hand to stop him.

"In spite of the minstrel's impressive testimony, we must find that there is not enough evidence to convict Zuban. Certainly, his testimony absolves Javik; but we cannot order your son's death on an identification made on a dark night by a frightened minstrel. We must..."

"Wait, Lord Tahsla!" A tall man with a bow and quiver stepped into the light.

"Who are you, and why do you interrupt?" Tahsla demanded.

"My lord, I am Challa, the archer. May I speak?"

"Speak, Challa," Tahsla agreed.

"Gunna could not have caused the blood on Zuban's underwear because she was not a virgin last night."

Again, the crowd gasped; and Gunna cowered at her father's feet. Kamar starred at the warrior in disbelief.

"Why did you not come forward earlier?" Tahsla demanded.

"I feared the wrath of both Lord Browdat and Lord Kamar, sir. I also wanted to protect the lady Gunna, but I could not bear to see Zuban go free on false evidence. I felt I must say that I have lain with her before Zuban."

"And I, too," another man stepped forward.

"And I," a third offered.

"Great Zhou!" Kamar swore. "Is there no one you have not

lain with in this village?" he swore at his daughter.

"I'm sorry, Father," she screamed as the tears flowed freely down her cheeks. "Zuban said he would kill me if I did not tell the story as he wished."

"Shut up, wench!" Zuban screamed.

The scene became chaos. The crowd growled angrily in response to the damning testimony and surged toward Zuban only to be held off by the warriors around him. Gunna sobbed hysterically at her father's feet while he swore even more violently. It took Browdat's gruff voice to calm the storm.

"Hear me! Hear me!" the huge lord demanded. The square fell silent.

The big warrior looked at his son with sad eyes, and his chin trembled as he opened his mouth to speak. "My son is guilty."

The crowd gasped in disbelief at a father convicting his own son.

"Tell us how you know that, Browdat," Tahsla commanded.

"Javik summoned me to see the evidence he and Sasha found when they were putting Zuban to bed. I saw the bloody underwear and Javik showed me the fly in the stone. Zuban knew none of this. He was asleep in a drunken stupor. After I awakened him, I asked him about the necklace; but I did not tell him about the fly. He told me the peddler had demanded a premium price for the item because it was flawless. He knows full well that amber cannot be considered flawless if it contains an insect. He had no knowledge of the fly."

"Father, what are you doing? You know I didn't kill anyone. This woman was a virgin, I swear it. Challa hates me. You all know that. It's all lies - all lies." His voice trailed off to match the silence of the stunned crowd. Only Gunna's sobs broke the quiet. The judges stared blankly at Browdat.

Zuban's gaze traveled from face to face seeking an ally, but each one was set in a grim scowl.

"Father...help me," he gasped.

"I cannot help you, my son. I thought I might be able to save you from death by telling only a part of the truth, but one look at this boy's hands told me I was wrong." Browdat nodded toward Margan. "I'm sorry, but I have to do the honorable thing." Tears streamed from Browdat's eyes as he turned from his son. Frieda rushed from the crowd to embrace her husband.

"My lord, you cannot condemn your own son. Say you lied," she pleaded.

"I will not, my wife. As much as I love you and our son, I will not lie to save him from the fate he deserves." Browdat turned to the judges. "He is yours to deal with now."

Frieda broke into a high-pitched wail. "My son, my son," she screamed as Browdat dragged her away.

Noticing the crowd was distracted by his mother's tragic scene, Zuban made a break for it, but two husky warriors soon subdued him.

"Lords, you cannot believe all of this!" Zuban shouted. "I am Zuban, son of Browdat. I have killed many enemies. Three Sentii heads now lie on Verna's altar. I am innocent!"

"Silence, Zuban," Tahsla commanded. Zuban's lip quivered, and the crowd waited in deadly silence. Tahsla, again, conferred with the other judges then turned back to the captive.

"Zuban, son of Browdat, this court finds you guilty of the rape and murder of Hella. We condemn you to death by the fire."

"No, no," Zuban cried. "I am the son of a lord. You may not burn me!" he screamed in abject terror.

Goldar leaned over to Tahsla and whispered in his ear. The old man nodded and turned back to Zuban.

"Goldar has asked mercy for you. You deserve the sword by

birthright, but by bringing such dishonor on Browdat's house, you have forfeited that privilege. However, we will leave the matter to Javik. He was the one falsely accused of your crime. What say you, Javik?"

Javik's mouth fell open. He looked at Zuban then back to the judges.

"I am but a boy. I have no standing in this court," he insisted.

"We have asked your opinion, and you must obey," Tahsla solemnly intoned.

Burning was what Zuban deserved. He had only seen one such execution in his short lifetime, and it made him sick. The screams of the dying man still came back to him in nightmares from time to time. If Zuban burned, he would have some time to contemplate Hella's pain and suffering before he died. It was only fair to Hella, but it was not in his heart to burden Browdat with the image of his son burning alive. The great warrior did not deserve that. He had been brave enough to convict his son out of his own mouth. Surely that counted for something.

"I say that Zuban must die by the sword," Javik spoke firmly looking the condemned man in the eye as he said it.

Zuban's knees buckled beneath him, and the warriors strained to hold him upright. "Thank you, Javik. Thank you," Zuban sobbed.

"So be it!" Tahsla pronounced the final words. "The execution will be here in the square when the sun stands overhead. Zuban! Take what time you have left to pray for your soul and to comfort your father. This court is dismissed."

Chapter 11

The crowd dispersed as the warriors led Zuban off to be held until his execution. Javik found Margan sitting at a table crying softly. He looked up when Javik put a hand on his shoulder.

"My hands are ruined, Javik. How will I live now?"

"Come with me. My mother is a good healer, and I'm sure she can do something." He helped Margan to his feet and led him over to Dana who was doing her best to console Frieda.

"Mother, will you help Margan?" Javik asked in a soft voice as he nodded towards the minstrel's hands.

"Of course, Son. Take him to the longhouse, and I will be with him as soon as I can." Dana returned her attention to Frieda. Javik led Margan to the rear door to avoid a confrontation with the grieving Browdat.

Dana tried her best to comfort Frieda, but she was inconsolable.

"My son will be killed like a common criminal," she wailed.

"Frieda, he dishonored your house," Dana pleaded. "He only receives a just punishment."

"I appreciate Javik saving him from the flames, Dana. Your son is a good boy, but so was my Zuban at his age. Where did I do wrong, Dana?"

"It wasn't your fault, Frieda. Each man chooses his own way in life. We can only show our children the right path. We cannot force them to follow it."

"I know what you say is true, but it doesn't help my shame and grief. Poor Browdat, he had such hopes for Zuban. Our other boys are all warriors to be proud of, but he thought Zuban would be a leader. He's crushed, Dana. I fear he won't recover." Frieda broke into uncontrollable sobs again.

"Let me take you home, Frieda. You need to comfort your husband now. We women must be strong at times like this."

"You're right, Dana. Help me home."

As soon as the women entered the longhouse, Javik approached his mother. "Mother," he whispered to her. "Will you look at Margan's hands? He needs your help desperately."

Dana turned to Frieda and said, "Frieda, I must help Javik's friend Margan. Will you be all right until I can return? It should only be a few minutes."

Frieda nodded her head in approval and put on a brave face for her husband's sake. "Go help the minstrel. He's suffered wrongly."

Dana followed her son back to her room to find Margan sitting on a straw pallet staring at his swollen hands. He looked up as they entered but said nothing.

"Let me see your hands, Margan," Dana said softly.

The minstrel held them out for her inspection, and Dana winced at the sight.

"They will need much care, but I think I can cure them. You must stay with me until they are healed."

"I cannot pay you or Lord Browdat for my keep," Margan admitted.

"I will share my food with you," Dana said. "Perhaps you can earn your keep by singing for the lord?"

"I cannot play, lady," Margan said as he held up his hands to show the damage.

"Your voice is not burned. The songs will be enough until you can play again. I think Sasha can play a little. Perhaps you can teach him some of your songs."

Dana moved to a shelf full of clay jars and carefully blended the contents of several into a small bowl. Returning to Margan, she spread the paste over his palms.

"That feels better already, my lady," Margan smiled.

"We must wrap them well. Javik, get me the bolt of white cloth in that cabinet, over there." She pointed to a large, wooden cabinet on the opposite wall. Javik found the cloth and brought it to his mother who wrapped Margan's hands carefully.

"There! We must apply the salve daily and change the bandages every other day. Do not let me forget," she nagged Margan.

"I have only one problem, madam," Margan said with a look of consternation on his face.

"What is that?" Dana asked.

"How will I be able to relieve myself?"

Dana laughed as Javik remembered her laughing while his father lived. It brought blessed relief from the heavy burden of the past night. "You will have to have one of the servants help you. If no one is around, find me."

Margan blushed beet red. "Lady! I would not embarrass you so."

"Don't be a fool! I have seen men before and wiped his bottom many times," Dana nodded her head toward Javik as she wiped the salve from her hands. She left the room to return to Frieda.

"Thank you, Javik," Margan smiled.

"It is I who must thank you," Javik said as he embraced the minstrel. If you had not come back to tell your story, I would be lying dead by now."

Javik looked up at the smoke hole in the ceiling. "When the sun is in the hole above, Zuban will die by the sword. Rest for a while. I will come for you when it is time."

"No, I have no stomach for such things. I'll stay here," Margan replied.

"I'll talk to you again afterwards, then," Javik patted the minstrel on his shoulder and left by the back entrance. He needed some time to himself to digest the events of the night. He walked into the forest and found a clearing with a convenient stump that made a fine stool.

The birds were chasing each other through the trees, and Javik knew they would soon mate. He felt the first stirring of manhood within him when he sat by the river with Hella, but there had been no time to enjoy such feelings. The terror he felt knowing he was about to die horribly drove all thoughts of women from his mind. Now that he was safe, he began to remember how lovely she was. Would he ever find another woman to equal her?

The sweet memory of the girl he knew for so short a time faded, and the thought of Zuban's execution took its place. Poor Zuban. He could feel pity for the wretch even though he hated him – to die so young and so shamefully. Javik was ready to die in battle, but he could not fathom being executed. How horrible Browdat must feel. His own flesh and blood was to be struck down in its prime for an act of cowardice and lust. Javik said a prayer of thanks to his father for instilling in him the sense of honor and integrity that kept even the thought of such actions out of his mind.

The crack of a twig behind him caused Javik to turn abruptly and reach for his dagger, but it was only Grazhda.

"Grazhda, you should not surprise people like that. If I had been a warrior, you might have been killed."

The old hag cackled merrily. "I do not fear warriors. It is warriors who fear me, but you are in no danger, son of Tolda. You have had quite and adventure this holiday."

"It is a sad holiday."

"Sad? How can it be sad when your enemy is soon to die a shameful death?"

"My father often told me never to be grateful for the misfortune of others."

"Tolda was a wise man, but he, too, was glad to see his enemies fall. Zuban's heads will rot away on Verna's altar, and the worms and crows will feast on his trophies, but Javik's wand will grow into a great tree, and the trophies he brings will not rot away. There is more to come on this holiday than you dream of, Javik. Remember Grazhda when you come into your true inheritance."

Javik was about to reply when a stag crashed into the clearing and caused him to turn away from the old woman. It bounded away swiftly, but when he looked back the hag was gone. He could only hear the sound of her shrill laughter dying in the distance.

Many things passed through the young man's head as he sat in the clearing contemplating Grazhda's remarks. What was his "true inheritance?" He had what little his father left him. The old woman made no sense. She was as crazy as everyone said she was, but he could not shake the nagging doubt in his mind. What did she know that he did not?

It was growing warmer by the moment, and Javik noted the nearly overhead position of the sun. It was time.

A crowd had already gathered around the posts that would have been Javik's fate but for Margan. Tahsla, Goldar, Browdat and the other warriors of the village were assembled as witnesses, but none of the women were there. Zuban was led in by two warriors and bound to one of the posts.

Zuban's eyes showed the effects of long hours of crying and his lower lip quivered in fear. Saliva ran from the corner of his mouth, and mucous dripped from his nose. He was naked from the waist up, and though the morning was chilly, sweat ran down his hairless chest.

Tahsla spoke. "Zuban, son of Browdat, you have been found guilty of heinous crimes that cry for your death in revenge. What have you to say?"

Zuban seemed to compose himself at this point and stood straight for the first time since he appeared.

"I wish to tell my father that I am sorry for dishonoring his house, and I ask Javik's forgiveness for making him appear to be guilty of my crimes." He turned to face Javik who nodded his agreement.

"I apologize to the village for bringing such sorrow upon it at a time when it should be merry. Finally, I pray Hella may forgive me. That is all I have to say." His head slumped back on his chest, and his body sagged against the ropes holding him to the post. His final statement consumed his last ounce of courage, but it was a good speech. Perhaps it would ease his father's pain a bit.

Javik looked at the big war leader, but he saw only a grim face. It must be taking every ounce of the great man's strength to maintain his composure in the face of his son's death. He only nodded agreement in response to Zuban's statement.

It was the custom of the Berglauni that the warriors of a village should draw lots for the duty of executioner any time such a penalty was called for. This lot fell to Mikka who now stepped forward carrying his long sword. As he approached Zuban, Browdat stepped forward.

"Here, Mikka. Use this sword instead." Browdat handed the warrior the family's ceremonial sword and took the warrior's weapon. "If my son is to die, his life blood should be shed by the sacred weapon of his clan."

Mikka hefted the ornate weapon and felt its edge. He nodded his approval to Browdat who resumed his position with the other warriors.

Mikka moved to Zuban and placed his hand on the victim's chest to find the heartbeat. Zuban flinched in response to the touch but did not open his eyes. Once more, Zuban summoned his last bit or courage to stand erect. As the cold point of the sword touched Zuban's skin, Javik saw a dark stain spread from Zuban's crotch. The crowd began to mumble, and Javik could see Browdat wince.

Mikka noticed the reaction and acted quickly. He thrust the sword into Zuban's chest directly below his hand. Zuban's eyes popped open in surprise as he sucked in a deep breath and strained against the ropes. He did not cry out, and his head remained erect as Mikka moved the sword to cut into the heart. Blood gushed from Zuban's mouth and nose, and he choked twice spraying his blood on Mikka. The warrior did not flinch but withdrew the sword and stepped back two paces. Javik was surprised to see very little blood coming from the sword wound. Zuban's head fell on to his chest – the blood pouring from his face and cascading down his body as it slumped against the ropes. He was still now.

Tahsla moved to the limp body and placed his hand on Zuban's neck for a moment. The only sound was the singing of the birds, so merrily oblivious to the tragedy below them. The crowd was as silent as Zuban's heart.

"He is dead," Tahsla pronounced. The crowd exhaled as one and began to disperse. There would now be two burials this day, and time was needed to prepare.

Browdat stepped to his son's body and wept openly. Goldar was with him, his arm around the big man's shoulder. Mikka wiped the sword clean and handed it to Browdat in exchange for his own.

"I am sorry I had to be the one, Lord Browdat," Mikka knelt before him.

"Rise, Mikka. You only did what you had to do. I hold no malice toward you," Browdat offered his hand to the warrior who took it in a firm grip before he embraced the father of his victim.

Goldar spoke. "You know my feelings, friend."

"You are a fair man, Goldar, and I'm glad you were one of the men on my son's tribunal."

Goldar embraced the big man before leaving the scene of the execution, fighting back tears.

Sasha appeared with another manservant.

"May we take him now, lord?" he asked Browdat.

"Yes, clean him up for burial. I will show you the things to be buried with him in a moment."

The servants untied the body and carried it back to Browdat's longhouse where it would lie next to Hella until time for the burial ceremony. Javik approached Browdat.

"Lord Browdat, I am sorry for the death of your son," he offered as he knelt down.

"Rise, Javik. Neither do I bear you any malice. My family has offended you greatly, and it is I who am in your debt now. I ask your forgiveness for my son."

Javik rose to face the great war leader. "You have it gladly, lord. My mother and I are grateful for your protection."

"You have that as long as I live. It is small payment for my son's wrongs against you." The war leader smothered the boy in a great bear hug, and Javik could feel the hot tears on the lord's cheek.

"Come, Javik. We must prepare for the burials," Browdat said wiping the tears from his face. In spite of all his efforts to hold them back, Javik's tears began to flow also.

"We must compose ourselves, Javik. You will soon be a warrior, and I am setting a bad example for you."

"My Lord, you have given me a fine example of what a war leader should be. Tolda, my father, often said that a man who does not cry when faced with a loss such as you have suffered is no man."

"You are truly Tolda's son, Javik. I think we men are sometimes too quick to hide our emotions for fear of being considered weak. There will be times when you are a leader of men when you must steel yourself against fear and sorrow, but those will be times of battle. There will be no battle today, only burials."

The big man and the young warrior-to-be walked side-by-side to the longhouse in silence.

The women were already busy preparing Zuban's body for burial. It had been cleaned up and his best clothes were laid out beside him. He looked so harmless and boyish lying there, but Javik remembered the bully he knew in life even though he felt some pity for Zuban. Browdat went into Zuban's room and returned with a helmet, sword, shield and several personal items to be buried with his son. It was then Javik remembered the pendant.

Tahsla gave him the amber necklace after the trial and Javik knew what he must do with it. He found Hella's body and stood next to her surveying the ravages of death. She was so pale now, and her skin was beginning to sag around her face; yet, she was still beautiful. "Oh Hella, I might have loved you," he whispered. "You were so innocent and wanted so little." He took the necklace from his purse and held it before her unseeing eyes. "You loved this trinket so much. Wear it in the next life and remember Javik when I come to join the wanderers under the earth." Javik tied the leather thong around her tiny neck and positioned the amber pendant on her bosom; then, he fell to his knees and wept.

* * * * *

The burials were finished, and the birds in the budding trees sang merrily as he walked down the path to the river. What did they know of sorrow? How lucky they are, Javik thought. He sat down on the same log he and Hella had shared and let the tears flow freely. They were as much for Zuban as for Hella. He had not liked Zuban, but he was still from Javik's village and the son of the lord who protected his mother.

The crack of a twig on the path behind him broke his melancholy, and he turned to see Browdat approaching. The big man had also been crying, though he had been a rock for Frieda during the burials. His voice was hoarse and weak.

"May I join you, Javik?"

"Yes, sir," Javik replied, moving over to make room on the log.

Browdat sat down and placed his arm around Javik's shoulders.

"We have both lost much this holiday. It was supposed to be a glad time, but it brought such sorrow instead."

"How is the lady Frieda?" Javik asked.

"She still mourns, and I cannot console her. I saw you go into the forest, and I decided to follow. Perhaps I can give you some comfort."

"It is I who should comfort you, sir," Javik protested.

"Yours has been a double loss – a niece and a son."

"The niece I still mourn, but I have no more tears for my son."

Javik looked at the scarred hand on his shoulder and placed his hand on top of it. "Zuban was drunk, sir. I'm sure of that. He would never have done what he did if he were sober."

Browdat pulled back his arm and turned away from Javik. "You're wrong, Javik. I failed to see my son's faults until it was too late. I could have changed him if I had taken a firmer hand in his upbringing, but I could not bear to discipline him harshly. He was a child of our older years and very precious to his mother. I'm afraid we both loved him too much and indulged him to excess. I hoped the responsibilities of manhood would change him, but he only got worse. I should have seen this coming."

Browdat buried his face in his hands. Javik thought he might cry, but the big warrior only brushed back his hair and stared at the river in silence.

"You were a good friend to my father, sir; and I am grateful to you for taking us in when he was killed. I'm afraid it is the only consolation I can offer."

Browdat smiled for the first time and turned to face Javik. "I have been thinking about this a great deal, Javik. Browdat sat for a moment searching for the right words. Finally, they burst forth as if from a broken dam. "I want you to be my son, Javik, and take the place of the one who dishonored my house. I want to adopt you and your mother as part of my family. There would be no inheritance for you. All I have will go to Ivan, my oldest son; but you will have my heritage as well as Tolda's. What say you?"

Javik was speechless. His father's heritage was significant, but that plus the honor of Browdat's house would place a heavy responsibility on his shoulders. He wondered if anyone should be asked to bear such a burden of expectations, but it meant he and his mother would be part of a lord's family and no longer wards of the King. Even Sigurd would have to acknowledge his status when he returned to the house of Tao Shan.

"Thank you, Lord Browdat," Javik almost stuttered. "I am honored, sir, and I accept if my mother is also in agreement."

"Good boy, Javik. The Lady Dana has already agreed." Browdat's face beamed as he, once more, enfolded Javik in a bear hug.

* * * * *

The remainder of Javik's time at home was clouded by the deaths of Hella and Zuban. Browdat seemed to recover somewhat, but Frieda still cried every day. Almost anything that reminded her of her son would cause the tears to flow. Dana tried to console her with the fact that Browdat had adopted Javik, and she now had a new son to care for, but it did not seem to help.

The day arrived for Javik to return to Tao Shan, and he was pleased to be returning to his lessons. The somber mood of Browdat's house had overshadowed the pleasure of seeing his mother and his old friends again. As he was saying his good-byes, Browdat approached holding a rather ornate dagger.

"Take this, Javik, my son. It has been in our family for many generations and earned glory for all who wore it. I want you to have it now." He held out the beautiful weapon in both hands.

Javik recognized the dagger. "Wasn't this Zuban's dagger?"

"Yes, he disgraced it; but I know you will restore its luster."

Javik unhooked his belt. With trembling hands, he removed his dagger and placed it on the table beside him. Taking the new weapon from Browdat's rough paws, he slid it carefully along the leather to its appointed position and re-fastened the belt. His eyes stayed riveted to the beautiful dagger for a moment, then a large hand turned his chin away. The look of pride on Browdat's face warmed Javik's heart. Now he was truly the great man's son.

"I am honored, lord," Javik bowed.

"You bow to me no more, Javik. You are my son now. Call me Father."

"Yes, Father," Javik almost whispered.

Browdat embraced his new son and held him at arm's length to inspect him.

"You are a fine boy. Learn well at Tao Shan's house so that you may bring honor on the names of Tolda and Browdat."

"Yes, sir...I mean, Father," Javik happily corrected himself.

Margan was waiting by the door as Javik and his mother walked out. The bandages on his hands were fresh, and he seemed to be able to move them more freely now.

"Your mother is a miracle worker, Javik. By the next time you see me, I will be playing again."

"I hope you will stay that long," Javik laughed.

"Lord Browdat has asked me to be the minstrel for his house. I will be here a long time."

"Then I will look forward to hearing you sing my praise as a warrior," Javik chided.

"I already have composed a song about you and Hella and Zuban, but I dare not sing it for some time to come."

Javik embraced the minstrel who returned the hug as best his bandaged hands would allow.

"Farewell, Javik, son of Tolda and Browdat."

"Farewell, Margan the minstrel. When I am a warrior, I will bring you the gold you deserve for saving my life."

"You owe me nothing, Javik. All I ask is your protection and your friendship."

"You have that forever," Javik smiled.

Dana interrupted their farewell. "It is time for you to go, Javik."

"Yes, Mother. Goodbye Margan."

"Study hard at Tao Shan's, Javik."

Javik and his mother walked together down the path to Tao Shan's longhouse.

"Are you content with us being part of Browdat's house now, Javik?"

"Yes, Mother. I know of my new father's regard for you, and with Zuban gone, I have no fear for your safety."

"Will you be happy to stay at Browdat's hearth and to wait for our own hearth until after you are a warrior?"

"I think I can wait now. We have been more fortunate than I could have imagined, Mother. The gods must truly smile upon us."

"Yes, Javik, Zhou is good."

They walked on in silence a while before Dana waved a tearful goodbye to the son who made her heart warm with pride. "Tolda, you have taught him well," she whispered to the soft clouds above.

Chapter 12

Javik opened the door of Tao Shan's longhouse to find an empty room. Evidently, he was the first one back. The memories of the spring festival made him shudder. What horrible things happened during what should have been a festive time. He placed his things in their designated spots inside the cubicle he shared with Noka. How trivial this was, he thought. What did it matter where he placed his tunics or foot wrappings? He was alive and Zuban was dead; what else mattered? Browdat's house still rang with the sobs of Frieda and the servants, and he was worried about the polish on his boots. He was about to go in search of the other boys when Noka appeared in the doorway.

"Javik!" he shouted as he dropped his burden and ran to embrace his roommate, nearly knocking him down in the process.

"I heard about the killing in your village, and they said you'd been executed, but here you are! I'm so happy to see you!"

"I'm glad to be here. The god of death was so close to me, I could smell his breath."

"Tell me all about it. What happened? Some amber peddler said a young boy, one of Tao Shan's pupils, was to be killed by the death of a hundred cuts, but he did not stay to see it. He said he feared they would accuse him of the murder and left the village as soon as the body was discovered."

"That amber peddler saved my life, in a way," Javik said.

"How could he do that?"

Javik told his story as Noka sat on the straw pallet with wide eyes and half-open mouth.

"What an adventure! The other boys will be green with envy."

"It was a horrible experience. Watching a man die is not something to brag about."

"Still, the others will want to hear the whole story, too. I can't wait for tonight."

At that point, Sigurd entered the room and all conversation stopped.

"I see the rumors of your death are not true, Javik. In my village we heard you'd been executed. Too bad they were only rumors."

The smirk on Sigurd's face made Javik want to plunge his dagger deep into that arrogant chest, but Tao Shan appeared behind Sigurd causing Javik to think better of the idea.

"Javik! Come into my apartments," the mentor commanded.

Sigurd turned at the sound of the voice and made way for Javik to follow the master.

Tao Shan was silent until they were inside his private rooms.

"Sit down, Javik," Tao Shan indicated a wooden chair, and Javik complied.

"I heard what happened in the village. Is there anything you wish to tell me?"

"No, master. It was a very sad time, and I'd like to forget it."

"Don't ever forget it, Javik."

The old man's eyes were as grim as Javik had ever seen them, and his voice rang with such gravity that Javik started at this statement. Surely, such things should be put into the past as quickly as possible.

"I don't understand, Master."

"Browdat did a courageous thing in condemning his own son. You should learn from that, but you should also learn a lesson about men. Men must sometimes be punished severely, and it is the poor leader who flinches from this duty. Examples must be set so that others will not follow in the footsteps of the criminal. War is a terrible thing, but when you command warriors you must be sure they will obey. Even one man shirking his duty can make the difference between defeat and victory. When you are in command, Javik, many will follow you because you have been given authority. Many more will follow if you are a good leader, someone who demonstrates the honesty and integrity you showed during the ordeal. But even the basest of men will follow because they are more afraid of you than the enemy. Do you understand now?"

"Yes, Master," Javik whispered as he bowed his head. Was this what it meant to be a leader? Had his father been like this? Must men be flogged and executed to achieve discipline? Perhaps he should become a hermit and find a place deep in the forest where men would not bother him, and he would not have to bother with them?

Tao Shan seemed to sense the boy's thoughts. "A leader who shrinks from disciplining his men is weak. He takes the easy way. It is hard to lead, Javik; but there is nothing more thrilling than having men follow you into battle. Nothing is more satisfying than the respect of your fellow men, and that is only gained through strong leadership. I feel sorry for any man who follows all his life. He may achieve great things in many ways, but he never knows the true bond between a leader and his men. Lead, Javik; and know the respect and love that only strong leaders know."

Javik looked up at the wrinkled face. How many deaths had those eyes seen? They reflected a hundred scenes of pain and suffering.   Yet, they also glowed with a pride transcending tragedy. He had seen the same look in his father's eyes when his men cheered him and raised toasts to him after raids. The confidence of Goldar, and the royal manner of the King gave credence to Tao Shan's words. Javik made up his mind then and there he would lead well when the time came to do so. He wanted what these men had, and anything less would be failure of the most awful kind.

"I understand, Master."   Javik responded with a new firmness in his voice and a light in his eyes that made the old mentor smile.

"Did your father ever speak to you of the animal spirits?"

"Yes, Master. He told me which spirit resides in each animal."

"Did he ever ask you to follow one of those spirits?"

"He did. He told me to always follow the example of the eagle."

"Why did he choose that animal spirit?"

"The eagle is a very dignified bird. He is the master of the air and moves where he pleases. His keen eyes see all below him, and he swoops upon his prey with blinding speed and total surprise. My father said I should learn these lessons from the eagle."

"Tolda was wise, but I will give you an animal spirit to follow also, if you will permit me."

"Certainly, Master. Which spirit is that?"

"I give you the wolf, Javik."

"The wolf?" Javik was surprised by his master's selection. No one followed the wolf spirit.

"Don't be shocked. The wolf has many lessons to teach a

warrior. Study the wolf's actions carefully, and we will speak of it again in the future. Now go and join the others." Tao Shan smiled secretly as Javik left the room. This boy would outshine his father; he was sure of that.

Javik started to cross the sand floor when he heard Sigurd's voice.

"Javik, come here," the boy called.

Javik looked up to see Sigurd and two of his friends on the other side of the arena. He moved toward them ready to defend himself.

"What do you want, Sigurd?" Javik asked wearily.

Much to his surprise, the older boy embraced him warmly then quickly stepped back with a smile curving his mouth. "I embrace you now as an equal, Javik, son of Browdat; but that does not mean that I have any higher opinion of you."

Javik didn't quite know how to respond to this turn of events. "Go to hell, Sigurd," was all he could manage.

Javik was almost angrier at Sigurd's condescension than he had been at his contempt. To Sigurd they were now equals in status but not in standing. Javik winced at the memory of his defeat by this arrogant boy and vowed he would change that situation as soon as possible.

"Be on your guard, Sigurd," Javik pushed between clenched teeth. "I have looked death in the eye, and I now fear no mortal."

Sigurd stood for a moment stunned by the remark. Javik pushed his way past the three boys and returned to his room.

Chapter 13

The next weeks were spent on more weapons and tactics training. Each boy became an expert with sword, bow and pike. Javik took to the sword immediately. His father was an excellent teacher, but Tao Shan's servants proved to be much more formidable than even his father. Javik guessed that each one of them had once been a great warrior in his own right.

The lessons Javik hated continued at an even greater pace. He was grateful when geography and history replaced math and writing. A very old man seemed to appear out of nowhere to teach these subjects. Javik had not seen him before in Tao Shan's house, and one of the other boys said he came from a village far away. He was incredibly old with hair the color of snow and a long beard reaching nearly to his waist. His face was as wrinkled as tree bark, and when he opened his mouth, only a few teeth showed, but his eyes were steely gray and declared an intolerance for nonsense that any boy ignored at his peril.

"My name is Bandor, and I have lived for over 80 winters. I have fought my share of battles, but the scars are now hidden in wrinkles. Any boy who ignores my teaching will find he is doubly the fool. First, he will feel the cane of Tao Shan, but more importantly, he will feel the sting of death later in his life when he blunders into a situation he could have avoided had he paid close attention to me. Learn well, young warriors. We will start with geography."

Bandor ignored the collective groan from the boys and pulled down a large map from the ceiling.

"This is Gaida, the land where all men live." He used a pointer to indicate a large mass of land surrounded by what appeared to be symbols for water, fish and monsters of horrible aspect.

"It is surrounded by a vast salt sea called by different names in different countries." The pointer tapped six names spaced around the massive continent.

"Here is Berglaundia." Bandor tapped the pointer near the center of the continent on a space tinted pink to contrast it from the rest of the map.

Javik thought his country was quite small. It never occurred to him how large it was with respect to other lands. Some of the lands to the north were much larger – almost three or four times the size of his. It suddenly dawned on him that his people were in great danger should such large nations decide to invade. As if anticipating Javik's thoughts, Bandor explained the problem.

"Don't let the size of these other nations fool you. Here we have Sentius, the land of our enemy the Sentii," he tapped the map north of Berglaundia. "It looks quite large, but most of it is desert or dry plains and unable to support large populations. The Sentii are nomadic people who have few large cities. They live by herding sheep and horses."

Noka's hand rose to ask a question.

"Yes, Noka," Bandor recognized him.

"Sir, how is it that the Sentii can keep horses in a desert? Horses need much grain and water."

"Good question. They have many wells in the desert in places known only to them. These wells also have stores of grain hidden in the ground near them. This part of Sentius," Bandor pointed to an area shaded in green, "is quite fertile. The horses are raised, and the grain is grown there."

"Are those the mountains that shield us from the Sentii?" another student asked pointing to a series of marks on the map.

"Yes they are the Mestra Mountains. This peak, called Verus, is the home of Zhou, the protector god of the Berglauni. Notice this land to the west." Bandor pointed to an area shaded in purple. "It is Wallandia. Wallandia is a land quite similar to Berglaundia. In fact, they are closely related to us since many of our families can trace their ancestors back to the time when King Gustav and his brother Mildor quarreled over the throne of Berglaundia two hundred years ago. Mildor was forced into exile in the land of the Wallas along with his loyal followers. The Walla were a very primitive people who lived by hunting and gathering wild berries, nuts and roots. They had no steel weapons or armor, and they lived a tribal life. Mildor and his men slaughtered them nearly to a man, but they spared the women and children. Over the years, they inter-married and produced a nation from the loose tribal bonds of the conquered peoples. They are now almost as strong as the Berglauni from which they came."

"My family can count members in the royal line of Wallandia," Sigurd boasted.

"I'm sure several of the boys here can say the same, Sigurd if they but searched the archives. The records are quite clear for nearly every family in Berglaundia." Bandor smiled at Sigurd, but Javik felt the old man was just a bit peeved at the snob.

So, many in Berglaundia are related to the Walla. That fortune teller was impressed by my Wallan coin, and she said I'd find Wallandia someday. I could be a Wallan prince and never know it. That would make Sigurd mad if I were. Javik snickered at his thought.

"Is something funny, Javik?" Bandor asked.

"No, sir. I'm sorry, sir."

Bandor turned back to the map, but there were more questions.

"Have you ever seen the great salt sea?" another boy asked.

"Oh yes, it is quite a sight. The waves crash upon the rocks making a sound louder than thunder in some places while in others they wash gently upon sparkling beaches of golden sand. As far as your eyes can see there is no end to it, and it is filled with frightening monsters able to consume a grown man in one gulp."

"Oohh," the boys responded in unison.

"Yet, there are some people, like the Aropeans here," he tapped the map on a blue patch on the coast, "who venture out into the sea in boats to catch the smaller fish."

"Are they boats like the ones we use on the lake?" Noka asked.

"No, they are much larger. If they were so small as our boats, the monsters would devour boat, man and all."

"Do they use lines or nets?" another boy asked.

"Both, but mostly nets. They make large catches and bring them back to shore to smoke or dry the fish for use during the winter months. They also sell the dried and smoked fish to other nations in trade."

"My mother has a necklace she says is made from sea creatures," Sigurd inserted.

"Yes, they collect the shells of sea creatures that wash up on the shore and make many beautiful things from them."

"Where is amber found?" Javik asked.

"Here, far to the North." Bandor pointed out a large land bordering the great sea. Many rivers crossed it running from a large range of mountains to the South. Javik calculated that it would take several weeks of hard marching to reach that land, and he understood why amber was so valuable.

"The people there call themselves Ruzz and speak a very strange language. I've never been there, but I have talked to several of them who make their living by selling amber in our land," Bandor explained.

"We are surrounded by mountains," one of the boys observed.

"Correct! These to the south of us form a large circle with the Mestra Mountains creating a natural barrier against invaders. This is the Sachan range, and it is almost impassable from the south. This has kept the powerful Tallans from invading Berglaundia. The passes are quite narrow and closed nearly the year round. They are only open for a few weeks in the summer when Tallan traders come to sell us the sweet fruit they grow there and trade for gold and precious stones."

"My father says the mountains do not protect us from Wallandia," Sigurd inserted.

"He is right, Sigurd. Here is the high moor country of Wallandia." Bandor pointed to a break in the mountains. "The land is rocky and not fertile. It serves as natural boundary between our nations along with the river Callistra, which the Wallans call the Walla. Armies can certainly march across the moors easily if they are well supplied, but the river is a formidable barrier. It is often very high and always very swift running."

"Show us the master's country," Harld asked.

Bandor moved his pointer to the far eastern part of the continent and indicated an area marked "Unknown Territory."

"We know little about this part of our world except for the information Master Tao Shan and his fellows have provided for us. We know the great ocean also laps on its shores, but only this small part," he indicated an area marked in light brown, "is known to Tao Shan."

"How did the Master come to Berglaundia?" one boy asked.

"You must get him to tell you that story." Bandor smiled at the request, knowing Tao Shan was very guarded about his past.

The days went on with the boys learning about the nations bordering their own, and Bandor telling them of many wonderful and miraculous things in those strange lands. Javik found the stories fascinating, but had no urge to travel outside of his own land to see them. Still, it was good to know of the lands beyond the mountains, particularly the Sentii and Wallan lands. Perhaps someday he would see a good deal of Sentius.

Chapter 15

The summer waned too quickly, and the time of Mauhad approached too slowly for the boys at Tao Shan's house. The mentor would soon announce which of the students qualified for the manhood trial. Each boy hoped his name would be posted on the master's door at the appointed time.

There was little time for conflict between Javik and Sigurd now. On top of an already heavy schedule, Tao Shan began pushing his physical conditioning program to the next level. The boys could barely move by the time they sank into their beds in the evening.

At last, the day came for the announcement. As was his custom, Tao Shan posted the names of the boys selected for Mauhad on the door to his rooms at sunrise. None of them needed to be awakened that morning. Javik found himself behind a cluster of eager boys scanning the list.

"I'm on it!" Harld shouted with glee as he danced into the center of the arena.

"You're on it too, Sigurd," Noka intoned in a monotonous voice.

"I would have been shocked if I were not," Sigurd replied half bored.

"What about me, Noka?" Javik called.

"Neither you nor I are on the list, Javik," Noka's voice reflected the disappointment he felt for Javik. Noka knew he would not be selected, but he felt confident Javik's name would be there in spite of his short time with Tao Shan. Javik knew as much as any of the boys selected and was just as good with any of the weapons. Noka made his way out of the press to Javik's side.

"I'm sorry, Javik. I thought sure you'd be on the list."

"It's all right. The master is wise. I respect his judgment." Javik said the words, but he didn't believe them. He felt betrayed, and he was hard pressed to hold back the tears. It would be another year before he could take his place among the warriors.

As the selected boys celebrated, Javik wandered off into the forest to think. He had to get away from elation he could not share. His mind was deep in dark thoughts, and he barely noticed the movement in the brush to his left. He froze eyeing the spot. If it was a bear, he was as good as dead. He had only his dagger, and there were no trees nearby large enough to provide a haven. He fingered the dagger's hilt. He would not go down without a fight.

There was no more movement. Perhaps it had only been a fox or a rabbit? Javik started to move on when a figure broke from the brush and ran down the path. It was a young girl, but not like any girl he had ever seen before. Her black hair was wild and tangled with burrs and seeds. It streamed out behind her as she ran on bare feet over the hard pathway. Her dress was made of roughly sewn deerskins. He could not see her face.

Javik called to her, "Please, don't run away. I won't harm you."

The girl did not stop or acknowledge his shouts. Soon, she was out of sight. Javik was completely surprised by the sight of the strange girl who seemed to appear out of nowhere. Maybe she was a witch, like Grazhda, but he knew of no legends concerning a young woman dressed in buckskin. Who was she? What was she doing here?

He moved through the brush to the spot where he first noticed her movement. A stand of berry brambles was partially trampled down, and a roughly woven basket sat in the clearing half- filled with the sweet, red fruit. He picked it up and surveyed the work. It was not like any weaving he had ever seen, and there were no markings on it at all.

"She'll come back for this, I think," Javik said to himself as he eyed the woods around him for a good blind. He spotted a tree whose trunk offered enough width to hide his body and a limb at the right level. Carefully covering his steps as he moved, Javik made his way to the tree and climbed to the spot where he would wait for his prey.

It seemed he was there for hours. The limb pressed into the arches of his feet causing him to shift more than he thought prudent, and the insects attacked him unmercifully. He felt his full bladder calling for relief, but he dared not in case the girl could smell his scent. She seemed more a wild animal than anything else. He was about ready to climb down when he heard a twig snap to his right.

Javik peered around the tree and felt a sharp pain as something slammed into the back of his skull. Stars swirled inside his head as he toppled from the tree limb and fell in a heap on the brush below.

He didn't know how long he was unconscious, but when he awoke, the pain was still intense. His head throbbed as he pulled himself to one elbow and felt the damaged spot tentatively with his other hand. A plaster of dried mud and spongy moss met his explorations. Someone had applied a poultice to his wound, but who? He sat up and looked around him for some sign of his assailant, but all was quiet. The basket of berries was gone, and there was no sign of any other person.

He took stock of himself. Other than the ache in his head, he was uninjured. The heavy brush cushioned his fall from the tree enough to prevent broken bones. It was then he noticed his dagger, Zuban's dagger, was missing. Whoever hit him must have taken it. Was it the girl? The basket was gone, but anyone could have taken it for the berries. A thief must have seen him and spotted the expensive dagger. Browdat would kill him for this.

Javik rose unsteadily to his feet and let the mists clear from his mind. He checked the sun angle and calculated he'd been unconscious for over an hour.   The place where he fell was trampled down by whoever tended to his head. There were no boot marks, only the prints of small, bare feet leading off into the forest. He followed them for a moment but soon lost them at an outcropping of rock. Puzzled and sore, he returned to Tao Shan's house.

The master was there to greet him when he arrived. "Come in to my rooms, Javik," Tao Shan ordered, but then noticed the blood on his tunic. "What happened to you?"

"I don't know, Master. I was walking in the forest when I saw this wild girl. She ran from me, but left her berry basket behind. I hid in a tree to wait for her thinking she would surely return for the basket. I heard a sound, and when I turned to investigate, something hit me on the back of the head, and I fell from the tree. When I awoke, the basket was gone along with the dagger Lord Browdat gave me, and there was no sign of her. I trailed her for a short while, but lost her tracks on some rocks."

"Let me have a look at you," Tao Shan ordered as he moved behind Javik.

"It has been expertly dressed. Whoever did this has an

excellent knowledge of healing."

"Ouch!" Javik reacted as Tao Shan pulled at the moss.

"Sorry, but I think I have something that will do you more good than this moss." Tao Shan called for a servant to bring a bowl of hot water and some bandages.

"Who could it have been, Master? She was not from the village; I'm sure."

"I don't know. I have heard tales of an old woman who lives in the forest and has the power to see the future, but no stories about a wild girl."

"That's Grazhda. I saw her just before Hella was murdered and again just before Zuban's execution," Javik spoke with a casual air. Many people of his village had seen Grazhda.

"Where did you see her?" Tao Shan asked with a note of curiosity in his voice Javik had not heard before.

"The first time, I was deep into the forest looking for a staff for the goddess Verna and ran into her. She showed me the sapling to cut for my offering."

"I was in the village the other day," Tao Shan remarked. "They say that one of the staffs offered to the goddess has sprouted leaves. They say also it is yours, Javik."

"Mine, that's good news indeed, sir. It's a sign from Verna that I will have good fortune." Javik was almost jubilant as the servant returned with the water and bandages. Tao Shan busied himself soaking off the moss poultice and cleaning the wound. He spoke as he worked.

"This looks like a sling wound, but a good slinger would have killed you if he hit you at this spot."

"How can you tell it's a sling wound, Master?" Javik asked.

"A club would have left a different mark. This mark is concentrated but not the deep hole from a sling stone. The slinger did not intend to kill you, Javik – only to make you unconscious."

"I thank him for that," Javik agreed.

"I'm curious, what did the old woman in the forest say to you?" Tao Shan asked.

"She only said that I would know what it meant to have Grazhda's gratitude. Then she showed me which tree to cut for my staff and vanished."

"You may have a powerful ally in that old woman, Javik," Tao Shan mused. "Do not take her blessing lightly. You may need her help sometime, and when you do, no one else will be able to do for you what she can."

"You speak in riddles, Master. What do you mean?"

"You will know when the time comes. You will know. Tell me of your second encounter with her."

"I had gone into the forest to think about Zuban's death when she appeared. She said something good would happen before the holiday was over."

"And, did something good happen?"

"Browdat adopted me as his son. That was certainly a good thing, but I don't know if that's what she meant."

"Sorcerers and fortunetellers never make precise statements. I've taught you that already, but this Grazhda has a reputation for making accurate predictions. I think Browdat's adoption is what she had in mind."

"I also encountered a woman at the festival who looked at a Wallan coin I found and said I would find Wallandia one day just as I found the coin. She told me the story of one of their kings, but it made no sense to me."

"Which king, Javik, do you remember?"

"It was Umbra, or Ungric, or something like that. I paid little attention since I knew she was a charlatan."

"Could it have been Umbric?"

"Yes, that's it, Umbric. She said Wallandia was cursed because of his sins, and the curse would not be lifted until a stranger was crowned king."

"I see," Tao Shan spoke automatically as if his mind were miles away. "It is an old legend, but one many in Wallandia believe." He changed the subject quickly. "I think we are ready to do the bandages now."

Tao Shan inspected the cleansed wound and grunted his satisfaction before moving to a shelf of jars and boxes. He scrutinized each item before selecting two jars. Pulling a pinch of vile looking weeds from one and shaking out a handful of green powder from the other, he dumped the mixture into another bowl and began to grind it with a pestle made from deer antler. Next, he added water until a soft paste formed.

"This will heal the wound faster than the moss, though it would have healed well in any case," Tao Shan spoke as he smoothed the paste into the wound. Javik winced but did not cry out. If this were a test, he would be sure to pass it.

"I called you in here to talk with you about Mauhad, not to dress your wound. Were you surprised when your name was not on the list?"

"Yes, Master. I felt I was ready for the test," Javik answered truthfully.

"You are as ready as any of the other boys, but I held you back to teach you more than they know."

Javik could not turn his head. Tao Shan was busy wrapping the bandage around it to hold the plaster in place. "But master, I need to join the warriors so that I may avenge my father."

"The Sentii will wait. You have much promise, Javik. I want to give you the benefit of all I know, not just enough to get you through Mauhad."

Javik knew the old man was sincere, and another year in his

school would give him knowledge few of his friends would be able to acquire after many years of experience. He should be grateful to Tao Shan.

"I thank you for allowing me to learn at your feet, Master. May I ask one favor?"

"What is it?"

"Will you also teach me some of your magic?"

Tao Shan threw back his head and laughed merrily. "Javik, there is no magic. I will teach you all I know, but that does not include any incantations or special potions. Magic is the refuge of charlatans, but knowledge is more powerful than any magic."

Javik blushed a bit at being the target of the Master's laughter, but the old man comforted him quickly. "Don't be embarrassed, Javik. I let people think I know magic to keep them a bit on the frightened side. You will learn to do the same thing, I promise."

The glow returned to Javik's cheeks, and he sprang from the chair.

"Master, I respect your decision. If you think it is best for me to learn more, who am I to question you? Now, I must go and congratulate the new candidates."

"You'd better take it easy for the next two days. I don't think you have any internal damage, but we'd best make sure. You may go now." Tao Shan stood aside as Javik felt the bandages around his head.

"One thing more, Master. My dagger was stolen by whoever hit me. How many stripes will I get for that?"

"None, Javik. I will have Lin bring you one of ours. Go now and join the celebration."

Javik left Tao Shan's quarters but lingered just outside the common room. The old man knew something Javik didn't about Grazhda, but he also seemed reticent about explaining it.

Perhaps later on the master might be willing to disclose more. He shrugged it off as another of Tao Shan's secrets. He was only happy the loss of the dagger would not mean an ache in his backside.

Chapter 16

The beer flowed freely in the boy's quarters as Javik entered. Most of the others were several mugs ahead of him by now. Noka was the first to notice Javik's bandage.

"Ho, ho, ho," Noka laughed. "Didn't she like your kisses, Javik?"

"I'm afraid I never got that far," Javik smiled knowing Noka was joking, but unknowingly referring to a real girl.

Noka looked puzzled and asked, "You mean a girl actually gave you that?" Noka pointed to the bandage. The rest of the room fell silent awaiting Javik's reply.

"Yes, at least, I think it was a girl," Javik tried to be evasive.

"Where would you find a girl around here?" Sigurd snorted. "I think Javik means he ran into a she bear."

"She hit like a she bear, but she was a girl sure enough," Javik countered.

"Tell us about her!" several boys shouted in a fugue-like chorus.

"I saw her in the forest today picking berries. She was a wild looking thing, barefoot and dressed in buckskins."

"Was she pretty?" one asked.

Javik was ashamed to admit he hadn't seen her face, so he made up a description he thought appropriate to the occasion. "She was more beautiful than any of you could imagine. Her hair was jet black, and her skin was fair as the snow. She had breasts the size of melons."

"I'm off to the woods in the morning at first light," Boder shouted.

"She was looking for me, Javik. Why didn't you tell her where to find me?" another chided.

"How did she come to wound you?" Noka asked.

"I came upon her while she was picking berries. She ran when she saw me, but she left her basket of berries. I decided to use it as bait and hid in a nearby tree to catch her when she came back for it."   Javik saw the anticipation in his fellow student's faces and was about to drag out the narrative a bit longer to build the suspense when Sigurd broke in.

"Then you jumped on her and raped her," Sigurd ended the commentary for Javik.

The boys broke into uncontrollable laughter, but fell quiet when Javik shouted, "That's not how it was at all, Sigurd. Unlike you, I am a gentleman."

Again, the boys roared with laughter.

"I give up, Javik," Sigurd pleaded. "Tell us how you charmed her into splitting your skull."

"I had no chance to use my considerable charm on the girl. She crept up behind me and hit me with something before I knew she was there. Tao Shan thinks it was a rock from a sling. I was up in a tree, so she couldn't reach me with a club."

"Wow! There's a wild girl out there, men," Harld's voice rose with wonder. "Maybe we can hunt her down and tame her to serve us?" he laughed.

"I don't think you'd have much luck with this one. She covered her tracks pretty well and lost me at some rocks. She knows what she's doing," Javik said.

"She's just a girl," Sigurd snorted. "She may elude Javik, but she'd better watch out if she runs into me."

The other boys laughed heartily emboldened by the beer.

"Do you scum find that funny?" Sigurd rose to his feet but wobbled a bit in the process. Boder pulled him back into a chair.

"Have another mug, Sigurd. You're in no position to do justice to any woman right now," Boder laughed.

The evening continued in drink and song, but Javik was only half into the celebration. After two mugs of qush, the strong ale of the Berglauni people, he left the party for the crisp air outside. His head was still throbbing a bit, but Tao Shan's potion was beginning to have a numbing effect on the area.

The full moon shone brightly through the trees that would soon be turning color again. It had been almost a year since his father's death, and he thought of the tall, muscular man who taught him so much. He thought how terrible he must have been in battle yet remembered how tender he was with the woman he loved. He remembered listening as the council debated the issues of the village and how the other men would fall silent to hear what Tolda had to say when he rose to speak. He would be like his father every way he knew how. Maybe this was what Tao Shan had in mind by holding him back? Javik knew he had much to learn. Perhaps another year with the master would help him gain the skills a leader of warriors must have.

"Are you all right?" A soft, heavily accented voice as delicate as the moonlight called from behind him.

Javik spun around to see only black forest and underbrush.

"Who said that?" he called.

"I didn't mean to hurt you. I only wanted my berries."

"Come out! Show yourself, and give me back my dagger! It's a family heirloom."

"I see you are not hurt so badly that you cannot bellow like a bear. I tried to cleanse and bind your wound, but I see someone else has helped you also. Your dagger is very fine, but I need it more than you do right now. Think of it as your gift to me. You can easily buy another."

Javik strained to see into the darkness. The moonlight bathed everything in a soft, silver glow, but the voice was coming from a section of the brush the moonlight did not penetrate.

"I'm sorry I shouted at you," Javik tried a softer tone. "Let me see you. I won't harm you." He scanned the shadows for a shape but saw nothing. "I have so many questions. Who are you? Why do you live in the woods?" Javik called.

"I just wanted to make sure you were alive and well. Now that I know you are, I will go. Perhaps we will meet again, Javik?"

"Wait, how do you know my name? Tell me yours. Come out where I can see you." Javik's calls were in vain. The forest was silent, and he could detect no movement in the brush. This girl was a master at moving through the night. Perhaps he could find her trail in the morning.

"Who are you yelling at?" Noka called out from the doorway of the longhouse. "I could hear you over the noise of these drunks." Noka moved out to stand beside Javik.

"She was here, Noka. Just now, she was here; and she spoke to me in a voice as soft as the fur of an otter. I must know who she is."

"We'll look for her tomorrow. Come, have some more qush tonight," Noka pleaded.

Javik joined his friends in their search for happy oblivion and dreamed of a wild girl.

Chapter 17

The next day, Javik was excused from the endurance run because Tao Shan said he must not exercise strenuously for a full day after a severe blow to the head. Javik had, however, obtained his permission to walk in the forest to maintain his conditioning. The master smiled knowingly at this request, sure that the boy was anxious to be in pursuit of the wild girl.

As soon as the boys left, Javik scoured the brush where he'd heard the girl's voice the night before. He found no tracks, but it dawned on him she might have used the trees to get close to the longhouse. He had used that trick many times himself. He widened his search area and found the same tiny footprints. They led deep into the forest.

Javik returned to the longhouse and packed a knapsack. He filled a water skin and drew a new dagger from the armory. While he was there, a longbow caught his attention, and he checked it out also, tying a quiver of arrows to his knapsack. Using the unstrung bow as a staff, he set off in search of the mysterious girl.

The trail led deep into the foothills of the Mestra Mountains. Javik had only been there once. His father showed him some of the passes leading to the country of their enemies and pointed out spots where ambushes were best laid. When the tracks reached rocky ground they vanished, but Javik knew how to find the girl's trail. He carefully checked each patch of moss and lichen for any disturbance. Those plants were very delicate and retained damage for a long time. It was not long before he found the trail again.

She has the cunning of an animal, Javik thought. *I must track her like a mountain sheep and not like a human. The sheep will rest watching its trail, and so will she.*

He scanned the rocks above him for a likely observation point and found several. She could be behind any of those rocks watching him even now. Undoubtedly, she had an escape route from all of them allowing her to vanish into the mountain unseen. No, he could not chase her down. Only a trap would work, someplace where he could lie in wait for her, someplace she would have to go every day. Her home was, most likely, a cave somewhere, but she would have to cook which meant a fire and the need for firewood. She would have to go to the forest for that, but it was quite possible she had an ample store in the cave allowing her to hole up for weeks if need be.

"What about water?" Javik mused. "If there was none in her cave, she would have to go to some source on a regular basis." Javik began a search for streams.

He found several, but none of them yielded any indication of human visitation. "What a fool I am," Javik scolded himself. "Anyone can follow a stream to its source and look for signs. It would be a sure give away. A rain pool is what I should be looking for."

He changed his search pattern but found no pools. He was about to give up and return to the longhouse when he noticed a colony of Marmots in the rocks above him and to his left. The little creatures needed water as much as humans, which meant there was some source of it nearby. Javik climbed toward the colony and found what he was searching for – a crystal clear pool of water nestled among several large boulders.

A narrow ledge led off to the left, and the smoothness of the rock told him it had been traveled often. This was her water source. All he had to do was watch it, and she would eventually come. He found a hiding place and waited.

The sun was now directly overhead, and the rocks around him began to absorb its rays raising the temperature of his body proportionally. Javik drank heavily from his water skin, and the wild girl's sling wound began to throb. She would have to come for water soon or he would be forced to find shade. A scuffle of rock brought him to full alert.

A mop of black hair appeared around the last rock blocking his view of the path, and beneath it was the most beautiful face he had ever seen. Her skin was like bleached parchment, but her lips were an almost unnaturally vivid red. Deep, black eyes searched the area for danger as she sniffed the air for scents. Javik had been careful to pick a spot downwind from the pool, but he was not sure if some part of his scent still lingered near it.

Satisfied there was no danger, the girl moved to the pool and began to fill a water skin made from the hide of a mountain sheep. Her eyes constantly searched the rocks around her. She was as nervous as a mountain cat, and Javik hesitated to startle her by speaking. If she sped off along the ledge, he would be hard pressed to follow her with any haste. She was small and agile while his bulk would require considerable caution to avoid a nasty fall. He decided on another tactic.

Gorse were not native to the mountains, but the small birds were common almost everywhere else. Javik had learned to imitate their call, and he calculated she would be curious on hearing the song of gorse in this region. Cupping his hands around his mouth, he produced the mournful cry of their mating season.

It had the desired effect. She stiffened and listened intently. Again, Javik made the call, only this time he used their usual song. The girl cocked her head to one side while her face took on a puzzled look. Leaving the water skin by the pool, she began to climb carefully toward Javik. She made no sound at all. Her bare feet caressed the rocks and tested each foothold carefully before she let her weight down fully.

If he startled her now she might fall. He had to wait until she reached a place of safety yet far enough from her path she could not retreat easily. When she came to a small plateau he judged the time was right.

"So, I have found my little nymph of the forest," he said softly.

The girl started and turned to retreat. Javik rose from his hiding place.

"Wait! Don't run. I won't harm you. I came to thank you for taking care of my wound."

The girl turned and recognized him. "How did you find me?"

"I am a good tracker, and Tao Shan taught me well the ways of both animals and men. I found your water source," Javik indicated the pool.

The girl looked past Javik scanning the rocks for others.

"I came alone. You have nothing to fear from me," Javik guessed her concern. "Are you hungry? I brought some food." He held up his knapsack.

She licked her lips and leaned toward Javik then resumed her defiant stance. "I have plenty of food. I don't need yours. You have thanked me, now go away."

"You don't speak like a Berglauni. Where are you from?"

She thought about this question for a while before answering. "I will not tell you. If you knew that, you would send me back."

Javik thought about her answer. She must be some kind of fugitive, but what kind? Obviously, she was not evading Berglauni justice. She was foraging too close to his village and taking too many risks. "Are you a criminal?" he asked.

"No, I am innocent. Please go and leave me alone."

"I must know who you are and why you hide in the mountains. Maybe I can help you. My master, Tao Shan, is a very wise man and has some influence with the King. If you tell me of your trouble, I will seek his advice on your behalf."

"Are you a slave too?" she asked in amazement.

"A slave," Javik laughed. "No, I am a student in Tao Shan's longhouse. We call him 'Master' because he is our mentor. Is that the trouble? Are you an escaped slave?"

"And if I was, would you not see that I was returned to my master? Now that you know of my pool, I must move everything." A tear escaped from one eye and created an even whiter track as it slid down her already pale cheek.

"Don't worry. I'm not interested in taking you back to your master. You are in Berglauni territory now, but even if your master were a Berglauni, I would not betray you." Javik smiled warmly at the pathetic wretch below him. She was dirty and unkempt, but her beauty shone through it all with a radiance that dazzled his senses.

She sat down on the ledge. "Perhaps I can trust you. How is your head?"

"Much better today. Tao Shan said your poultice was quite good, but he changed it for one of his own."

"I did the best I could with what I had. I'm glad you weren't badly hurt, Javik."

"How do you know my name?" Javik asked.

"I heard the other boys calling to you in the forest. I've been watching all of you for some time." She blushed a bit but recovered quickly. "I needed a new knife, and I hoped to be able to steal one of yours." Her voice resumed its independent tone.

"The dagger you took from me was a gift from my adopted father. If he learns I lost it, he will beat me severely. It also has a good deal of sentimental value. Would you be willing to trade for another one?" Javik pulled Tao Shan's standard issue dagger and offered it to her.

She looked at Javik's dagger hanging by a thong from her leather belt. "This one is quite pretty, but I do need a sheath. Give me your dagger and sheath and your food, and I will give this one back to you."

"Done!" Javik smiled. "But, you have to come up here to get it." He began to thread the sheath off his belt.

The girl thought for a while then climbed toward him. When she reached his side she handed the dagger to Javik and snatched the other one from his hand with surprising quickness.

Now that she was close to him, Javik could smell her scent. She had obviously been washing regularly, but there was no hint of soap or the perfumes the women of his village often applied to themselves. The impression was one of the forest itself. She was clever enough to hide her scent with something natural.

"I haven't eaten yet. We can share the food for lunch, and you may keep whatever is left. I brought plenty," Javik assured her.

He produced a loaf of bread and a wedge of cheese from his knapsack and watched the girl lick her lips in anticipation as he cut a slice from the loaf and capped it with a hunk of cheese. She reached for it eagerly, but he drew it back.

"First your name. I must call you something," Javik insisted.

"My name is Allana. Give me the cheese, please," she begged.

Javik handed her the cheese and bread. Allana took a large bite from the chunk and closed her eyes as she chewed. "It has been so long since I tasted good cheese," she spoke with a mouth full of the delicious stuff.

"How long have you been out here?" Javik asked.

"Here in these mountains for almost a year. Before that, another year on the Sentii side," she pointed in the proper direction.

"Were you a slave to the Sentii?" Javik asked.

"Yes, one of their war chiefs bought me at their slave market in Bendar."

"I have no love for the Sentii. They killed my father," Javik's face grew stern.

Allana stopped eating and stared at the change in Javik's demeanor. "You must hate them as much as I do. I'm sorry, Javik."

"Why did you escape?"

"My master's wife hated me. She beat me at the slightest offense. There were other reasons too, but you don't need to hear them."

Javik smiled at her. "Let's not speak of the Sentii. Eat some of the bread. Tao Shan's kitchens are wonderful."

"My water skin!" she almost panicked. "I left it down there."

"Have some of mine," Javik offered her his skin, and she drank deeply before resuming her repast. Her hunger betrayed her as she ripped a large mouthful of bread from the loaf with her teeth.

"Did you make your clothes?" Javik asked.

"Yes, my old ones wore out ages ago. This is made from

deer hides." She almost modeled the dirty skins.

"You are very resourceful, but how did you manage to kill a deer? You have no bow."

"I have this." Allana produced a leather thong with a wide spot in the middle.

"A sling? You killed a deer with a sling?" Javik was skeptical.

"No, I drove away the wolves that killed it. I even killed two of them in the process. They made a warm coat for the winter."

"I can't place your accent. You are not Sentii and not Berglauni, but you don't speak like any of the other foreign people I have ever heard."

"I am from Gorgos. It's an island in the great sea. A fierce tribe of seafarers conquered my homeland when I was a little baby. I've been a slave ever since. I don't remember anything about it. I only know what the woman who raised me said about it." Allana wolfed down the remaining cheese and bread and drank heavily from the water skin. "Is there any more?"

"I have more, but you'd better take it easy. Too much rich food could be harmful to you after your diet of berries and roots," Javik cautioned.

"I have meat too. I kill when I'm hungry."

"I have some sausages, but we would need a fire for that," Javik offered.

"We can't build one here. I have seen Sentii around here from time to time. If they find me they will take me back for the reward." Allana lifted one sleeve of her buckskin dress and revealed a tattoo on her left shoulder. A serpent twined around a hoop marked her as a slave.

"You must build a fire where you live. We could go there," Javik suggested.

"You ask too much, Javik. I don't trust you that much yet. Give me your knapsack and let me have one hand width of sun travel head start before you leave this place. I promise I will come to you again soon. Look for me at the berry bush where you first saw me. We will talk more then." Allana rose and held out her hand. Javik handed her the knapsack. She slipped it over her shoulders and adjusted the straps to fit.

"Until we meet again, Javik." Allana made her way back to the pool and her water skin as easily as any mountain animal then vanished around the rock where she first appeared.

Javik sat in the sun watching the spot and feeling a new surge in his being. He remembered feeling something like this with Hella, but now it was much stronger. The wild part of her called to the deep center of his being. He remembered feeling somewhat the same way when he saw a fine stag on his first hunt. The only difference was he had no urge to kill her only a burning need that seared his brain and left him with an ache in his loins he did not understand. He hungered to see her again, but he was true to his word and did not try to follow.

Without the burden of the knapsack he moved much more easily. Only the quiver impeded his progress now, and that was almost nothing. He descended from his perch to the floor of the valley and looked back at the spot. He burned every detail of the location into his mind. There was no sign of any place Allana could use as a shelter, but she was there somewhere. He thought he could sense her eyes upon him at that very minute. Instinctively, he waved toward the rocks before turning for home.

Chapter 18

Javik returned to the longhouse and found the boys back from the endurance run. They lay sprawled across beds and leaning against walls still breathing heavily from the exertion.

"Look who's decided to join us," Sigurd smirked. "It's Lord Javik."

"I was excused today because of my head," Javik answered.

"Well, it's not everyone who can be felled by a snip of a girl. Such horrible combat truly ranks an extended rest." Sigurd and his cronies laughed heartily at their own joke.

"Until you've been hit by a rock from a well-aimed sling, I wouldn't say too much, Sigurd," Javik shot back.

"Oh? Perhaps you would like another lesson in the ring?" Sigurd's voice oozed confidence.

"Look Sigurd, my head is throbbing like a drum, and I have no wish to quarrel with you right now. Look me up when my head is healed, and I'll be happy to accommodate you." Javik walked past the bully to his own bed and pulled off his boots.

"Where did you go today?" Noka sat down on the end of Javik's bed.

"I found her today, Noka." Javik's voice boiled over with elation. "We even talked for a while and ate together. She's so beautiful. Her hair is like a raven's feathers and her eyes are obsidians. She moves with the grace of an elk, and her skin is white as snow. I love her, Noka, and I must see her again or die of loneliness."

"What a formidable creature! You speak as if she were a princess instead of a wild hermit living alone in the forest."

"She hides in the forest because she's an escaped Sentii slave. She fears someone will send her back for the reward if she shows her face in the village."

"She should know the Berglauni and the Sentii are bitter enemies," Noka said.

"She trusts no one. Maybe I can get her to trust me enough to bring her here. I'm sure Tao Shan would take her in as a servant."

"You'd best speak to him first, Javik. He would know the law in these matters, and there may be no alternative to returning her."

"I'll speak with him after dinner. Right now I need some rest." Javik lay back and closed his eyes, ending the conversation.

* * * * *

After dinner, Javik approached Tao Shan. "Master, may I speak with you in private?"

"Certainly, Javik. Come into my rooms." Tao Shan led the way and indicated a seat for Javik. "What do you want to tell me, Javik?"

"Do you remember the wild girl I told you about?"

"Of course, what about her?"

"I found her today in the mountains. She's an escaped Sentii slave, and ..."

Tao Shan interrupted him. "This is a serious matter, Javik. Escaped slaves must be returned, even to our enemies."

"Even to the Sentii?" Javik's heart fell. There was no way he could take this lovely girl back to the dirty bed of some Sentii dog. If they had not managed to find her by now, she could probably avoid Berglauni capture also unless he aided the search party by pinpointing her location, and he was not about to assist in her capture.

"Even to the Sentii. If we are to have any hope of retaining our own slaves, we must respect the rights of other peoples in these matters."

"She is a fine girl and doesn't have the manner of a slave. I couldn't stand to see her given back to the Sentii. Those swine killed my father."

Tao Shan rubbed his chin and remained silent for a moment. Javik fell silent also, knowing he should wait on the master to complete his thought process before he spoke again.

The master studied his pupil. The signs were unmistakable. Javik was in love with this wild girl and would not rest until she was either his or she rejected him outright. The fact that she let him approach her at all told Tao Shan the latter prospect was not likely. He remembered his own adolescence and knew the boy would be a hopeless case until the matter of the girl was resolved.

"There may be a way. Is she a Sentii herself?" Tao Shan asked.

"No, she claims to be from an island called Gorgos in the great sea."

"Gorgos?" Tao Shan's eyebrows raised in surprise. "The Gorgons were a very refined people until they were slaughtered by the Voldunee. Travelers tell me the island is just a mass of ruins now, populated mostly by goats. She must have been little more than a baby when it happened."

"She says she has no memory of the island," Javik inserted.

"Well," Tao Shan continued, "there is an exception for

foreign born slaves. She could be won in combat. You would only have to kill her master to claim her for your own, but you are not yet considered a warrior."

"You could do it for me," Javik spoke with an air of hope his master could not ignore.

"So, you would pit me, an old man, against some fierce Sentii warrior so you could have a girl?" The glint in the old man's eye told Javik he was not really scolding him.

"I didn't mean to place you in danger, Master. You would only have to go with me. I would do all the fighting."

"You are ahead of yourself, Javik. I need to speak with this girl before we do anything. Do you think you could get her to come here?"

"I doubt it, sir. She trusts no one but me, and I'm not sure she trusts me that much."

"Then we will go to her. Do you know the way?"

"Yes, but she said she would contact me when she was ready to speak again."

"Very well. Let me know when she contacts you."

Javik left for his bed and some much needed sleep, but Tao Shan sat staring at the fire. A time long ago arose from the mists of his mind, a time when a young slave boy sought refuge from his captors in the camp of strange bearded men with long, heavy swords. Their fierce looks and harsh language struck fear in his heart, but even the vilest death at their hands was better than a slave's life. The fearsome men laughed at him and tossed him about for sport until one of them took him to his fire and spoke with him in a language they both understood.

The next day, this huge man placed him in front of the shield line and called for his owner to come forth and battle for his property. When no one appeared, the warrior claimed the boy as his own slave. It was the beginning of a new life for Tao

Shan. He learned the ways of the warriors his people called barbarians and found they were as refined as his own race. After he grew to be a man, they granted his freedom, and he eventually became a war leader among the Tallan.

During a raid on the Berglauni capitol city, he was wounded and left behind. Because of his valor in battle, the father of the man who now held the Berglauni throne spared his life. His service as a mentor for Berglauni boys help repay the mercy shown him long ago. Now Javik asked that another slave be freed. He had come to have such great hopes for this boy, how could he deny him?

* * * * *

Every day, Javik checked the berry bush clearing for any sign of Allana, but none appeared. His head healed rapidly, and he was back on Tao Shan's rigorous training schedule, leaving him little time for anything else. He was beginning to wonder if she was hurt or ill, or if the Sentii had finally found her and taken her back into slavery. The image of her wild hair and soft, white skin haunted him at night. He had to see her again, but he knew a trip into the mountains would be useless. She would have found a new water source and, perhaps, even a new hiding place. Waiting on her to contact him was his only option.

It was another two days before he saw the berry basket in the middle of the clearing. It was her signal, to be sure; but how should he respond? He moved to the basket and picked it up. A row of berries beneath it formed an arrow pointing to a large tree some distance off. Javik filled the basket with berries and followed the arrow.

At the tree, he found another arrow carved into the bark pointing to a large fallen tree on the edge of a meadow. He almost ran to the spot. Once there he saw a line of stones pointing to a boulder on the other side of the meadow. She was clever. She would be watching the meadow to see that no one accompanied him.

The walk across the meadow seemed to take forever. Javik was hungry for the sight of Allana, and he imagined her laughing by his side and sharing the delights of the forest. He finally reached the rock and found no other signs, but there was no Allana.

"Did you come alone?" the soft voice with the thick accent was unmistakable.

"Yes, I'm alone. Where are you?"

The girl jumped down from a nearby tree limb startling him. "Right here," she laughed.

"You are worse than a mountain cat, Allana," Javik said as he regained his composure.

"Thank you for bringing my berries. I was afraid you'd not know to fill the basket."

"Allana, I want you to speak with my master, Tao Shan. He thinks there is a way to free you from the Sentii."

"You mean he wants to collect the reward," Allana sniffed as she popped several berries into her mouth.

"No, he is a good man, a wise man. He can help you if you'll talk to him."

Allana swallowed the fruit and studied Javik carefully. "You really trust this man, don't you?"

"As much as if he were my father," Javik replied.

"Where would he want to meet?"

"You may name the place. He only asks that it be fairly open."

Allana's eyebrows raised in skepticism. "An open place where a trap could be easily set. Is that it?"

"No, I don't know why he asks that, but he has a good reason, I'm sure."

Allana thought for a long time. "Do you know the clearing near the place where the small stream falls from the cliff?"

Javik thought for a moment, mentally scouting out the terrain near her old water pool. "Yes, I know it. The one with two fallen trees that make an archway."

"That's the one. Bring him there at noon tomorrow, and I will speak with him. You may not see me, but I will be there. Just the two of you, understand?"

"Just the two of us," Javik assured her.

"Very well. I'll be there. Now, turn around and count as high as you know how."

"But, I just got here," Javik protested.

"What more is there to talk about now? We will talk tomorrow. Turn around. You can count, can't you?"

"I can count well over a hundred numbers," Javik boasted.

"Good! Use all of them." She placed her hands on his shoulders and turned him to face the meadow. Javik felt the warmth of her grasp through his tunic. It penetrated into his very soul and created strange and wonderful thoughts. He began to count.

"One, two, three, four..." He continued to over sixty before turning to look after her. There was no sign she had ever been there.

Back at the longhouse, Javik informed Tao Shan of the arrangements.

"Good, we will find out some things we must know before we go any farther. How long will it take to reach this place?"

"Only an hour's fast walk, Master."

"Then we will leave after morning training. I will put Ling in charge of the afternoon session while we are gone. Your fellow students will appreciate me more after a session with Ling. We will travel with no weapons so she will not fear us. Only daggers, is that clear?"

"Yes, Master, but..."

Tao Shan cut him off with a motion of his hand.

"It is more important that she trust us than to be prepared for possible Sentii raiding parties. If we are careful, we should be in no danger."

"I understand, Master." Javik said it, but he didn't really understand. Tao Shan always erred on the side of caution. It was folly to venture that close to Sentii territory unarmed.

Javik spent the remainder of the day studying the maps in the large classroom. Berglaundia was so much smaller than the other countries around it. He marveled that his land was still free and not part of Wallandia or Sentius. He traced the lines indicating mountains and remembered old Bandor's lessons. These mountains saved his land from invaders, and Allana lived in these mountains.

A vision of the girl flooded his mind and blocked out all other subjects. How beautiful she was even with unkempt hair and dressed in animal skins. He tried to imagine her with brushed hair and fine clothes, but he couldn't get past an image of her standing naked before him. He had never seen a naked woman before, but the boys all had stories of spying on the women while they bathed in the river during the summer months. Tolda forbid Javik to join these forays on pain of a severe beating, and he'd complied, but he still longed to explore the unknown territory of women. That night he dreamed of Allana. He held her close in his arms, and they kissed warmly. The morning came after a delightfully fitful sleep.

Chapter 19

The early training session seemed to last forever. Javik was still excused from heavy exercise, but he kept up with the other boys on those parts where Tao Shan indicated he should join in. Noka caught up with him when the session ended.

"Have you seen your wild girl anymore?" Noka asked.

"Only in my dreams, but I hope to see her again today. You must not tell anyone about this, but she's an escaped slave. The Master thinks there's a way to free her, and I hope he's right."

"If there is a way, the master will find it. I think he'd better find it quickly, though, or you will float away on a cloud of bliss. You made several mistakes today, and your eyes are like vacant windows. Some might say Javik is in love."

Javik punched Noka's arm only half playfully.

"If you say anything like that to anyone but me, I'll beat you senseless, Noka."

"It is true, isn't it?"

"Yes, but Sigurd and the others would make my life miserable if they knew."

"They all suspect it now, the same as me. I'm surprised Sigurd hasn't said something before now."

"Sigurd has a new respect for me now that I am Browdat's adopted son, but I'm sure he's only waiting for the right moment to unleash his dogs."

At that moment, Tao Shan appeared with a knapsack and handed it to Javik.

"This is our lunch. The kitchen was generous, and it's enough for three people, so you may carry it for us."

"Thank you, Master." Javik responded with the only words he knew to be acceptable under the circumstances. Any protestations would have earned him a stripe from the master's rod.

"Good hunting, Javik," Noka called after them.

As they walked through the forest to the designated meeting place, Javik brought up the subject bothering him nearly as much as Allana.

"Master, you told me to study the wolf, and I've given that much thought, but I don't think the wolf can teach me anything."

"Tell me what you know of the wolf, Javik."

"Well, he is a cowardly animal who skulks through the forest and often eats carrion. His voice is a mournful dirge in the night, and he avoids contact with man."

"You are correct in what little you know, Javik, but you have missed much about the wolf."

"Tell me more about him, Master. I want to understand why you told me to study him."

"The wolf is a very clever animal. He avoids man because man is his only deadly enemy. He respects his enemy, and that is the first lesson to learn. Do not listen to those who call the Sentii stupid or the Wallans primitive. All men are formidable, and each has his own special talent. Never underestimate anyone."

"I see that point, sir, but what else do you find favorable about the wolf?"

"The wolf does not count on his own strength alone. There are no heroes among wolves. The pack is more important than any one member. The pack can take down a deer or a moose, and no wolf could do that alone. They cooperate in their kills with each one contributing his special talent. This is an important lesson for us. We must learn to use each man's talent in concert with all other men's talents. A group of men can accomplish more than any one man is capable of. The wolf teaches us that."

"I never looked at the wolf that way before."

"Another thing, the wolf mates for life. When you hear its sad cry in the night, it is probably one who lost a mate, crying from loneliness. You will understand that aspect of their behavior much better when you are older."

"I think I know something of that feeling now, Master. I mourn for my father at times, and I can appreciate how a man would miss his wife."

Tao Shan smiled at the boy and patted him on the shoulder. "I believe you can, thanks to this wild girl, but there are many more lessons the wolf can teach you besides love. This is why I would have you study another year. Any common warrior could dismiss such a notion as foolishness. I would have you able to look beyond and see the truths as a leader must."

Javik blushed, and quickly changed the subject.

"The meeting place is just beyond that hill, Master."

"You go to the left, and I will go to the right. Move slowly and check for any sign of treachery. If you see anything, give the call of the elk, understand?"

"Yes, Master."

Javik circled warily, watching every footstep to avoid snapping a twig or prying loose a stone that might roll down the hill to alert an enemy. He had the hardest part. His route was up the steep hill, and the brush was thick. Thorns cut into his hands as he carefully pried back the bushes to look for tracks.   Every few steps he stopped to listen, but only the natural sounds of the forest came to him.   At last, he reached the top of the hill where the sound of the waterfall drowned out all others.   From this point, he could survey the clearing below and the area around it.   There was no sign of trouble.

In a few moments Tao Shan appeared in the clearing and signaled for Javik to join him.   Javik waved back to show he understood.   The path back down the hill was easier since silence was no longer required.

"Where is your forest nymph?" Tao Shan asked as Javik joined him.

Javik checked the sun angle.   "It is noon.   She should be here by now."

"Perhaps the Sentii managed to find her after all."

"Oh no, Master.   She's much too clever for them, but she is as shy as a mouse and can hide equally as well."

"Oh well, we'll wait here for a while.   Might as well have some of that lunch while we're waiting."   Tao Shan pointed at Javik's knapsack.

Javik unshouldered his burden and opened the pack to find a very substantial lunch.   He had just passed the cold chicken to Tao Shan when a disembodied voice called, "Is there enough for three?"

Javik's face lit up at the sound.   "Where are you?"

"I'm where I can see you, but you can't see me.   Are you alone?"

"It's only the two of us, and you can see we are not armed," Tao Shan shouted to the sky where the voice seemed to be coming from.

"I'll be right down."

The men heard no sound, but in a few moments Allana walked into the clearing.

"I assume you are the Tao Shan Javik spoke of," Allana said. "I didn't expect you to be so old."

"Allana!" Javik scolded.

"It's alright, Javik." Tao Shan smiled and shook his head to indicate he was not offended. "And you must be Allana, I didn't expect you to be so beautiful."

"Javik says you are a wise man, and you may have some way of freeing me from my bondage. Is that true?"

"I have several ways to accomplish what you and Javik wish, but first, I must have some information from you. Who is your Sentii master?"

"His name is Grucheau, he is a war leader of the Sentii."

"I know of him. He is a formidable man. How long ago did you escape?"

"Almost two years ago now."

"Why did you escape?"

Allana's face turned red and she looked at the ground. "I'd rather not say with Javik here."

"Leave us, Javik. This may be very important."

Javik bristled at being left out of the conversation. "I think I have a right to hear her story if I'm to help in her rescue," he protested.

"Javik, there are some things a woman wants to keep private. One more word from you, and you'll feel it in your backside tonight. I'll call you when you can return."

Javik walked from the clearing grumbling to himself about women.

* * * * *

After what seemed an eternity to Javik, Tao Shan called him back and the boy sat down near Allana. He noticed her face was red from crying.

"Has my master made you cry, Allana?"

"No, Javik. He has been very kind to me. It's just that what I had to tell him was very sad to remember."

Tao Shan broke in. "Javik, I told Allana the wisest course of action would be for me to buy her from her current master. Of course, that would mean she would be a slave to me. I tried to assure her she would be treated fairly, but she distrusts me. Will you tell her how my servants are treated?"

Javik was not prepared to have Allana trade one master for another no matter how kind her new owner might be.

"But Master, I thought our goal was to obtain her freedom."

"In due time, Javik. I think someone might be willing to take her for a wife someday, and I would not stand in the way of her happiness, providing her husband was willing to buy her freedom. Now tell her that she would not be mistreated in any way." The old man gave Javik a sly wink.

It took Javik a moment to digest the remark, but it dawned on him what Tao Shan had in mind.

"It's true, Allana. The master has many slaves, but they live as well as any free man in his longhouse."

"Javik left out one important point, Allana. All of my servants are also instructors. You must be able to teach my students something useful to a warrior." Tao Shan grinned broadly as he tapped one finger on the back of his head indicating the place where her sling stone wounded Javik.

Suddenly Allana's eyes glowed with understanding. "I could teach your students the sling," she beamed.

"Then it's settled. You will come to my longhouse and teach sling. Let's have some lunch now."

The three of them ate heartily and quenched their thirsts from the pool below the waterfall. Javik felt as light as a feather. He studied everything Allana did, the way her hair swung when she walked, the movement of her body beneath the deerskin dress, the way she moved her hands, and the way her fingers tapered from root to tip. This was truly a remarkable girl.

Allana also felt a heavy burden removed from her shoulders. This Tao Shan seemed to be a good man, and he was too old to want her physically. She would be happy to teach sling, and it would put her close to Javik.

She didn't know what drew her to Javik. He was attractive to look at, and he had a warrior's body, but he did not yet have the hard edge of the warrior. Every time she thought of him as a man, the softness of his youth broke the spell. He was still a boy.

Tao Shan washed the residue of lunch from his hands and turned to Javik and Allana.

"You might as well come back with us, Allana. It will take a few days to settle your situation, and you would be more comfortable in the meantime."

"No, I will stay in my cave until everything is arranged. Should something go wrong, I will still be free."

"As you wish. Come, Javik. We must get back before your fellow students try Ling's patience too much."

Javik lingered a bit and spoke to Allana. "I will come for you when the Master has arranged everything. Look for me."

"I will wait for you, Javik."

Tao Shan and Javik left Allana standing in the clearing and turned toward home. On the way back, Javik questioned Tao Shan.

"Won't it take a lot of gold to buy Allana from the Sentii?"

"I think not. The way she described the situation, Grucheau's house is probably much more peaceful with her gone. She will probably not cost much."

Chapter 20

Tao Shan sent Ling into Sentius to find Grucheau. Ling once lived among the Sentii, and spoke their language fluently. He assured Javik they would have an answer in a few days at the most.

Javik returned to the normal training routine and found Sigurd to be as obnoxious as ever.

"Well, if it isn't the master's pet back to join the rest of us miserable wretches."

"We were on serious business, Sigurd, and it's none of your concern."

"Ooooh, serious business, eh? It couldn't be something to do with that wild girl who nearly killed you, could it?"

That's no concern of yours, Sigurd."

Sigurd turned to his toadies. "I'll wager he had to have Tao Shan along to show him how to service the wild thing properly. Perhaps he held her down for Javik?"

His friends howled with laughter.

Javik felt the rage burning brighter inside his chest and remembered the advice from both his father and Tao Shan. He tried to put out the fire, but the embers still smoldered. The cold, calculating look in Sigurd's eyes told him the bully was only trying to pick a fight, and a smirk began to wrinkle his lips warning Javik the challenge was near.

"Perhaps you would like to learn your place again? Even if

Lord Browdat adopted you, you're still longhouse filth with a clean face."

"Beware, Sigurd. You step too close to the edge of my patience by questioning my father's judgment," Javik fixed the boy in his glare and rested his right hand on his dagger.

Sigurd's face went pale, but he recovered quickly. He wrapped an arm around Javik's shoulders and hugged him firmly.

"I was only joking with you, Javik. Please tell the Lord Browdat that I and my family have only the highest regard for *him*." He emphasized the word to give the clear impression that Javik was not included in his "highest regard."

Tao Shan summoning the students to a session of strenuous calisthenics interrupted the boy's confrontation.

* * * * *

It was three days before Ling returned. Javik could hardly keep his mind on his duties that day, but finally, Tao Shan broke the suspense.

"Sit down, Javik. Ling has bad news. Tell him, Ling."

"Grucheau, the girl's master, no longer looks for her. He thinks she died somewhere in the forest, but his servants told me he would pursue her if he knew she was alive. They were sure he would never sell her, and he would insist she be returned to him." Ling knew his news was not what Javik wanted to hear.

"But, I thought his wife hated Allana," Javik said.

Ling continued. "Grucheau's first wife died childless, and he has a new wife who has also proved to be barren. He mourns the loss of Allana because he knows she was fertile."

"Fertile? How would he know?" Javik asked.

Tao Shan picked up the conversation. "Allana told me she

carried Grucheau's child when she escaped. That was the part she didn't want you to hear."

"We could not let Allana return to be a brood mare for some Sentii stallion," Javik protested.

"We can talk of that later," Tao Shan said. "There is something else Ling has learned, something more important than your wild girl, Javik. Tell him, Ling."

"A Berglauni shield emblazoned with a red eagle hangs on the trophy wall of Grucheau's house, Javik. I have seen that shield many times. It was your father's."

Javik's brain took a moment to absorb the meaning of this information. It could only mean Grucheau was his father's killer. Now he had even more reason to want Allana free of him. He decided to rely upon Tao Shan's wisdom in this matter, but he filed Grucheau's name away in his mind for later action.

"What can we do, Master?"

"If he has stopped looking for her, and he thinks she is dead, it is safe for her to come here. I feel no obligation to return her now."

Javik's heart felt like a war drum pounding in his chest. Allana could come to Tao Shan's longhouse, and he would be close to her all the time.

"Oh, Master. May I run to tell her this good news?"

"Patience, Javik. You may go in the morning. Just remember she is still a slave. If I do not return her to Grucheau, she must be my slave. That is our law."

Javik had not anticipated this turn of events. If Allana were Tao Shan's slave, he would have to buy her from him to have her as his bride. It might take years for him to gain that much gold.

"I was hoping she could live here as a free woman," Javik said.

"Javik, where is your honor? She is a slave, and the law is the law."

Javik knew he was right. No man could call himself honorable if he flouted the law. Yet, Tao Shan also taught him the law was not wise enough to cover all circumstances. Surely, this was one of those times when the exact letter of the law need not be observed and honor retained. There had to be some way to free Allana. He needed time to think, and in the meantime, she would be safe in Tao Shan's house.

"I will go to her in the morning, Master."

* * * * *

The next morning, Javik set out for Allana's hiding place. He rehearsed his speech over and over. Still, he was not sure she would agree to this plan. She seemed amenable at the last meeting, but there was no guarantee she had not changed her mind. He had been around women long enough to know they could be mercurial.

He reached the spot just below the cliff where he found her watering pool and gave the call of the gorse. He never saw Allana though he scanned the cliff face carefully, but he soon heard her voice behind him.

"What news, Javik?"

He turned to see her peering cautiously from a stand of yew at the edge of the clearing.

"It's alright, Allana. I'm alone."

The girl moved from her cover as she scanned the area for any signs of treachery. She approached Javik and stood staring at him with a questioning look.

"Well?"

"Grucheau isn't looking for you anymore. He thinks you are dead."

"That's great news. Doesn't that mean I'm free?" Allana's face lit up, and she seemed to stand a little straighter.

"No, if he knew you were alive he'd demand your return. One of my master's servants talked to members of his household staff and discovered that he mourns your loss. His first wife died without giving him a son, and his second wife is also barren. He knows you are fertile, and he would have you bear his children."

Allana's eyes narrowed and her mouth twisted into a grim frown.

"I didn't want to tell you about that, but now that you know, also know I would not have that devil's children if he were the last man alive."

"Don't worry about that. Tao Shan will not send you back to him, but you cannot be free as long as Grucheau lives. My master offers you shelter in his longhouse as his slave if you will teach his students the sling. Please say you'll accept."

Allana turned away and walked two steps toward the forest. Her anger passed into a mood of pensiveness. She turned and walked back toward Javik then retraced her steps several times before answering.

"Yes, I will accept his offer. I've grown tired of this wild living. It will be good to have decent clothes and a hair brush again."

Javik fought back the urge to jump with delight. He must be the reserved and emotionless messenger until she was safely in Tao Shan's house.

"I'll help you carry your things back if you like," he offered.

"There are only a few things I must get from my hiding place. Wait here, and I'll return soon." The girl vanished into the forest while Javik seated himself on a nearby fallen log to wait.

Allana returned with Javik's old knapsack on her back and carrying another large bundle under her arm. "I am ready now," she announced.

Chapter 21

The presence of a female in Tao Shan's house created quite a disturbance since all of the servants were male. The first problem was her appearance, which required considerable improvement to meet Tao Shan's standards. This was the first instance where Allana's stubborn mind rammed squarely into Tao Shan's wall of discipline. She welcomed the hot bath, but rebelled strongly against the male clothing. She only relented when she learned the master burned her buckskin dress while she bathed.

Once clean, her hair hung to well past her waist, and she refused to braid it or pile it up on top of her head. She announced she would wear it as it fell, but Tao Shan would have none of that. It took three muscular servants to hold her down while another cut off the shining black tresses to shoulder length. When the job was done, Javik marveled at the improvement. The wild mop of hair had done a great job of hiding her natural beauty.

Her face was attractive before the haircut, but now it shone with a delicate radiance Javik had not noticed before. Her cheeks were well defined and placed high upon her face, much like Tao Shan's, but her eyes were round and soft in direct contrast to the master's heavy-lidded orbs. Her nose showed the most change. Before, it was hardly noticeable, but now it set off her other features without distracting from her appearance.

It was small and fragile looking, and the nostrils flared pleasantly when she was angered. *She's so beautiful. Surely, what I feel now is love.*

Her buckskin dress hid the shape of her body, but the male clothes accentuated her slim waist and long legs. The tunic covered her small bosoms and nearly hid them from view. For the first time, Javik noticed she was nearly as tall as he. Perhaps it was the boots instead of her bare feet?

Her sleeping arrangements were the next problem. She could not bunk with the boys, all of the servants were male, and Tao Shan was certainly not willing to share his rooms. The only solution was to build her a room of her own at the end of the longhouse. While it was under construction, she made do with a tent. Tao Shan placed an armed servant on guard nearby to discourage any "animal" urges of the other males in the household, particularly Javik. . He'd notified the boys that anyone feeling the need of carnal attentions from the girl should notify him so that he could cane those feelings into submission.

The boys were excited about the prospect of a female in the longhouse. They descended upon Javik for more information.

"Tell us about her, Javik. You can't keep her all to yourself," Harld prodded.

"She was a slave to the Sentii and escaped into the mountains. I happened to find her one day and told the master about her. The master offered to take her in as his slave. She will teach the sling. She's very good, as you can tell by my wound."

"We know all about your wound," another boy interrupted. "Tell us more about the girl."

"She comes from an island in the great ocean called Gorgos. The master says a fierce seafaring people destroyed it years ago. That's all I know about her," Javik said.

"Except that she's a good shot with a sling," Sigurd laughed, as he and his cronies joined the discussion.

"Did you kiss her?" Noka asked.

"Ohhhh," a chorus of knowing sounds greeted this question.

"No, she is a wild thing who moves like a cat and vanishes faster than a chipmunk. I could barely get close enough to speak with her, let alone kiss her," Javik explained with a note of disappointment in his voice.

"But you were alone with her twice," Noka blurted out before thinking.

"So, Javik is not only an easy sling target, he's bashful as well," Sigurd teased.

"She was the bashful one. At first, she was afraid of me, but by our second meeting, she acted as if I might be able to get close to her someday. I must admit she claimed my heart the first time I saw her, and I was afraid to move too rapidly for fear I might lose her forever," Javik explained.

"She would have found me a different sort of man," Sigurd boasted. "I'll wager I could have seduced her on the second meeting."

A burst of disbelieving laughter erupted from the boys in spite of their fear of retribution from the bully and his companions.

"We all know that you are well loved by the women," Dava mocked. This boy was from Sigurd's village and knew him well.

"Tell us of his conquests," Noka shouted.

Dava stepped forward as Sigurd turned red and seethed. He could not afford to start a fight at this time and jeopardize his status as a candidate for Mauhad. Dava knew that, or he would not dare embarrass the bully.

"You should have seen him during the festival. All of the girls were swooning over him." Dava made a sighing noise and clasped a hand over his heart in mock admiration.

Sigurd instinctively lunged for his fellow villager, but his friends restrained him.   Javik smiled inwardly at Sigurd's obvious embarrassment.

"How many did he take?" Verd egged him on.

"Sigurd is very selective," Dava feigned dignity. "Only the best for him. He chose to take Gerda, the queen of the village."

"Is she beautiful?" Noka asked.

"Beautiful?" Sigurd jumped in on the discussion. "She is a paragon among women. Her golden hair shines like the sun, and her green eyes are soft as the spring grass in the meadow."

"Ahhhh!" the mock admiration of the boys only made Sigurd's face redder.

"As I said, only the best for Sigurd," Dava continued.

"Tell us the rest!   Tell us!" the boys pleaded as Sigurd smoldered.

"Well, Sigurd the lover lured her into the forest on the pretense of showing her a bird's nest. They were not gone long when Gerda returned alone. Naturally, I was concerned about Sigurd."

"Naturally," the boys agreed among themselves.

"I went into the forest and found him doubled over holding on to his private parts and moaning like a tortured man. He also had a large red welt on his face. When Gerda's slap wasn't enough to force his retreat, she knew where to strike next."

The room erupted in laughter while Sigurd sat scowling at his fellow villager.

"One day we will re-live this moment, Dava, and we shall see who laughs then," Sigurd's voice was black with rage.

"Relax, Sigurd!" Harld said. "We have all been slapped, and Javik has been wounded!"

Another round of laughter ran through the boys, but Sigurd

only stomped from the room with his two mates close behind. Slowly, the boys returned to their normal routine.

By dinnertime, Sigurd was taking the ribbing good-naturedly and even giving back as good as he received. Allana was nowhere to be seen, which gave Javik pause until Tao Shan assured the group the girl was properly fed and would be given her duties the next day. He emphasized that her duties would in no way involve service to any of the boys.

After supper, Javik lay back on his bed and thought of Allana. He would have to find some way to free her. His mother would certainly take her in at Browdat's longhouse, and she could teach Allana all she needed to know about being a woman. He loved this girl and would not rest until she was his. She was safe now with Tao Shan, so all he had to do was convince her she should love him in return. He fell asleep and dreamed of the beautiful, raven-haired girl.

Chapter 22

The next day, a much more presentable Allana, dressed as a student, stood before Tao Shan. She was not sure what this man would require of her as his slave, but she knew that anything would be better than her life with the Sentii. The strange, yellow skinned warrior seemed to be kind, but Allana kept up her guard in case he proved to be putting up a front. He didn't chain her at night, and his security was almost non-existent. If she felt there was any risk to herself, she could always go back to the mountains.

"What shall I do with you?" Tao Shan asked. "You must earn your food here, or I vow I will sell you to the next slaver who passes through."

Allana's mood did not change. "I have been a slave before and escaped. I can do it again. If you don't want me here, I will go back to the mountains."

"You will do as I command, or I will make good my vow, and you will not see Javik again," Tao Shan looked her squarely in the eyes and noticed a slight waiver in her resolve. It was true; she had feelings for the boy just as Javik had for her.

"Yes, Master," Allana responded more meekly than any time since entering his presence.

"Good! Now, as I remember, we spoke of you teaching the sling to my students?"

Allana already knew most of the house servants doubled as

teachers in his school. From her limited observations since coming to Tao Shan's house, she deduced most of them were warriors in their own right at one time; yet they served this man and taught his students. They must owe him a great debt, but it dawned upon her that she, also, owed him a great debt. She was still a slave, but she realized slave status meant little in Tao Shan's longhouse. She was treated as well as any paid servant. Only the tattoo on her shoulder branded her as different from the others.

"Yes, Master, I could teach the sling."

"True, but teaching sling will not take that much of your time. What else could you do for me?"

"I could serve you otherwise by mending clothes. I am skilled with a needle, and I've noticed that many of you wear clothes with shoddy seams." She pointed to a particularly sloppy repair on Tao Shan's tunic.

"Yes," Tao Shan acknowledged as he shifted the garment to hide the offending work. "Banda was once a sail maker, but skill with the softer fabrics seems to elude him. If he were not such an excellent archery instructor, I would have sent him on his way long ago." The master rubbed his chin and considered Allana's offer. "Show me your skill with the sling, and I will decide after that if teaching and mending is enough."

"I have it here, Master," Allana produced the leather thong from her purse and patted a pouch of stones hanging from her belt. "Show me a target."

Tao Shan led her outside to the archery range. He had seen slingers in action and knew they could be effective provided they had some protection from the enemy's archers. A bow had more range, but the stone from a sling had the impact of a crossbow. He stopped at what he considered a good distance from the targets, considering she was only a woman, and turned to Allana.

"Strike the gold from here," he commanded.

Allana smiled confidently as she fitted a smooth stone to the pouch on the thong. The task Tao Shan set for her was well within her range. She whirled it only once before loosing the missile. Almost at the same time, a loud "splat" sound called Tao Shan's attention to a hole in the middle of the gold circle. He whistled softly as he moved to inspect the damage. The stone had gone completely through the matted straw backing of the target. This might have been a lucky shot.

"Now from here," Tao Shan walked back several paces beyond the previous spot. At this distance only the best male slingers could be accurate.

Allana judged the distance. It would be a long shot, but she'd made such shots before. This time she swung the leather thong several times before releasing the stone. She smiled broadly as it impacted just on the line between the gold and red circles.

"Very good!" Tao Shan instinctively clapped the girl on her back in congratulation. "I wonder that Javik is still alive after his encounter with your sling."

"I did not want to kill him. I used a soft stone and threw it with less force."

"Show me how you did that," Tao Shan asked.

Allana fumbled through the pouch and produced a large stone. "See Master, this stone will crumble when it strikes anything offering resistance." She passed the stone to Tao Shan who turned it over in his palm and hefted it to test its weight.

"Sandstone," he announced as he handed it back to Allana.

"Yes, most of my stones come from stream beds, but I must make these stones from larger pieces." She fitted the missile to the sling and swung it slowly before releasing it. The rock hit the target with a soft thud and splattered into a thousand pieces without penetrating the canvas.

"Formidable," Tao Shan complimented. "If you can put five straight rocks in the gold, I will give you no other chores than teaching and mending."

Allana smiled and selected five small stones from her pouch. In rapid succession, she landed all five in the gold circle.

Chapter 23

Javik was not the only one to notice the change in Allana, brought about by a haircut and new clothes. Sigurd suddenly realized what he had written off as a wild animal was a remarkably attractive woman. The fact she was also a slave, and someone who should be doubly impressed with his breeding and wealth, gave him the confidence to approach her after his first sling lesson.

"Let me introduce myself, Allana. I am Sigurd of the house of Odum."

"I have heard of you Sigurd." Allana didn't look up from inspecting the slings the boys used for practice that morning.

"I want to compliment you on your skill with the sling. I've never seen the weapon used before, but I'm sure you exceed even the best men."

Allana looked up from her work and studied the boy. He was not bad looking, and he had money and a good name, but several of the boys had already warned her about him. His confident smile reminded her of the look Grucheau had when he forced himself upon her. Sigurd saw her only as an object of desire, and probably considered that a tryst with him would be a favor to Allana. Yet, he was being complimentary.

"I am no match for a good male slinger, but I thank you for your compliment."

"Perhaps you might be willing to spend some extra time

with me. I would really like to master the sling."

Allana read his mind easily. The lessons would probably be in some remote spot, and he would conveniently bring along a skin or two for when they wanted to rest. She would be safe in refusing his advances because Tao Shan had given the boys strict orders concerning her, but it might be amusing to play him along for a while. He would have to obey her wishes concerning any intimate contact since Tao Shan would have his hide if he raped her.

"Very well, when would you like to have an extra lesson?"

Sigurd's eyes lit up with anticipation, but he stammered a bit as he tried to think of an appropriate time and place. He wasn't prepared for a positive response.

"Well, ah, I think, ah, tomorrow after lunch. I know a meadow where we could practice on some tree stumps."

"Then, tomorrow after lunch it is. Bring your sling and gather some stones. You know what kind we need, don't you?"

"Oh yes, I will bring plenty of stones." Sigurd had no idea when he would find time to gather stones for the practice session, but he gave the only answer he could.

"You must excuse me now, Sigurd. I have a lot of mending to finish before the evening meal." Allana gathered up her slings and stone bags and disappeared into the longhouse.

Sigurd stood for a moment studying her walk. A familiar warm surge rose from his loins and sent his heart into a spasm of activity.

Javik noticed Sigurd talking to Allana, but felt confident her feelings for him were the same as his for her. After all, Sigurd was a boor, and everyone made sure Allana knew he was a bully and a snob. Javik went on to his next assignment feeling very sure of his position. He wasn't so confident when he saw Sigurd and Allana heading off into the forest after lunch the next day. The fact that Sigurd carried a large bundle under one arm was also disturbing. From its size and bulk, Javik deduced it was probably a roll of furs to use as ground cover. He decided to follow them.

As they walked through the forest, Sigurd took advantage of his captive audience.

"My house is one of the finest in Berglaundia. My father is a war leader and a valued member of the King's council. King Olgar rarely makes a decision without consulting him."

"I'm sure he is a fine man." Allana tried to find something good to say in spite of her amusement at Sigurd's indirect approach. He was handsome enough in his own right, and he had no need of impressing her with his family's position. Even though she was sure she would turn him down if he made an advance, he was not hard to look at.

"He is, and my uncle is master of the King's archers. We keep a large household, and even our slaves live better than most Berglauni."

"Is that an invitation, Sigurd?"

"Why no, I was just telling you about my family."

"Oh, I thought that you might be wanting to buy me from our master."

"I have not completed Mauhad, and I may not own slaves, yet."

"But, you might want to own some afterwards?"

"Never you, Allana. I would not bring you to my family's house as a slave." Sigurd knew he was in very deep, but he realized that his last remark dug the hole even deeper. There was no possibility of his family accepting a former slave as his wife, and he suspected Allana knew this as well as he did. He tried to find an easy way out.

"You have a fine situation here at our master's school. You are a respected teacher, and you have your pick of the students, if you wanted any of them."

"Oh, there are one or two who might interest me." Allana's smile told Sigurd he was possibly one of them.

"I suppose Javik is at the top of that list."

"Not necessarily. Javik is a fine looking boy, but there are others just as handsome, and many are richer." Allana felt a twinge of guilt offering false hope to Sigurd, but the game was fun. She would enjoy seeing him squirm later.

They walked on in silence until Sigurd announced, "The meadow I spoke of is just over the next hill."

* * * * *

Javik found it easy to trail the pair. They were too absorbed in each other to notice him, and he stayed well back while they were walking. If they stopped, he would move closer and more caution would be required. When they entered the meadow, he found a large tree affording an excellent view though he could not hear them very well.

* * * * *

"Well Sigurd, what target did you have in mind?"

"I think that stump over there, the one in the open."

"Good choice. Did you remember to bring your sling and some stones?"

"Oh yes, right here." Sigurd produced the leather sling and a small bag of stones.

Allana weighed the bag in her hand. "This isn't very many stones for a practice session."

"I thought you could show me your release technique. I'm having trouble getting my stones on target. They keep sailing off into the air."

"I think you're holding the free end too loosely. Let me see your grip."

Sigurd grasped the sling as Allana taught them, and she took his hands in hers to test the positioning of the fingers and the strength of his grip. The touch of her hands sent shivers up his spine. Though her hands were rough from living so long in the wild, they were still delicate. The warmth of her touch almost made him sweat. He moved closer until their bodies touched at the hip. Allana pushed him away roughly.

"Not so close, Sigurd. I can see very well from here." She grasped his hands again leaving more room between them.

"Sorry, I thought you wanted me closer."

"Your grip looks good. What you must remember is that the stone comes out of the sling on a radial line, not a tangential line. If you release too early, the stone will go high of the target. Try one or two, and I'll watch your release."

Sigurd cast the first stone and deliberately released it late. Allana only nodded and said, "Try another."

He released the second stone early, and Allana moved toward him.

"No, no, no. You must learn to be consistent as well as correct." She took his hand and positioned it where the stone should be released. "Here, here is where you should release. Does your body tell you anything about this position?"

"My body tells me that it's proper position is close to yours." Sigurd grasped Allana around the waist and pulled her to him.

"Sigurd! Stop that! Our master will be angry with you."

"One kiss and I will be satisfied. Is one kiss too much to ask?"

"Sigurd! No!"

* * * * *

At this point, Javik could stand no more. He burst from his hiding place and descended upon Sigurd before he was aware of the attack. He wrapped one arm around Sigurd's neck and began to close off his air. Sigurd reacted very quickly, but this time Javik was prepared for his move. The attempt to throw Javik over his shoulder failed, and the boys fell to the ground with Javik's arm still strangling Sigurd.

"Javik, what are you doing?" Allana screamed at the struggling boys. "Stop! Stop it now."

The boys froze in position and turned their eyes on Allana without saying a word.

"You're both acting like children. Javik! Let loose of Sigurd."

Javik relaxed his hold on Sigurd's throat, and started to regain his feet when Sigurd pulled him back to the ground and rolled on top of him.

"Sigurd! You're in enough trouble as it is. Get off Javik."

Sigurd gave Javik a shove and stood up glaring at his rival. Javik stayed on the ground and pulled himself up on one elbow.

"I thought he was attacking you, Allana. I was only trying to help."

"I didn't need your help to handle Sigurd, but why were you following us in the first place?"

"I was afraid Sigurd might harm you."

"What nonsense!" Sigurd said. "I would no more harm this girl than myself. You're a fool, Javik."

Javik jumped to his feet and lunged toward Sigurd. Allana stepped between them with a speed that startled both boys.

"I've had enough of your male egos, both of you. Javik, I'm grateful to you for bringing me to Tao Shan's house, but don't mistake my gratitude for affection. Sigurd, if you wish to own me, you must vent your anger on Grucheau, my Sentii master, not Javik. I'm going back to the longhouse now, but I want both of you to promise that it ends here."

"This will not end until I have my satisfaction on Javik," Sigurd said. He drew himself up into a haughty pose and folded his arms across his chest. His mouth curved into a confident smile.

"It will end now, or I will inform Tao Shan of your actions." She turned to Javik. "Yours too, Javik."

Javik realized a severe caning awaited both of them if Allana did inform their master of the incident. He was also somewhat demoralized by Allana's words. Was he so stupid that he completely misread her feelings for him? He had to admit his experience with girls was very limited. Perhaps he had mistaken gratitude for affection. It was obvious now she cared nothing for either of them.

Javik spoke with sincere humility. "It's over for me, Allana. I apologize for acting like a jealous fool."

The words seemed to soften Sigurd. He looked at Allana's stern face and decided she would make good on her threat if he didn't make some gesture toward Javik. He extended his hand.

"A woman isn't worth even one stripe from our master, Javik. I forgive you."

"Forgive! You forgive me!" Javik threw himself at Sigurd, and the two landed in the grass rolling over and over. Allana only watched and sighed in resignation that boys would always be boys. She turned from the fight and left the meadow.

Sigurd managed to gain the upper hand and was about to ram his fist into Javik's face when he noticed Allana striding into the forest.

"Damn, Javik. She's going to tell the master about us thanks to your temper."

"My temper! If you weren't such a snob you could have just shook hands and it would have been over, but you had to *forgive* me."

Sigurd stood up and offered his hand to Javik to help him rise.

"I'm sorry, Javik. I can be an awful boor, I know. Let's go home. We've both blown any chance we may have had with Allana."

Javik took the offered hand and pulled himself to his feet. He dusted the dirt from his clothes and looked at Sigurd. The boy had an expression of genuine chagrin on his face for the first time since Javik met him.

"Do you have any feelings for her, Sigurd, or are you just looking for a conquest?"

"I don't know, Javik. I started out here only with the thought of having her, but she is a remarkable girl even if she is only a slave."

"I thought she cared for me, but her words just now convinced me she does not."

"I don't know why we should bother with her. We're in the same boat, you and I. Neither of our families would let us take a slave girl for a wife."

Javik hadn't considered that part of the problem. In his own mind he was still Javik, son of Tolda, and free to have any woman he wished. Now that he was Browdat's adopted son, his marriage would be a matter of family alliances with dowries and land settlements in the bargain. He suddenly felt a companionship with Sigurd.

"Sigurd, I'm not used to being on your social level yet, but I understand what you're saying. Let's go home."

The boys walked back to the longhouse, and they were relieved when Tao Shan was not waiting for them with a stiff hickory rod.

Chapter 24

The long, boring summer of geography and mathematics ended, and the time for Mauhad was fast approaching. Allana seemed to be ignoring all of the boys' attentions. She kept herself busy teaching them how to use a sling and mending a mountain of clothes for the residents of Tao Shan's longhouse. The forest was, once again, ablaze with autumn as the time for the harvest festival approached.

While the rest of the village was busy harvesting crops, the five boys Tao Shan selected for Mauhad became rock hard and ready for any challenge. In honor of the harvest festival, Tao Shan recessed the school for the week. Much to Javik's surprise, Tao Shan asked him to take Allana into his village for the celebration. As they walked the short distance, Javik tried to mend fences.

"I'm glad you're coming to my village for the festival, Allana."

"It was Tao Shan's idea. He didn't want me to be left out of the celebration, and he thought Browdat's house would welcome me."

"I will welcome you even more. By the way, I haven't thanked you for keeping my fight with Sigurd a secret."

"I saw no point in either one of you taking any more of a beating than you were giving each other."

"Just the same, I'm grateful."

The walk continued in silence for a while, then Allana spoke, "Tell me about the house of Browdat."

Javik filled her in on the household and the tragic events of the spring festival. Allana seemed to absorb his words like a sponge, and she tried to read the information back to him.

"Let me see if I have this straight, Javik. Your father was a war leader of the Berglauni who was killed by the Sentii, and his name was Tolda. You and your mother were given to Lord Browdat as wards of the King, but Browdat adopted you when his son, Zuban, was executed. Your best friends are Berda and Karl, and Browdat's wife is named Hella. Is that all right?"

"No, Hella was murdered by Zuban. Browdat's wife is named Frieda. It'll be easier once you have faces to put with the names," Javik assured her. "How do you like living in Tao Shan's longhouse?"

"Tao Shan is a good master," Allana said.

"He's a wise man and, really, very kind. I'm lucky to be his student. When my father was killed, I didn't think I would ever be able to pass Mauhad."

"Tell me of this 'Mauhad'. I've heard nothing but that ever since I came to Tao Shan's house, but no one's told me what it is."

"It's our manhood test. Each year, at the harvest festival, fathers must present their sons to the village elders as candidates. If a boy has no father, like me, his mentor must present him. If he has no mentor, he must find some man who will speak for him. The elders question each candidate before he is accepted, but everyone passes that part of the trial. The hard part comes when the boys are sent out into the forest to live for an entire week on their own."

"That's not much of a test," Allana sniffed. "I've lived on my own for two years. Perhaps the Berglauni would accept me as a man?" Javik sensed that she was only half joking. The hint of sincerity in her voice belied the laugh accompanying the statement.

"If it was only that, it would be easy. The hard part is evading the warriors sent to find you. The boys are sent out in the evening, and some of the best men in the village are sent out the next morning at dawn to bring them in."

"Sentii warriors looked for me, and they never found me," Allana bragged. "I don't see what's so difficult about your Mauhad."

Javik shrugged his shoulders and walked on in silence. It was true, this remarkable girl managed to accomplish everything any manhood candidate of the Berglauni would be asked to do. Javik consoled himself by believing that a Berglauni hunting party would have been much more effective at finding one slave girl than a whole host of Sentii warriors.

As they entered the fields before the village stockade, Javik could see the grain sheaves standing in golden piles throughout the black soil of the fields. Men and women were busy loading them on wagons for the trip to the threshing floor. Many of them greeted Javik warmly as he passed.

"How nice it would be to have a family and friends," Allana said.

"You will have my family, such as it is; and I am your friend," Javik replied.

Allana smiled at him with that glow he had come to love, and his heart melted. Only the call of Karl and Berda could penetrate his trance, and he was almost sad to hear them.

"Javik! Javik!" they called from the gate then raced to meet him.

Allana held back as the three greeted each other with a love she had often seen between the boys of Tao Shan's longhouse.

She envied their close relationship, but she knew these juvenile ties would melt quickly once they began to realize their desire for females.

"I want you to meet Allana," Javik turned his two friends toward the girl. "She serves at the house of Tao Shan." He made the introductions.

"Does Tao Shan take female students?" Berda asked.

"I am not a student. I'm one of his servants...and an instructor," Allana added quickly.

"You're dressed like a student," Karl observed.

"Tao Shan has no women's clothes in his longhouse," Allana explained.

"What do you teach?" Berda asked.

"She instructs us in the use of the sling," Javik inserted. "You should see her, Karl. She can drop a sparrow from a limb at thirty paces."

"Ooohhh," Karl was truly impressed.

"It was the only weapon I could hide while I was a Sentii slave. One of the other women taught me to use it. I got quite good at it, too."

"Come with us," Javik commanded. "I have to take Allana to my mother, then we can catch up on what's been happening in the village since the spring festival."

Allana wanted to stay with the boys, but she understood why Javik was leaving her with his mother. Tao Shan told her to obtain some women's clothing during her visit, and gave her some money for that purpose. Javik would be no help in this task.

"Mother! Mother, I'm home!" Javik called as he entered Browdat's longhouse.

Allana was impressed by the tall, dignified woman holding her arms open to embrace her son. Allana thought the older woman had held her looks well, while Javik noticed that the change in her status from ward of the King to mother of an adopted son had created some improvements in her clothing and grooming. She was truly as much a lady now as she had been when she was Tolda's wife.

"Welcome home, Son." Dana embraced her boy then held him at arm's length to study the changes the summer wrought. "You are more muscular than last spring, and I think you've grown half a hand." She rubbed her fingers across his chin. "Is this a beard I feel?"

"It's so light no one knows I have one," Javik apologized.

"It will soon be dark enough if you shave it regularly." Dana rubbed her son's chin playfully then noticed the slim looking boy behind him was actually a girl.

"Who is this?" Dana indicated Allana.

"This is Allana, Mother. She was a slave to the Sentii, but she now serves Tao Shan."

Allana bowed to Dana. "I am honored to meet you, Lady Dana."

"Rise, Allana. You are not a servant here." Dana lifted the girl's chin and surveyed her carefully. "You are a lovely girl even in boy's clothes. Would you like to have something more flattering to wear?"

"Yes, Lady. I lived in the wild for so long I've forgotten how lovely a woman could be until I saw you."

Dana smiled. "Your time in the wild has not dulled your ability to flatter. I am an old woman and pale beside you. Come, you may have some of Hella's things. You are close to the same size, and I can alter what does not fit. Excuse us, boys. I'm sure you three have much to talk about without having women around."

"Where is Margan, Mother?" Javik asked before she could

leave. He often thought of the man with the twisted back and mellow voice who sang his father's praise so well and saved him from a cruel death.

"He's gone on his way. His hands healed nicely, and he thanked me for helping by composing a song about me. He promised to come back one day and sing it for you." Dana saw the disappointment in her son's face. "He hasn't forgotten you, Javik. He will be back one day. Come, Allana, we will leave the boys to their own devices."

The boys watched as Dana led Allana back into the women's section of the longhouse.

"Javik, your staff is alive!" Karl said. "It was the only one that lived."

Javik remembered the sapling old Grazhda picked out for him as a gift to Verna during the spring festival. The fact it lived through the summer was a significant omen of great things for Javik. The legend was that such a man was destined to be a leader of the Berglauni people.

"I heard from Tao Shan. Let's go see it," Javik said as he prodded his friends toward the doorway.

The sacred grove of Verna was lush and green even in the throes of autumn. The altar was washed clean by the summer rains, and the necklaces and clothing that previously hung on the goddess' statue were gone. In the area reserved for staffs several dead sticks surrounded one green, living sapling whose leaves were just beginning to show traces of bright red. Javik walked to it and touched the shining leaves.

"It is true," Javik whispered as he marveled at the sight. "It lived."

"It's a mighty omen, Javik," Berda said. "It means you will be a great leader of our people and bring much wealth and happiness to the Berglauni."

"If I ever get the chance," Javik sighed. "I am not to go on Mauhad this year."

"That can't be so," Karl was surprised. "You were almost ready when you went to Tao Shan last year."

"I know. I thought so, too; but the master wants me to spend another year with him."

"Does he know what he's doing?" Berda asked.

"He's a very wise man. I must trust his judgment even though I don't agree with it. There's enough time to be a man in my future."

"Perhaps not," Karl's voice held a note of foreboding.

"Why do you say that?" Javik asked.

"There is talk among the men that we'll soon be at war with the Wallans," Berda said.

"But, I thought the Sentii were our worst enemy," Javik protested.

"There's no love for the Sentii here, but the Wallans have threatened to invade the province of Harcha if the Berglauni do not grant them unlimited hunting rights there. I've heard my father say the King will never give them what they want," Karl explained.

"It would mean boys our age could be pressed into service as porters and camp attendants if we don't pass Mauhad," Berda said.

"I have not trained for a year with Tao Shan to carry someone's shield for him," Javik said.

"That's why I was sure Tao Shan would select you for Mauhad," Karl said. "My father says we will need every able bodied man in the country to defeat the Wallans."

"A war, and I will serve as a porter," Javik slammed a fist on Verna's altar and fought to hold back the tears. He was as much a man now as anyone his age and more so than many who passed Mauhad last year. Tao Shan was to blame for this, and Javik would confront him after the festival, if war were truly imminent. Until then, he would wait and see which way the winds blew. Browdat would know the truth if anyone did.

Karl put an arm around his friend. "It's okay, Javik. At least we'll be together, just like always."

"Yes, we'll have some fine adventures together," Berda added.

His friends' support was little consolation to the budding warrior.

Chapter 25

Dana led Allana to a trunk in the women's rooms and opened it, revealing a stash of dresses. "These were Hella's things. Did Javik tell you about her?"

"Yes, Lady. It was a very sad story. I hope the lady Frieda has recovered from the loss of her son."

"She still mourns both him and Hella, but she will be glad to see Javik. Now that he is her son too, he can give her much comfort." Dana pulled out a lovely white top and blue cover garment. "Try these on, Allana."

The girl removed the boy's clothes, and Dana admired her figure, as she stood nude before donning the undergarment. She was a beautiful girl. Perhaps Javik would find her attractive. He could free her from servitude, marry her, and she would be a great asset to his hearth. She sighed inwardly, knowing that her boy was destined for greater arrangements now that he was Browdat's son.

The female clothing made a remarkable difference in Allana's appearance, but Dana studied her to determine what was still missing. "It's your face," she announced after a while.

"What about my face, Lady?" Allana asked striking an indignant pose.

Dana laughed at Allana's reaction. "Your face is lovely, but as lovely as it is, it needs a bit of help. Come with me."

Dana led the girl to her own room and sat her down next to

a shelf of jars and bottles. "A woman must have some help from alchemy to look her best," Dana explained. "The trick is to do it so a man thinks it's all natural." She rubbed various ointments and powders on Allana's face and painted around her eyes and lips. From time to time she stood back to analyze her work then returned to add more or redo what was already done. Allana began to tire of the process, and was about to protest when Dana pronounced success.

"There! You're even more beautiful, and I didn't think it was possible. Come see!"

Dana led her to a piece of polished brass, and Allana marveled at the image. She was beautiful. This image was not at all like the one she saw reflected in the forest pools. Dana had worked a miracle.

"You need some jewelry," Dana announced as she opened a small chest and selected several bracelets and a bead necklace. She showed Allana how to wear them and stood back glowing with admiration. "Tonight you will have every boy in the village falling at your feet."

"There is only one boy I want at my feet, Lady, and that is your son," Allana blushed.

Dana's face softened as she spoke. "If my Javik does not think you are the loveliest thing he has ever seen, I will beat him senseless."

"You must not tell him of my feelings, Lady."

"Of course not, Allana. That shall be a secret between us women."

A smile spread across Allana's face as the two women hugged.

* * * * *

Browdat sat in the council meeting drumming his fingers on

the table. All of this talk was useless. The Wallans would move as soon as they had the King's answer, and the Berglauni were in no position to stop them unless they mobilized at once. Every man and boy in the kingdom would be needed to turn back the Wallan horde. There would barely be time to hold the Mauhad before the army would have to move. The talk wore on until midday when the king closed the discussion with a motion of his hand. He stood silently and drew his jewel-encrusted sword, placing it on the conference table before him.

"My lords, it will be war with the Wallans, but we must prepare before I send our answer. Each of you will return to your lands and muster every able-bodied man. When your forces are ready, send word to me and move to the agreed-upon places. May Zhou help us."

The lords left for home in somber mood. All of them had seen war, and none of them wanted to sacrifice a generation of Berglauni on that bloody altar; but there was no choice now. The Wallans must not be allowed to take the best hunting grounds in the kingdom.

Browdat rode into the village and directly to the council house. The word of his coming preceded him, and the house was packed with men. He strode to the center of the group and made his speech.

"Warriors, the King has decided on war."

A spontaneous shout of exaltation rose from the assembled men, and Browdat mourned the fact his people were so eager to die.

"You captains know what to do. Alert your men and have them ready to march immediately after the Mauhad. As you muster your units send word to me. We will ride for Wallandia Moor the morning after the Ceremony of Manhood."

The men departed in a jubilant mood, but Browdat's

thoughts were dark as he walked toward his longhouse. Javik met him before he had gone half way.

"My lord father, is it to be war?" Javik asked.

"Yes, Javik. It is war. We will march immediately after Mauhad. Are you ready for the test?"

Javik lowered his eyes. "Tao Shan has not recommended me."

"What! That's ridiculous. You're as ready as any boy in the village." This news did not improve Browdat's mood.

"I accept his decision, Lord, but it will be hard to bear another's pack when there is glory to be won."

"I won't have you held back," Browdat said. "I will speak with Tao Shan." He turned to one of his servants. "Go to the mentor's house and bring him here. Tell him nothing but that I wish to speak with him."

"Yes, Lord." The soldier turned and ran toward the horses.

"We will see about this," Browdat blustered as he stomped into the longhouse.

Behind him, Javik felt a surge of hope brighten his mood. If anyone could change his master's mind it would surely be Browdat. With any luck at all, he would not be a porter in this war.

Frieda saw the look on her husband's face and immediately understood the situation.

"It's war, isn't it?" she asked.

"Yes, we have no choice, wife."

She embraced her husband as she fought back tears. How many times had she seen him ride off into danger? Too many, she was certain. He always returned. He usually rode back, but there were several times he arrived on a litter. She felt he was tempting the gods by risking his life in battle at this age, but he would never sit behind the fray and watch. The huge man knew only one way to lead – from the front of his men.

Dana bowed to her lord and protector. "We welcome you home, Lord."

"Dana, you look well," Browdat complimented, then noticed Allana.

"Who is this lovely girl?" he asked.

"This is Allana, my lord. She was a Sentii slave but now serves Tao Shan." Dana pushed a somewhat frightened Allana toward Browdat. The girl knelt before him.

"Rise, Allana," Browdat managed only a whisper. The striking beauty of this girl overwhelmed his senses. "It's not hard to tell why that old scoundrel wanted you. You are welcome in my house."

"Thank you, Lord," was all Allana could manage. The fierce aspect of the man coupled with his huge frame magnified the sense of awe engendered by his status as a Berglauni war leader. Her old habits as a slave had not yet died out completely.

"You must be hungry," Frieda spoke. "Come to the great room. I've prepared some food."

Javik approached Allana and almost stumbled over his own feet in the process. "I didn't think anyone could improve on your beauty, but my mother has transformed you into a goddess."

Allana almost blushed, but she recovered quickly and smiled at Javik. "Why Javik, I never knew you could say such nice things."

* * * * *

As the family ate, the talk was of nothing but war. Allana sat next to Javik and said little. She was used to her place as a woman and a slave – her opinions were unimportant.

"What say you, Allana?" Browdat asked. "Will the Sentii join with the Wallans?"

Allana was completely taken aback that such a powerful man would ask her opinion. She felt humility was her only logical response. She lowered her gaze and spoke softly. "Lord, I am a mere slave girl. I know nothing."

"Nonsense! Who was your master?" Browdat roared.

"My master was the lord Grucheau, sir."

"Grucheau! He is one of their war chiefs. You must have heard something around his house."

"I have not been in his house for almost two years, sir. I escaped from his village and hid in the mountains to be free."

Browdat looked at the girl in amazement. "A little slip of a girl like you? You hid in the mountains for two years, and the Sentii did not find you?"

"That's true, Lord," Allana replied meekly.

"The Sentii never found her, but I tracked her down in one day, sir," Javik boasted.

"Only after I knocked you out of a tree with my sling and stole your dagger," Allana added.

The family laughed merrily, and Browdat looked quizzically at the girl and then to Javik. "How did Javik find you if you eluded the Sentii for two years?"

"He tracked me to the cliff hiding my cave and set an ambush at my water hole."

"I'll be damned!" Browdat roared even louder. "You are a true son of mine, Javik. If this girl is not worth trapping, I don't know what is. She's finer than prime ermine," he laughed loudly.

Allana blushed even redder than Javik at the big warrior's praise of their worth.

At that moment, Tao Shan entered the hall.

"Greetings, Lord Browdat," the old man said.

"Tao Shan! Welcome! Sit down and eat," Browdat commanded.

"I have eaten, Lord, but I will have something to drink," he looked at Frieda who signaled a servant. A mug of qush was placed in front of the mentor. "What do you wish, sir?" Tao Shan knew the answer to this question by the look on Javik's face.

"My son, Javik, tells me that you did not recommend him for Mauhad. What is your reason?" Browdat asked.

"He is ready, sir, but Javik has the makings of a war leader, and I would take another year to train him in the ways of a leader."

"You know there is to be war with the Wallans?" Browdat asked.

"I assumed as much from the activities of the men as I approached the village," Tao Shan answered.

"I want my son to be in the war as a fighter, not as a bearer. If you will not nominate him for Mauhad, I will do it as his father." Browdat's speech was not a request but an order.

"Lord Browdat, I cannot in all good conscience nominate Javik for Mauhad. True, he is ready both physically and mentally, but I would let him see this war from the rear so he might better appreciate the next year's lessons."

Javik burned to say something in his own behalf, but he knew he must be silent. Any protestation on his part would only serve to confirm Tao Shan's decision to hold him back as immature.

* * * * *

Dana listened with a sense of fear gripping her heart. She had already lost her husband to war, must her son be sacrificed so soon? Still, he would be a man someday. She could not hold back time, and Javik would go the way of all men in spite of her protests.

* * * * *

"I know you mean well, Tao Shan; but in this case, my feelings must overrule your wisdom. Javik must be a part of this war." Browdat knew the mentor was right, but he also knew Javik would be humiliated if he sat safe in the rear while his peers were in the thick of the fighting.

"Of course, I must bow to your wishes. You are his father," Tao Shan said. "Perhaps you would be willing to send Javik back to me after the war is over?"

"How could I do that? He would be a warrior then and not a boy in training."

"In my homeland, a young man often spends time as the apprentice of an older man. Though the custom is not observed among the Berglauni, I see nothing in your culture that would prohibit such a thing."

"How could he earn a living and keep his own hearth if he were with you? It would be humiliating for a warrior to be seen as a student after he had been to war." Browdat fought to control his rage.

"My lord, Javik will not be in a position to set up his own hearth until he has captured a good deal of gold from his raids. He could live in your house and come to my house for training each day," Tao Shan offered.

"He would have duties here, if he were in my house," Browdat reminded the mentor.

"But, could his duties tolerate, say, three mornings a week?" Tao Shan turned to Javik. "Javik, I know you hope to set up a hearth so your mother may be the head of her own household, but would you be willing to let her remain with Lord Browdat for another year in order to learn how to lead men?"

Javik looked at his mother and then at Allana. Now that he was a son of Browdat, his mother's situation was not so critical; and he would have to win a great deal of gold to purchase Allana from Tao Shan. He could only do that as a war leader entitled to a triple share of any booty. It would make sense to learn as much as he could from the master.

"Yes, if my mother will agree," Javik answered.

"With all my heart," Dana added quickly.

"At what cost?" Browdat scowled.

"None to you, Lord. As a man, Javik would have to pay his own way," Tao Shan smiled.

"I'm afraid I have no gold, Master," Javik said.

"You will earn it. You will earn it," Tao Shan assured him. "My price will not be too heavy a burden upon you. We will speak of that later."

"Then it is done," Browdat roared. "I will nominate Javik for Mauhad immediately." He summoned a servant and sent him to the council house with the name of Javik to be added to the list of boys for Mauhad. After the servant left, he shouted for more qush.

"This calls for a toast," Browdat said as the tankards were filled, including one for Javik and Allana.

The giant warrior rose and raised his tankard on high. "To Javik, the new Hammer of Zhou."

Javik rose proudly and raised his tankard toward Browdat. The smile on Tao Shan's face brought waves of pride surging through his chest. He did not see the tear fall from his mother's eye or the frown beginning to turn down Allana's mouth.

Chapter 26

The Mauhad began at dawn. The boys selected were herded into the village square for calisthenics under the watchful eyes of several warriors. Any boy failing to keep up with the rigorous pace received a severe tongue-lashing and a demand for even more strenuous activity. One by one, they were escorted into the great hall for interrogation by the village elders.

Javik's turn was early, and he was glad to be free of the physical demands. In spite of the chill air, his tunic was already wet with perspiration. Mikka, Zuban's executioner, escorted Javik. It was hard for Javik to refrain from conversation with the muscular warrior, but he knew that at this point in the ceremony any sound on his part would only result in a solid blow for his insolence.

The great hall was dim. Only a few torches burned, casting flickering shadows around the room and giving it an eerie appearance. Smoke from a small fire in the center of the floor curled slowly up to the ceiling vent hole adding an aura of mystery, while the constant pounding of a small drum added a degree of solemnity to the situation. Buran, the law keeper, Tahsla, the village elder, and Goldar were seated behind a table on the other side of the fire. Behind them a statue of Zhou, protector god of the Berglauni, loomed over the proceedings. Old Banda, the priest of Zhou stood to Javik's left just outside the ring of light from the small fire. This was Zhou's ceremony, and it would be conducted with all of the solemnity and secrecy associated with the high god.

"Who comes to be tested by Zhou?" Tahsla intoned in a quavering voice.

"I bring Javik, son of Tolda," Mikka replied.

"Javik is also son of Browdat," the big war leader thundered. Javik saw Mikka cringe a bit at his own forgetfulness.

"It is noted," Tahsla answered. "Come forward, Javik, son of Tolda and Browdat."

Mikka pushed Javik toward the fire and whispered, "Kneel before the elders."

Javik knelt just within the circle of the firelight. The elders he knew so well from previous encounters were now disembodied voices in the darkness.

"Answer me! What is the duty of a warrior to his village?" a voice he recognized as Buran's asked.

"A warrior must give his life for his village," Javik answered.

"Answer me! What does a warrior owe to his family?" This was Goldar.

"The protection of his arm and loyalty unto death," Javik spoke clearly. Tao Shan had coached him very well, and he knew he must give these answers exactly.

"Answer me! What does a warrior owe to himself?" Javik knew Tahsla's voice well. It was burned into his memory from Zuban's trial. He hesitated, Tao Shan had not prepared him for this one. There was no standard reply, and his mind raced to formulate the answer he thought the elders wanted.

Buran would want him to say something about obedience to the law. Goldar would look for an answer reflecting his duties as a warrior, but Tahsla was a different matter. What would an elder look for in his answer? He hadn't talked with the old man before and knew little about his background except that he was once a fierce warrior. He remembered his actions and words at the trial, but they only proved he was wise and had the benefit of many experiences. What would Tao Shan expect him to say? The mentor never discussed this with any of the boys.

"We are waiting for your answer, Javik," Tahsla prodded.

Javik finally decided the answer must be his own. Only he could say what he owed himself. The realization hit him instantly – he knew the answer all along. He pulled himself up to his full height though still kneeling.

"A warrior owes himself his honor," Javik spoke proudly. *If this is not the answer they're looking for they can go hang themselves,* he thought. *In the end, a warrior must live with himself, and he can only do that if he's satisfied he always did the honorable thing.*

A low murmur was the only response from the assembled men. He did not see Tahsla nod to Banda, but he did see the priest step into the firelight.

"Priest of Zhou," Tahsla intoned. "Is our God satisfied with these answers?"

Without a word, the priest stepped toward the fire and threw a handful of powder into the flames. Javik recoiled from the bright flash of light, but regained his composure quickly.

"Zhou is pleased, lords," Banda replied, and Javik thought he saw a faint smile on the somber man's lips.

"Rise, Javik, son of Tolda and Browdat. You will now be returned to your fellow candidates to await the final decision of this council."

Mikka lifted Javik to his feet, placed a large hand on his shoulder and spun him around. With the flat of his sword, he slapped the boy across the bottom propelling him toward the exit of the common house.

Back outside, Javik was again subjected to the hazing of the warriors while the other boys were questioned. He couldn't wait to ask Karl and Berda what questions were put to them. The ordeal lasted until well into the afternoon because of the number of boys being tested. At long last, Goldar emerged from the common house and called the boys to attention.

The boys selected for Mauhad lined up in ranks before Goldar in the central square. There were thirty-six in all. No man wanted his son left out of the coming fight, and every boy of proper age had been nominated. Javik stood next to Karl and Berda. He knew most of the other boys by name but not by association.

"Candidates for Mauhad," Goldar's voice was sure and strong. "You have been nominated for the manhood test of the Berglauni, and you have all been questioned by the elders to be sure you are qualified for this ordeal. Now you must go to your mentors and prepare yourselves. Return here when the sun sets. Dismissed!"

The boys ran in all directions. Javik headed for Browdat's house where Tao Shan waited in a room by himself. He looked very somber, almost as if he'd expected Javik to fail and was only waiting confirmation from the boy himself. Javik knelt before him.

"How many questions were you asked?" Tao Shan's tone was even more menacing than his looks, and Javik thought he must surely have failed.

"Only three, Master."

The mentor's face began to melt into a smile, but he resumed his stern appearance almost instantly. "What was the last question?"

"They asked me what a warrior owed to himself," Javik answered.

"And your answer was?"

"I said a warrior owed himself his honor, Master." At this point Tao Shan smiled broadly and clapped a wrinkled hand on the boy's shoulder.

"You have answered well, Javik. I would like to think my training had something to do with it, but I think your father was the one who instilled this answer in your soul. Well done."

"Thank you, Master. I was afraid I had not passed the test."

"You did well, Javik. Now we must get down to practical matters. You may only take three items with you. What will you take?" Tao Shan asked.

Javik had given this subject much thought in years past and responded quickly.

"My hunting knife," he said.

"A good choice," Tao Shan affirmed.

"A water skin and my fire tools," Javik finished.

"Not good choices," Tao Shan replied. "You will not dare risk a fire, so why bring fire tools? Water is everywhere in the forest; why burden yourself with a bulky water skin? No, Javik, take this." He handed the boy a salla, the signaling whistle used by the Berglauni.

"But, who would I want to signal, Master?" Javik was dumbfounded.

"You Berglauni possess a very valuable resource. Only your people can hear the confounded thing. I think you all must be part dog since they can hear it also. Just remember that there are times when it is better to be found than not found."

Javik took the salla and placed its thong around his neck.

"The other thing you will need is this." He produced a leather pouch filled with spanga leaves. "They will be hard to find this late in the year. I have saved these for my candidates. I gave each one a bag full before they left for their own villages.

This one is mine. I knew what Browdat wanted when he summoned me, so I brought it along."

Javik tied the bag to his belt. "Thank you, Master. I should have thought of that myself."

"You are still young, Javik. A year from now I would not have had to do this for you. Now you must know what my other students learned just before they left my house."

"The meaning of the markings on your door," Javik's face brightened as he recalled the mysterious runes.

"Yes, they are a proverb in the ancient language of my people." Tao Shan produced a stick of charcoal and wrote the seven strange symbols on the door of the room from top to bottom in a vertical line.

Tao Shan pointed to the first two symbols. "These say, 'Wise is a man who knows himself.'" He moved his hand past the next three. "And these say, 'Great is the man who is true to his word." The mentor placed the charcoal on a table and turned to Javik. "Now you are ready for Mauhad."

"But Master, what are the other two symbols?" Javik asked.

"I will tell you when you return from Mauhad. Now go and make Browdat and me proud of you."

Javik knelt before his mentor. He knew he should not have tears in his eyes at a moment like this, but it was impossible to hold them back. The memory of his father flooded his mind with emotions too strong to repress. Tao Shan and Browdat had provided him with all the things Tolda would have wished for his son. He owed all three of them more than he could ever repay. "I thank you for all you have taught me, sir. My father looks down from Zhou's throne and thanks you also."

"Rise, Javik! You have a new father now, and it is he you must honor from now on. Go, boy!"

Javik ran back to the square to join the other boys. The sun was setting, and dozens of torches illuminated the gathering place. Karl looked at him quizzically.

"Why are you taking a salla, and where's your water skin?" Karl asked.

"Tao Shan told me to take one and leave the other," Javik smiled, confident in the wisdom of his mentor.

"Are you sure you heard right about which was which?" Karl asked.

Javik only smiled. Goldar's voice interrupted their conversation.

"Line up for inspection!"

The boys lined up as before, and several of the village warriors searched each candidate to be sure they were not hiding some object other than the three they admitted to. Mikka was puzzled by Javik's bag of leaves.

"The forest is full of leaves, Javik," the warrior smiled.

"Not this kind, sir," Javik smiled back. Mikka evidently was not aware of the power of spanga leaves.

After the search, Goldar spoke again. "You will soon be free to leave. You may wander anywhere you like and hide as you see fit. The warriors will begin their search for you at dawn. You may not return to the village until after sunrise on the eighth day. Any boy who is caught will be tried before the council. If he is found wanting, he will not pass Mauhad. Are there any questions?"

Silence greeted the war chief as he scanned the rows of eager faces. "Go!" he shouted at the top of his lungs, and the boys sprinted off into the forest.

Javik felt a surge of energy. It spread from his shoulders to his legs only stopping at his gut for a moment to tie it in knots. He ran faster than he ever ran before. He must not fail this test. Death would be preferable to failure, but he had a plan. He knew where he was going. Allana's hideout in the mountains must be near the waterfall. If the Sentii could not find her there, his own people would not find him. There may even be some things there he could use. He sprinted down the path he knew would lead him there.

Mauhad was deliberately set for a time of the full moon. It made it more difficult for the boys to evade their pursuers, but it also gave the candidates some light for the first night when they would be running at full speed to put some distance between themselves and the village.

He thanked Tao Shan for his rigorous training program. He was covering the ground easily at a lope that would put him near the falls before midnight. He listened for the sounds of other boys and was glad none had taken this path with him.

His lungs did not begin to burn until he heard the sound of the water cascading down the rocky cliff. He pulled up in the clearing where he and Tao Shan met with Allana and sat down to catch his breath.

The moonlight played upon the dancing water creating luminous splotches spinning merrily as they vanished into the black pool at the bottom of the falls. Javik sat mesmerized by the scene until his breathing returned to normal.

Her hiding place must be somewhere between here and the drinking pool I found, Javik thought to himself. He climbed the face of the rocks next to the waterfall and found a promising ledge. It was narrow, but the bright moonlight made the trip no more dangerous than during the day. Soon he recognized some landmarks from his initial search for Allana, but there was no sign of a cave in the rocky hillside. Allana had found a wonderful hiding place, to be sure. He decided to find a place to sleep and resume his search in daylight.

As he rested against a large rock, thoughts of Allana rushed into his head. The transformation of her appearance under the guiding hand of his mother was miraculous. She was a lovely girl in her wild state, but her beauty exploded once she was dressed as a woman should be. He must have her for his wife, but winning her would be a difficult task. She had been alone so long she may not need any companionship now. He would do his best, but he knew he was only a novice when it came to women. He leaned back against the rock and allowed his mind to go blank. The long run and the sweet thoughts of Allana helped him drift off to sleep quickly.

Chapter 27

The chill of the pre-dawn hours aroused him from sleep. He was shivering cold and immediately began exercising to generate some body heat. The dull gray of the sky would soon give way to bright day, and the men from the village would be out in force. He must either run or hide very soon.

The rays of the morning sun took a long time moving over the hills and into the valley, but Javik was able to find Allana's drinking pool in the shadowy light. He worked his way back along the ledge leading from it, but found only a dead end at the face of a solid rock cliff.

"It has to be here somewhere," he voiced his frustration.

He could hear the sound of horses in the brush below him, and he knew the men had tracked him at least as far as the falls. From that point, they would not be able to use their skills since he had been traversing solid rock ever since. He would be safe for a little while yet, but they would soon begin systematically scouting the rocks.

Javik worked his way back toward the pool, but stopped dead in his tracks as he saw the first rays of the morning sun glint from something just ahead and slightly above him on the rock face. He moved closer and saw it was a metal object of some kind. The climb to it was not difficult, and he soon reached the spot to find a piece of a broken knife blade lodged in a small crevice.

Allana must have dropped this when she cleaned out her hiding place to go to Tao Shan's house. Her cave should be above here, he thought.

He strained his neck to see above him, but the rock receded too quickly. He would have to climb higher. After only a few meters, he saw it.

It was a small opening. He was not sure he could fit through it, though the tiny Allana would have had no trouble at all. He had to try it. The men would be upon him at any moment now if he stayed in the open.

The cave entrance was a tight squeeze, but by removing his tunic and belt and shoving them in ahead of him, Javik was able to wriggle into the cave. It was pitch dark, but the small amount of light from the entrance showed him it was large enough to almost stand up. Allana would have been able to walk around easily.

The signs of human habitation were unmistakable. Rocks had been re-arranged to form tables and shelves, and the pieces of wood she used as hooks and hangers for her equipment lay scattered on the floor. Her hurried departure caused her to leave things as they fell. The cave went back much farther, but it was pitch black beyond the small circle of light from the entrance. He could see some firewood in one corner, but a fire was out of the question until he could determine where the smoke went. He smiled knowing Tao Shan was right about leaving his fire tools behind. The only sound was a soft rush of air far back in the darkness.

"I can't move during the day with the men on my trail. I might as well rest here until dark." Javik found a bundle of animal skins Allana probably used for a bed and made himself comfortable. If the men found him here, they would have to be super-human. He thanked Allana for finding such a clever hiding place. He was sure he would be safe here until it was time to return to the village, and this contentment lulled him into a deep sleep.

Javik awoke late in the afternoon with hunger gnawing at his insides. He knew the first day or two would be the worst, but if he wasn't running, he would not need much food to carry him through the ordeal. The spanga leaves would help when he began to wear out, but he would save them as long as possible. He crept to the opening of the cave and listened.

The men had moved on. There was no sound of horses. Javik reasoned that they would fan out from the clearing by the falls and scour the mountain face for any sign of him. If that failed, as he knew it would, they would cover the possible exits from the area. Any source of food or water would be remembered as a possible ambush site. He would have to find food on the mountain itself if he ate at all.

Thirst compelled him to risk poking his head from the cave entrance. He had taken no water since before leaving the village. The excitement of being on Mauhad kept him running in spite of his thirst, and the need to find Allana's shelter dulled his urge to drink. Now that he was settled in, he felt the dryness in his throat. It had been tolerable for a while, but now it was driving him mad. If he did not drink soon, he would be screaming for water.

The trail below was empty, as was the rock face as far as he could see. The most likely spot for the men to post themselves was the top of the hill housing his cave. He rolled to his back and found that a small overhang hid his head, but by peering around it, he could see the summit easily. Allana was no fool. From this position she could easily survey the likely hiding places of any attackers. His trained eye scanned those spots and found no one on guard.

Javik slid out on the ledge creating more scratches and bumps to add to those he collected making his entry. He crept cautiously to the pool. The view from the ledge commanded an excellent sweep of the entire valley below. There was no sign of pursuit, but he sat for a while contemplating his homeland. The dark forests were everywhere, but small villages lined the rivers and the now barren fields broke the monotony of the landscape. He could see his own village in the distance, and he wondered if Allana ever sat here and longed to return to civilization. His parched throat interrupted his reverie, and he lay down to drink from the pool.

The water was cool and quenched his thirst instantly. He drank until he could hold no more, remembering Tao Shan's advice to drink deeply whenever he could. The absence of pursuers gave him courage to go a bit farther afield in search of food.

The rocky ground yielded little of nutritional value. He did find some hard berries growing on thorny, hardscrabble stems. Tao Shan called them chan-trea, but his people's name for them was strangleberry. The mentor showed the boys how to squeeze the pulp from the center and discard the poisonous hulls. He cleaned off the entire stand and still felt hungry, but he knew it was enough to keep him going. After another drink he returned to the cave.

The berries and the water combined to create a strong urge in his bowels, and he wondered where Allana had relieved herself. The light of the morning was gone from the cave, and it was now almost completely black inside. He felt his way cautiously back into the darkness. The wind sound he'd heard earlier seemed to grow in volume as he moved deeper into the cave. The ceiling dropped lower and lower as he went. Soon, he was on his hands and knees to avoid smashing his head on an exposed rock or stalagmite. He had crawled only a short distance when his hand dislodged a rock. To his surprise, he heard it ricocheting as it dropped down a crevasse.

He moved his hand forward cautiously and found only empty space, but he felt the cool breeze moving past his arm. There was a strong updraft in the crevasse, and he now knew the cause of the eerie sighing sound. He reached out carefully and felt solid rock facing him across the crevasse. Using his hands as measuring tools, he marked the distance from the cave floor to the vertical wall. The crevasse was no more than four hands wide.

Javik pulled back to solid ground and felt the wall in front of him. It dropped down vertically, but a spot a bit to his left felt smoother than the rest of the rough surface. He moved over to it and found a large rock on the cave floor worn smooth also. He turned around and sat on the rock with his back against the smooth wall. His behind was over the abyss, and he instantly knew this was Allana's toilet.

It was a very clever hiding place. Not only was it almost impossible to see unless you knew it was there, it also had the advantage of a toilet that would not betray the refugee with its stench. She also had to have some place for a fire. There was no way she could survive the winters without one. The crevasse must have acted as her chimney.

He continued his groping explorations until he felt what he thought was ash and burned wood. He rubbed his hands in the residue and moved to the light of the entrance. The gray ash and black stains of the charcoal were proof of her fireplace. He moved back to the spot bringing some of the stored wood with him. He stacked the wood carefully and fumbled for his fire tools before remembering he did not have them. Perhaps Allana left something to start a fire with?

Javik groped the floor around the area of the fire finding nothing. He sat back against the cave wall in disgust and hit his head on something. Reaching up carefully he found a large limb wedged into the rocks. As he explored the smooth wood, his hand touched a pouch hanging by a thong from one of the stubs. He pulled it down and took it to the light. It was filled with flints. Evidently, Allana saw no need to bring along extra flints when she abandoned the cave. To Javik, they were a welcome sight. His knife blade would serve as the steel he needed to make sparks for igniting the tinder. If only he had some tinder.

He found some dried moss Allana stored for some unknown use and soon had a red glow going in the small bundle. He had some light at last. He moved the small package of light to the wood and blew on it softly. The red glow turned into a yellow flame licking up at the small twigs. The twigs caught in a blue flicker, and soon a small fire lit the inside of the cave.

Because the wood was extremely dry, there was little smoke. Javik watched as the wisps from the fire migrated to the back of the cave and up the shaft of the toilet. If it had not betrayed Allana, it would surely not betray him.

Javik looked around him at the home Allana made for herself. On one wall, charcoal markings showed a calendar. On the other, was a drawing of a man's face. Javik drew closer only to see himself. He had looked into mirrors many times, and he recognized his hair, but it was the eyes that clinched the identification. Allana had used some type of paint to color them green just like his own. His mother told him green eyes were rare among the Berglauni, and he should be proud of them.

Evidently, Allana had been tracking him for some time before he found her. *She loves me,* he thought. *She's loved me for a long time, and I never knew.*

A warm sensation flowed over his insides as he pictured he and Allana together as man and wife. This was the woman for him. He vowed then and there that he would have no other.

In the new light, Javik searched the cave more thoroughly. Not much was left of any value, only some skins and a few bones that might prove useful. He managed to find a pile of stones for her sling and a large rock she must have used for blocking the entrance to the cave.

It suddenly dawned on Javik that it was getting dark. The light from his fire would be visible through the entrance. He pushed the rock into the opening, and filled the chinks with skins and some of the dried moss.

Javik fluffed up the pile of skins to make a bed and relaxed. If Allana had managed more than two years, he could do seven days here easily. He fell asleep and dreamed of the wild girl who drew his portrait.

Chapter 28

The fire was nearly out when Javik awoke. He added the last of the wood and blew it back to life. The air in the cave was remarkably fresh since the draft from the latrine crevasse was constantly sucking fresh air in from the cave opening. He could see no light around the stone and calculated it must still be dark. He would need more firewood, and this would be an excellent time to collect it. At the same time, he could search for food. He moved out of the cave pulling the stone up into the entrance as far as he could. Some firelight still showed around the stone, so he used his tunic to fill in the gaps.

The air was cold and stung his bare chest as he moved along the ledge to the pool. He drank deeply once again before climbing down to the forest floor.

Suitable wood was not hard to find in this part of the forest. No one lived nearby, so the fallen branches lay where they fell. He remembered seeing his mother use a skin to carry firewood, and one of the skins from Allana's cave served him well. In no time, he had all he could carry.

Food was another thing entirely. He found some mushrooms, a few plants that were good raw, and some nuts. All of this went into his pants since the skin was full of wood. He wondered how Allana managed so well by herself. The climb up the rock face was a bit more difficult carrying the wood and shifting the food in his pants legs, but he managed.

Safely inside the cave once more, Javik congratulated himself on his strategy. He only had to wait until the final day to leave his hiding place, which meant he only had to evade the searchers between here and the village. It would be easy. He fell asleep confident that his plan was sound.

* * * * *

For three more days, Javik remained in the cave going out for firewood at night. Water was easy, but the meager rations of food were beginning to affect him. He'd learned to control his hunger as Tao Shan's student, but his strength was beginning to wane. What little fat previously clung to his body was nearly gone now. Trapping a small animal or gathering more suitable plants would mean a risky trip during daylight, but he felt more food would be necessary if he were to evade the warriors on the last day. He decided on a dawn sortie.

The next morning Javik was out of the cave before the sun rose. He made it to the forest floor just as the first light crept over the crests of the hills around him. There was enough light now to spot the plants he needed, and he wasted no time gathering the new rations into one of Allana's old skins. He was about to return to the cave when he heard the snort of a horse. Javik hid himself as well as he could and watched.

"He's been here, all right," one voice called softly. "The firewood that was here two days ago is gone."

"Yes, Jundar, and some plants have been pulled up here. He's around here somewhere. Probably in a cave in that cliff."

Javik could see them now, and his heart began to pound so loudly in his chest he was sure the men could hear it. It was Jundar and Hulda, two warriors from his village. They quartered the ground carefully looking for more signs. Javik began to worry about his tracks. He had been lax in covering them up. The cave gave him a false sense of security.

"Do you see any tracks?" Jundar called.

"They're all over the place here. This must be where he comes down the rock face. The cave is probably just up there a bit," Hulda replied.

"He'll be holed up during the day," Jundar said. "He must have pulled up those plants just before sunrise. He's probably back in the cave enjoying breakfast right now."

"Do you suppose he can see us?" Hulda asked.

"It could be. I think we'd better act like we haven't found anything and ride off. Mikka is to meet us at the large sycamore tree. We'll form a plan with him to catch our little cave bat before Mauhad is over."

The two men rode off quietly, and Javik breathed a sigh of relief. His plan was now foiled, and he cursed himself for being so careless. Such experienced warriors would find the cave in short order now that they knew where to look. He climbed back to the cave and prepared his meal. It had little in the way of taste, but he knew it would give him the nourishment he needed and fill his stomach for the run ahead of him.

As he ate, he contemplated his next move. Now that his pursuers knew approximately where he was, they would find him easily before the Mauhad was over. He would have to leave the cave, but where would he go?

Javik smiled as a dangerous thought crossed his mind. He could go closer to Sentii country. He could follow the path leading through the mountain pass and on to the high desert of the Sentii. Their capitol city was not far away, but even the Sentii avoided the dry, desolate wasteland. Water would be his only problem. Tao Shan taught him the mountains squeezed all of the water out of the clouds on the Berglauni side leaving none for the Sentii plains. The location of Sentii water holes was a closely guarded secret, and even if he found one, it could be dry. If he drank deeply at the water pool, he might be able to stay in the desert for the remaining time. He decided to leave the cave immediately.

Traveling in the daylight seemed strange. He watched carefully to see that the warriors were nowhere around and tried to cover his tracks as best he could along the pathway. The climb was steep, and he used some of his spanga leaves to keep up his pace. Soon, the high desert of the Sentii spread out before him. He descended easily to the floor only to find a grisly totem marking the Sentii border. A badly decomposed head with two dead crows hanging below it sat atop a bloody pole. It was the Sentii warning sign, and Javik knew it meant death for any Berglauni found there. He felt his knees grow weak and a shiver ran down his back, but he calmed himself with the thought he would only be in the desert for one full day and two nights. The second morning he would head back to his village before dawn.

The desert's flatness gave him even more courage. Any Sentii patrol would be visible from a long distance giving him ample time to hide or return to his own territory. The thought suddenly hit Javik that he, too, would stand out like a beacon among the low scrub brush. He scanned the wasteland for possible hiding places and saw none. Then, he remembered something Tao Shan told them. To hide in the desert, one must burrow like the desert animals. The soil would be easy to dig, and a shallow grave would allow him to breathe through the sand if he kept some space above his face. It was perfect. He stepped past the grizzly totem and out onto the sandy plain.

Javik looked back at his trail and saw the tracks were easily followed. He pulled up a small bush by the shallow roots and smoothed the soil back over the depression. Using the bush as a broom, he swept his tracks away and walked backward toward a small clump of cactus that might be large enough to hide him if he lay flat on the ground. He decided to make his burrow there.

The sky was becoming more and more ominous as Javik moved toward the cactus. Tao Shan warned them that distances in the desert were deceiving, and he was beginning to understand just what he meant. The meager cover seemed to be as far away as when he started, and he had been walking for over an hour. A sound like the rumble of a thousand loaded carts on a stone road made Javik turn away from his duties of covering his tracks and look toward the center of the desert. A wall of brown dust was coming toward him at furious speed.

Bandor had spoken of the dust storms on the Sentii desert, but Javik often dozed off in his class. He now knew he should have paid more attention. He did remember it was important to find some kind of shelter and cover his head. He ran for the clump of cactus, but the storm beat him to it. Soon, he was wandering blindly in the storm searching vainly for someplace to shelter.

The sand clawed at his skin like a hundred cats and forced him to pull his tunic over his face to save his eyes and allow him to breathe without ingesting a pound of sand with each breath. He kept moving even though Tao Shan advised holing up in these storms. He had to find some kind of shelter.

Just when he was about to collapse of exhaustion, he felt the wind die a bit and pulled the tunic away from his face far enough to uncover his eyes. A gray mass of rock loomed in front of him blocking the wind. Javik thanked Zhou for his good fortune and dove under a small overhang.

The howl of the wind was deafening, but the rocks blunted

the force of the sand. It no longer stung his face, but it still filled the air around Javik forcing him to use his undergarment as a filter to keep from choking on the red powder. Was this how he was to die? His throat and lungs were burning from the sand he had already sucked in, and there was no water within a half-day's walk. Tears began to moisten his eyes, only adding mud to the other irritants trying to blind him. He said a silent goodbye to his mother and Allana. He would die here on the bleak Sentii plains, and he would never be found. Fatigue finally overcame him, and he fell into a fitful sleep.

* * * * *

Javik awoke to blackness so deep he thought he must be dead. Perhaps this was the underworld where he was to roam until eternity? Maybe his father would find him here and show him the ways of the spirits? He suddenly realized the darkness was due to the fact he was looking at the inside of his tunic.

It was difficult to move his arms. They seemed to be pinned to his sides by some outside force. With all of his remaining strength, he was able to push one arm free of the imprisoning sand and into the chill of the desert night. He used that hand to scrape away enough sand to pull the tunic away from his face.

The myriad of stars in the black, clear sky was a welcome sight as Javik rose from his temporary grave to survey the situation. He was not dead after all, but the ache in his throat told him he would need water very soon. Javik stamped his feet and rubbed his arms to restore the warmth stolen by the chill morning air. Soon, the sun would soon bring warmth, but water was his most immediate need. His clothes were covered with a layer of red grime, and his throat burned from swallowing the abrasive stuff. He must go back to the mountains to find water, but which way to go? He would have to wait for more light to determine the proper direction of travel.

"Will you never rise today, cursed scourge of this Zhou forsaken desert?" he muttered, but his anger did not hasten the sun's appearance, though he did feel warmer for the effort.

Javik berated himself for continuing to travel in last night's dust storm, but he justified his actions by telling himself he would not have survived without the shelter of the rock outcropping now beside him. It was certainly an excellent way to lose the warriors chasing him should they manage to track him to the desert. *Unfortunately, I have lost myself as well,* Javik thought.

It suddenly dawned on the boy that being lost was the least of his problems. He was, most likely, deep into Sentii territory, and if he were captured by one of their patrols, his head would soon be on the post marking the edge of Sentii lands. Until the sun rose, he could not tell how far he was from his own country or which way to travel. The morning chill bit deeply into his body while the dread of Sentii torture froze his soul. Had he survived the storm only to be a victim of his nation's deadly enemy? He listened for hoof beats in the silence of the pre-dawn, but not even the birds were stirring.

"Where is the sun?" he pleaded; then, as if in answer to his prayers, the first edge of the dull orange disk appeared between two peaks in the distance.

"Oh no," Javik moaned. "The mountains are so far away. I wandered much too deep into Sentii lands during the storm." Javik knew he could not make the journey back to Berglauni lands without water. He would surely die on the way back. He had to find water first. Javik climbed on the stones that sheltered him the night before and surveyed the area in the dull morning light.

Wispy curls of steam rising from behind some low hills to his left betrayed the presence of water in some form. Perhaps this was one of the hidden wells of the Sentii? It meant going deeper into Sentii country, but it was water.

Javik ran toward the mist and found a hot spring bubbling up from the ground and pouring over into a larger pool below the source. He moved his hand closer to the pool to test the heat, and almost cheered when he found it was not too hot to drink. Javik fell down next to the larger pool and drank deeply, clearing the dust from his throat before washing the caked grime from his face. The water had a harsh, mineral taste, but it was wet.

He looked at the pool longingly. There was no sign of Sentii patrols. Why shouldn't he take a few moments to cleanse himself before returning to safer land? He shed his clothes and lay down in the shallow pool letting the warm water wash the dust from the rest of his body and soak the pain from his joints. He was almost asleep when a dark form eclipsed the rising sun. A rough hand grabbed him by the hair and pulled him from the hot pool to a chorus of laughter from three men gathered nearby.

"Our sacred pool is contaminated by Berglauni fish!" the man roared.

They were Sentii. Javik knew them by their lisping accent when they spoke Berglauni and by the style of their high, leather boots. The tattoos on their bare arms were Sentii totems, but they were more than warriors. Black veils hung from the sides of their helmets and covered their faces. Only the cold, blue eyes typical of the Sentii showed above the heavy cloth. These were Sentii holy men, and they would kill him any minute now in the most horrible way imaginable. His mind raced to find some way out of this deadly situation.

"What brings you here, Berglauni?" A tall man, more slightly built than the others stepped from behind the warrior priests. He was not veiled, and the long, elegant sword slung across his back marked him as a leader. Only council members had such expensive weapons.

"He carries nothing but a bag of leaves, a hunting knife and this trinket that all of them carry." The short, ugly one had found Javik's clothes

"Tell me lad, why are you here?" the leader demanded.

Javik's mind raced. Should he tell them of the Mauhad? No, then they would know other warriors were looking for him. Suddenly, and idea occurred to him. He might be able to use Allana as a means of avoiding death.

"I am looking for a man called Grucheau." Javik saw the leader's face brighten and heard the other men mutter something in Sentii.

"You have found him, boy. I am Grucheau. Why are you looking for me?"

Javik had not expected this. He suddenly found himself face to face with his father's killer. It was hard to believe this man could defeat Tolda. He stood about a hand taller than Javik, but that would make him almost a hand shorter than Tolda. Certainly Tolda would have had a good ten kilos or more on this man, but looking at the flint hard, blue eyes it was not difficult to believe in his skill with a sword or any other battle weapon. His face was pinched, and his cheeks were sunken. A dark beard rimmed his jaw line, and lips almost as full as a woman's stood out in contrast to the rest of his face.

Javik felt his heart grow cold as he studied this man. Here was the chance to avenge his father, and he was in no position to do anything about it. He vowed Grucheau would not claim both father and son. He pressed forward with his plan.

Perhaps the opportunity for revenge would come later.

"You had a slave girl named Allana, and she ran away."

Grucheau grasped Javik by the throat and pulled him closer.

"How do you know this, Berglauni dog?"

"I know where she is. My master has her, and he sent me to find you. He wishes to buy her from you."

Javik felt himself growing weaker as Grucheau's grip cut off his breath. At last, he released Javik who fell to the ground gasping for air.

"She is not for sale, but I would have her back. Who is your master?"

Javik smiled inwardly. Ling told the truth, Grucheau still wanted Allana to bear his children. He knew he could not tell Grucheau who had Allana. Once he possessed that knowledge, he would have no need of Javik.

"My master has forbidden me to tell you his name, but I will take you to him."

Grucheau laughed heartily and his men joined in.

"Do you hear that, Karmou? He is forbidden to tell us his master's name."

"I think a few minutes in my tender care will convince him otherwise," Karmou said.

Javik knew he must not beg for his life. If death were his fate, he would face it bravely as his father had.

"My heart is prepared for death," Javik answered.

The Sentii around him applauded his courage openly, but even as they did so, he saw Karmou remove the cover from his long spear. The polished blade reflected the sun into his eyes and blinded him for a moment.

"Not here, Karmou," the leader commanded. "This is holy ground. We will take him into the desert. Give him his clothes."

"What about this, Grucheau?" The short, squat one handed a

small, bright object to the leader. "It may be valuable."

"They all have one. They call it a salla, and it has something to do with their false gods. It has no value, but you may keep it if you like."

The warrior priest dropped the salla into his pouch and prodded Javik toward his clothes with the point of a sword.

"Wait! My master bids you know that if I do not return safely, he will kill the girl."

Javik congratulated himself on being so clever. He had been searching his mind for some way to avoid his fate, and an old story his father once told came to mind. He used the same plot here.

"Wait a moment," Grucheau commanded.

The war leader stood with his arms folded, looking intently at Javik. It was as though he was trying to penetrate Javik's skull with his stare to see if he was telling the truth. Javik met his gaze squarely. Grucheau turned away first.

"Maybe you are telling the truth. I would not want to risk Allana's life for the simple pleasure of seeing your guts exposed. Do you know what happened to her child?"

Javik didn't know about any child. Perhaps this was a scheme to test his veracity.

"No, but my master would know if she had a child at one time. She had none with her when she came to us." It was the truth as far as he knew, and he hoped it would satisfy Grucheau.

The war leader studied Javik while he stroked his coarse, black beard. "She may have lost it in the wild or killed it after it was born," he said to no one in particular.

"Lord Grucheau, how do we know this Berglauni will not lead us into a trap?" it was Karmou again.

"We don't." He turned to Javik. "How were we supposed

to ride into Berglauni territory without being attacked?"

Javik's mind raced to find an answer. The storm provided an easy response.

"I had a white banner to signify your peaceful intentions, but it blew away in the sand storm along with my pack and water skin. If you have something white with you, you could use it instead of my flag."

"Who has anything white?" Grucheau asked.

"I have a bolt of white cotton cloth, but my wife needs it all," one of the others volunteered.

"I will buy it from you, Nulak. You can get her some silk instead." Grucheau reached into his purse and produced several gold coins.

"Lord Grucheau, this is too much," Nulak protested.

"A small sum if this boy can lead us to Allana. Make a flag."

Nulak cut a square piece from his bolt and fastened it to a spear. He handed it to Grucheau.

"Now we have our safe conduct flag. Tie the boy up, he will ride behind me."

Once dressed, Javik's hands were tied behind him. One of the Sentii brought up their horses, and the short one lifted him up behind Grucheau's saddle.

Javik's mind raced as the party headed toward Berglauni territory. They were unwittingly carrying him closer to the warriors sent to find him. They would not be looking for his pursuers, but they would still be wary upon entering enemy territory. He must find some way to signal. Javik suddenly hit on a possible solution to his dilemma.

"Please, sir, may I have my salla? It is a holy object to us, and when I swing it in the air it says a prayer to Zhou. I need to do much praying for my sinful life." Javik hoped they would believe the lie.

A roar of laughter erupted from the other men.

"By Grona, you must be a wicked boy indeed to have accumulated such sins this early in life," Grucheau said. There was just the hint of distrust in his voice.

"I have been very lax in obeying my mother and I have treated my brothers badly. I've caused them much pain that must be atoned for with many prayers. If you give it to me, I'll say a prayer for you also."

"Give it back to him, Karmou," Grucheau commanded.

Karmou grudgingly retrieved the salla from his pouch and untied Javik's hands.

"Here, boy. Say your prayers. You will need all of them if you've lied to us."

Javik swung the salla in a circle producing a soft buzzing sound. Grucheau's eyes softened a bit.

"Keep it, boy, and may your gods grant you many pleasures in the next life." Karmou tied Javik's free hand to the leader's saddle, and the band continued through the desert toward the mountains.

Javik's heart beat faster as the group moved closer to Berglauni country. Hopefully, the warriors sent to find him would be nearby. He swung the salla with even more energy as they approached the border. Javik prayed his pursuers were close enough to hear it. The Sentii patrol would be visible from a long distance as they crossed the flat, open expanse. If his people saw he was a captive, they could arrange an ambush.

It seemed to take hours to cross the desert, and Javik's arm was growing tired from swinging the salla. He scanned the mountains ahead, but there was no sign of his people. They must be too far away to hear the salla. He thought of his mother and Allana. Beautiful Allana, he would never have the pleasure of holding her in his arms. In spite of his efforts to keep them back, a tear rolled down one cheek. It mingled with the sweat from his forehead, and he hoped that none of the Sentii noticed it.

Karmou rode up to Grucheau.

"Grucheau, we must be wary of an ambush. The Berglauni will see us coming and set a trap."

"If the boy is not lying, we carry the signal they agreed to, but there is no point in tempting fate. Halt here."

The party came to a stop, and Grucheau unbound Javik's hand.

"Get down, boy. You will carry the flag ahead of us, but you must be on a proper leash."

Grucheau took the rope from his saddle horn and placed the loop around Javik's neck. He tightened it just enough to allow Javik to breathe.

"Now, walk in front of us. If there is any treachery, you will be the first to die." He handed Javik the spear with the white cloth flag.

Javik felt a bit more comfortable with a weapon in his hand, but he knew that a sharp yank on the rope would cut off his air completely. If it came down to it, he would bury the spear in Grucheau before he was killed. At least his father would be avenged, and Allana would be free of him even if he would never see her again.

The group passed into Berglauni territory, but Javik saw no sign of the pursuing warriors. His only hope was to continue on toward the village in hope of meeting some of his own people. The Sentii party grew increasingly watchful as they penetrated further into enemy territory. He could not use his salla now since it took both hands to carry the spear.

The low pass through the mountains was just ahead. The Sentii would be expecting an ambush there, and they would be doubly cautious until they emerged into the forest on the other side.

"I haven't seen any Berglauni yet, Grucheau," Karmou spoke softly, almost a whisper.

"If the boy tells the truth, we have nothing to fear, but keep your eyes open and your head constantly moving," Grucheau said.

The Sentii were moving in a column now along the narrow trail leading to the pass. The brush on both sides of the trail was low and dry. Javik saw no way an ambush could be laid here, but as he thought that, he heard a cry in the Sentii language that was cut off in mid voice by a terrible, gurgling scream. Grucheau turned to see what happened, and Mikka suddenly sprang from the ground beside Javik.

Mikka's sword cut the rope around Javik's neck before he sidestepped Grucheau's charge.

"Get into the brush, Javik!" Mikka called as Grucheau charged toward him, sword in hand. He shoved the boy out of the way just before he parried Grucheau's slashing blow. The horse and rider sped past them several meters before Grucheau could turn.

Javik stepped back into the pathway, but Mikka shouted at him again.

"Get out of this, Javik."

But Javik was having none of that. He pulled the rope over his head and braced the spear against the ground as Grucheau wheeled his horse for a second charge.

The sound of arrows flying and the screams of the other Sentii told Javik an archer was at work, but he dared not turn to see who it was. Mikka rushed past him to confront another Sentii riding to aid Grucheau, leaving Javik alone.

"Run, Javik! Hide!" Mikka commanded, but Javik stood

firm. This was his chance to kill the man who robbed him of his father, and he would have revenge or die trying. He may never see this chance again.

Grucheau bore down upon Javik with his sword held high. Javik knew the tactic. Grucheau would let the horse do the killing, if he could, only coming back to finish Javik off later. He was more concerned with the battle going on behind Javik.

Javik lowered the point of the spear so that it was directly in the horse's face. Even an experienced warhorse would not charge directly at such a target. Grucheau turned his horse to his left after the first charge. Javik surmised the horse was left footed and would shie to the left at the spear point. He was prepared to go either way, but his first instinct would be to move the spear to his left to catch Grucheau. If the horse didn't turn too far off course, Grucheau would parry the spear with his sword and riposte toward Javik. With no shield, Javik would have to move quickly to avoid a fatal cut.

The horse must have been in many battles, for it only moved a bit off course to avoid the spear point. Before Javik could adjust his aim, the horse's head was past the sharp metal. Javik was about to re-position the point for Grucheau when a sudden breeze caught the cloth and flung it into the horse's face. The charger reared up quickly, and the surprise move unseated Grucheau. His sword flew from his hand and landed in a nearby bush.

Javik saw his good luck and pressed the point of the spear into Grucheau's chest. As he rammed it home, he said, "This is for my father."

Grucheau's eyes still showed life as he struggled to remove the spear, but Javik used all of his strength to hold the warrior pinned to the ground. Grucheau finally fell back, and his hands dropped from the spear shaft. He stared at Javik.

"Who is your father, boy?" Grucheau gasped.

"I am Javik, son of Tolda, the Hammer of Zhou."

A smile spread across Grucheau's face as the light behind his eyes went out.

The noise of battle behind Javik stopped. He turned to see Mikka and two other warriors checking the Sentii saddlebags. Grucheau stirred, and Javik pushed even harder on the spear, but it was only the last death throes. He felt a rough hand on his shoulder.

"It's all right, Javik. You're safe now," Jundar soothed.

"You heard my salla, then," Javik asked as he relaxed his grip on the spear.

"We heard you an hour ago, and spotted the Sentii patrol heading this way. Fortunately, Mikka and Bundic were nearby, and we were able to arrange an ambush of our own. But I have one question, Javik. What made you bring a salla on the Mauhad?"

Javik smiled, "Tao-Shan advised me to take it. He said that sometimes on a Mauhad it is better to be found than not to be found. The master knew what he was talking about, didn't he?"

"You were wise to heed his counsel," Mikka said as he and Bundic joined Jundar.

"I have all of you to thank for my life," Javik sank to the ground and leaned against a rock. The relief at being in friendly hands once more finally released his emotions, allowing fatigue and hunger to overcome his brave front. "I need to rest a moment before we go back, please, and I would be grateful if you have something to eat."

Jundar smiled at the boy so obviously drained by the experience. He had evaded capture for six of the seven days, and would have made it back safely if not for the Sentii. Jundar doubted that he would be in any shape to travel after such an adventure. "You may rest for the space of one hand's sun travel, Javik. Bundic! Give him some of your rations."

The men cleaned their weapons and searched the Sentii for booty. Mikka returned with two purses and Grucheau's sword.

"These were well-heeled Sentii," Mikka said with a satisfied grin. "Oh, and these are yours, Javik." He handed Grucheau's sword and purse to the boy.

"More than that, Mikka," Jundar said as he lifted off Grucheau's helmet. "This one is the war leader Grucheau."

"Grucheau!" Mikka gasped. "You have killed Grucheau?"

"It was revenge for my father. Tao Shan's servant, Ling, saw my father's shield hanging on his trophy wall. Tolda is now avenged."

"The Sentii must know you killed him, Javik," Mikka said. "If it is a blood feud, they will not send any raiding parties after him."

"How will we do that?" Javik asked.

"I'll show you," Jundar said.

Jundar removed Grucheau's chain mail, then the heavy sheepskin undercoat to expose his chest. Using his knife, he carved Javik's name and Tolda's into Grucheau's breast using the Sentii alphabet. Mikka helped him drag the body to the edge of the desert where they tied it to the same post holding the Sentii warning totem.

"There, they will be checking this totem before he rots away, and they will know how he died. Off to home now, my boys – we must deliver Javik to a fate only a bit less dreaded that what the Sentii planned for him."

The men roared with laughter as they mounted their own horses. Javik was given Grucheau's horse to ride while each of the men led off another Sentii horse laden with its owner's weapons, gold and armor.

Chapter 29

The ride back to the village took most of the day. Jundar dumped him into a stockade holding seven other boys including Berda.

"I see they found you, too," Berda greeted his friend.

"Believe me, considering my plight at the time, Jundar was the most welcome sight of my life. That is, with the possible exception of Margan. They both saved me from a horrible death."

"What are you talking about, Javik?" Berda looked astonished. If Margan saved Javik from execution, what could have happened on Mauhad to equal that?

Javik related his adventure with the Sentii, how Jundar and the other men rescued him, and how he avenged his father's death.

"Javik, you are truly blessed by Zhou. What more can happen to you in your lifetime?" Berda said.

"At least this is the last day of Mauhad," Javik rationalized. "When did they catch you?"

"Two days ago. I made the mistake of building a fire. I think I would have frozen to death if I hadn't. It was almost worth getting caught to warm up. How did you stay out so long?"

"I found Allana's cave. She used it to hide from the Sentii, and it almost did the trick for me, too, but I was careless. I used too much firewood and didn't cover my tracks well enough," Javik admitted.

"That Mikka must be part dog," Berda sighed. "He said he tracked me every day even though I walked through a stream for a whole morning."

"They are good. Tao Shan tried to tell us how good, but I don't think I really believed him until now."

The boys' conversation was interrupted by a loud bellow.

"What in Zhou's name are you doing here?" Browdat's ruddy face glowered at Javik through the small window in the stockade door.

"I'm sorry, Lord Browdat," Javik lowered his head knowing his adopted father was enraged that his son was captured before Mauhad ended.

"Sorry! Now I'll have to go before the council and plead for you. I thought Tao Shan was a better mentor than that."

"It was not his fault, sir. I wandered into Sentii country and a group of their holy men found me. I had to signal Jundar with my salla so he and his men could rescue me, and..."

Browdat interrupted him. "Mikka told me all about it, and that puts a little better face on it. Rest well until tomorrow. I'll see you then."

Before Javik could add the part about avenging Tolda, the little window slammed shut, but the door opened to reveal several warriors carrying buckets and brushes.

"All you failures stand up," Mikka commanded as the others sat down their buckets. "Time to clean the stables."

A series of groans welcomed the news of the new task.

"Clean the stables?" Javik asked.

"They've been giving us such lovely tasks ever since I got here. Just be thankful you only have one night of this. Bort, there, was caught on the second day."

"And I now have women's hands from all the scrubbing," Bort replied showing Javik his rough, red hands.

The warriors marched them down the streets of the village to the jeers of the women and the ridicule of the men. Javik had never felt so humiliated in his life. Even Allana laughed at him as they passed Browdat's longhouse. His mother only smiled warmly, which made his heart jump a little.

As they cleaned the stalls, more and more boys joined them. The last bunch to arrive included Karl.

"That only leaves five out there," Javik counted up the tally.

"If they're as hungry as I am, they'll surrender by morning," Karl said. "When's dinner?"

"The slop won't arrive until we finish this," Berda said. "And it won't be your mother's cooking, I can tell you."

"Quiet, failures," one of the men supervising the cleanup commanded. "Save your breath for your chores."

Berda was right. The food was hardly recognizable and tasted like sweepings from the stable floors. The new boys dug into it with gusto just the same.

Before morning, three other boys joined the group. With each new arrival, the entire population of the stockade was roused and forced to sing a bawdy song about their lack of manhood.

My father never sired me,
And my mother was a sow.
My balls were never finished,
I can't be a warrior now.

When the time comes for the battle,
I will guard the baggage trains,
I will find my only glory,
In the digging of latrines.

Javik fell asleep as soon as his body relaxed on the straw covering of their makeshift cell's floor. He dreamed of Grazhda. The old woman was shrouded in a dark mist as she moved toward him. She seemed to be floating on the air, and cackled brightly as she stopped in front of him.

"Well, young warrior, you have your revenge, and so early in your career," she wheezed.

"I am not yet a warrior, Grazhda, and I'm afraid I've failed Mauhad," he protested.

"Nonsense. You will take your place among the great men of your land very soon. Now you know what it is to have Grazhda's gratitude."

"What do you mean?" Javik asked.

"Hah! Do you think the breeze that blew that cloth into the horse's face was a lucky wind?"

"You mean, you…" Javik was thunderstruck.

The old crone cackled even louder and began to recede away into the darkness.

"Farewell, Javik. I will be with you again one day. Farewellllllll." Her voice echoed into the distance, and Javik awoke with a start.

The boys were all asleep and snoring like a dozen hibernating bears. Javik shook the cold fear from his body. It was only a dream.

At the first light of dawn, Javik and the other boys were roused from what little sleep they were allowed and formed up in the square outside. They watched as one of the remaining boys ran from the forest and into the village gate. He was jubilant, and the captured boys cheered him wildly until two warriors leaped upon him, one on either side. The boy was led to the group and told to stand with them.

"But I made it," he protested.

"No, you were captured just before you reached the square, and the rules clearly state that you must reach the square," Mikka smiled. "Too bad."

The assembled crowd broke into laughter. Javik always wondered what was so funny about this part of Mauhad. The younger boys were confined to one of the longhouses near the far wall of the village during this portion of the ceremony, but he heard the laughter even there. He understood now why that precaution was necessary.

The one remaining boy saw the fate of his friend and decided to climb over the stockade wall to avoid capture. He had no better luck. Two men nabbed him as soon as his feet hit the walkway. He too, joined the group of failures.

The boys were marched back to the small prison stockade and told to wait for their turn to appear before the council. They were called in the order of their capture.

Javik found it hard to make conversation while he waited. Berda went before he did depriving the group of its most talkative element. He had to wring information from Karl.

"Where were you caught?" Javik asked.

"Not far from the village. I'd made my way back to a hiding place I'd scouted out months ago. I figured I'd make a dash for it this morning, but they found me last night."

"How did they manage to find you?" Javik asked.

"I think my stomach was growling so loudly they could hear it inside the council house. I don't really know, but they were waiting for me when I got close to my spot. They seemed to know where I'd be."

"I suppose they know all the good hiding spots near the village," Javik tried to comfort his friend.

"Javik, you're next!" a stern voice commanded.

Javik rose and walked to the waiting warrior. As the door

slammed closed behind him, the warrior placed a rope around his neck, bound his hands and placed a blindfold over his eyes.

"Follow where the rope leads," the warrior said as he jerked on the rope. Javik had little choice but to do just that.

The sound of chanting grew louder, and Javik knew they were close to the council house. He'd heard this before. Even though the younger boys were kept inside on this day, he heard the song faintly from his father's hearth. He thought of those past years.

He had seen the captured boys brought in and watched them perform the more degrading jobs of the village, but he was not allowed to know what happened on the last day or what went on inside the council house. He did know that almost all of the boys passed - captured or not. Each year only a few were held back to try again, and he only knew of one boy who never passed. The poor fellow left the village in disgrace, and no one had seen him since.

Javik felt confident he would pass, but what tortures awaited him inside that house? There must be something captured boys were subjected to in order to make them worthy of manhood even though they failed Mauhad, and it was surely a terrible price to pay. The morning air was cold, but he felt sweat run down his back.

The procession stopped as Javik responded to a heavy hand against his chest. The next sound was the guard banging on a door.

"Open to admit a candidate for manhood," the guard called.

The chanting stopped and the voice of Tahsla answered, "Send the candidate to his fate."

Javik was even surer some horrible trial awaited him when he heard the dread in that voice. The door opened, and he was led into the warmth of the building past the smell of hot men, stopping at what he presumed was the center of the floor.

"Lords and warriors, we have before us Javik of the house of Browdat, failed candidate for Mauhad," Tahsla announced.

"He shames the village," a chorus of men responded.

"He only managed six days of the seven," Tahsla added.

"He shames the King," the chorus answered.

"He was captured by our enemies and had to be rescued," Tahsla spoke again.

"He shames the Berglauni," the men chanted.

"Is there any here who would plead for him?" Tahsla asked.

"I, his father, ask the mercy of Zhou for my adopted son." It was the voice of Browdat.

"I ask mercy in the name of Tolda, the hammer of Zhou, now dead." It was Goldar.

"I ask the council to consider his excellent performance as a student." That was Tao Shan.

Javik felt better. With such illustrious men pleading for him, mercy was assured.

"The Council hears the pleas of these worthy warriors, but the grievous failure of this candidate must be acknowledged. Javik, son of Tolda and son of Browdat, what say you? Are you worthy to become a warrior of the Berglauni?" Tahsla asked.

Javik thought long and hard. The silence of the room seemed to close in on him like a collapsed cave. He could have avoided capture. He had violated one of Tao Shan's basic principles when he continued on through the storm. He knew he was not worthy. He knew Tao Shan was correct in keeping him back another year to learn more.

"I am not worthy, sir," Javik mumbled. A faint snicker ran through the room in response to his answer, quickly followed by shushing sounds. Something was up, but what?

"Men of the Berglauni host, do we accept this answer?"

Tahsla asked in a voice a bit cheerier than before.

"NO!" resounded loudly through the room.

Javik thought his knees might buckle at any moment. The blindfold and noose were removed and a broadly smiling Browdat was his first sight.

"My son," he beamed as he enveloped Javik in a bear hug.

Other hands loosed Javik's bonds, and a tankard of qush was pressed into his hand. Everywhere men offered their hands in congratulation. It suddenly dawned on him that he had passed. Tears of joy streamed down his face as he released the pent up emotions of the last several days. There must be some appropriate words to say, but he couldn't think of anything he considered worthy of the occasion. He turned to Browdat.

"My father, I hope I can be worthy of your love and Goldar's also." He turned to Tao Shan. "Master, you have taught me well, but I'm afraid I did not learn as well as you taught."

"Nonsense, Javik! You have earned your manhood in noble fashion."

"The new warrior must prove himself worthy in one final task," Tahsla smiled. "You must down that tankard in one draught."

The assembled men began to shout, "Toila, toila, toila," an ancient Berglauni word for good health and the standard toast of his people. They continued until Javik took the tankard from his lips and turned it upside down to show nothing remained inside.

A cheer greeted his success, and Browdat led him to a chair near his.

"The Council will come to order for the next candidate," Tahsla commanded. "But first, I must have a tankard myself."

A ripple of laughter greeted this announcement as a servant brought a fresh tankard to the elder.

"I thought I failed," Javik said, still amazed at the turn of events.

"That is what you are supposed to think," Browdat winked at him. "You must never reveal the secret of this ceremony to anyone. If you are asked how you passed, you may truthfully say that the pleas for mercy were effective and that you had to survive a most horrible test to meet the requirements."

"But I only had to drink a tankard of qush," Javik responded in bewilderment, somewhat amazed that the war leader would ask him to lie.

"But you had to drink it quickly and in one draught. Everyone knows that this is a horrible way to drink qush," Browdat smiled as he slapped Javik heavily on the back.

"Father, there is something important I must tell you."

"Not now, Javik. We must finish the ceremony before we can talk."

Tahsla finished his qush and called for quiet. "Begin the chant again," he commanded.

Javik picked up the words quickly and joined in the tune as the guard again pounded his fist on the heavy wooden door.

The rest of the candidates were as flummoxed as Javik had been and equally as amazed that they passed. After the final candidate, Tahsla announced, "Let the merriment begin!"

The door opened again, and a stream of women carrying platters of food paraded in. The large wooden tables groaned under the weight. Thirty-six hungry boys dove into the feast with abandon as the men held back a bit.

Javik was aching to tell Browdat how he avenged Tolda, but before he could speak, Browdat enfolded him in a bear hug.

"My son, you've made me proud. It's not every man whose son manages to kill a Sentii war leader and avenge his father's death before he officially becomes a man."

"Then you know."

"Of course I know. Mikka couldn't wait to tell us all about it. I'm surprised that any man here could keep from cheering you during the ceremony."

Tao Shan joined them smiling broadly.

"You are my finest student, Javik. Congratulations on becoming a man and avenging your father."

"Thank you, Sir. I could not have done any of it without your teaching.

Dana approached the men and dropped to one knee in front of Javik.

"I honor the warrior who avenged my husband," she said.

"Mother, you must not bow to me. I'm your son." He took his mother's hands and pulled her to her feet.

"Not any more, Javik. You are a man now, and a warrior, but may I have one last embrace?"

Dana held out her arms and Javik raced into them as tears streamed down both of their faces.

"Someone else is looking for you, Javik," Dana whispered in her son's ear.

"I must tell Allana the good news. Has anyone told her about Grucheau?" Javik pushed back from his mother a bit and looked around the room.

"She does not know yet. The women have been too busy to speak with the men until now. Go, tell her, Javik."

"Pardon me, lords. I have something very important to do." Javik ran off to find Allana while the men and his mother laughed heartily.

Javik found Allana serving food and took the tray from her hands.

"I must speak with you, Allana. I have important news."

"Javik! I'm busy serving now. Can't it wait until later?"

"No, we must speak now." Javik took her hand and led her out of the common house.

"What is so important that you must drag me away from my duties? I know you are a man now, but I am still a slave."

"You are no longer a slave, Allana." Javik watched her eyes as they searched his face trying to discern the source of this remark. They told of hope mingled with disbelief.

"Don't joke with me, Javik."

"It's no joke. I've killed Grucheau in combat, and you are now mine."

"I don't believe you. You're just saying this so that you may have your way with me."

"Wait here, I'll prove it to you." Javik was about to find Mikka when the warrior came out of the common house.

"There you are, Javik. Now that you're finished with the ceremony, you can keep these." He handed Grucheau's sword and purse to Javik. "The rest of his armor is at Browdat's house."

"Thank you, Mikka. I was just coming to find you."

"I'm glad I saved you the trouble. I see you are occupied with more important things." He winked knowingly at Javik.

Allana took the sword from Javik's hands and studied it carefully.

"This is his sword, but how did you get it?"

Javik told her the whole story while Allana sat in a state of shock.

"That means I am your property now." Allana voiced the words as if from a trance.

"No, Allana. It means you're free now."

"I cannot be free until I pay for my freedom. You cannot just say 'you are free Allana' and have it be so. You may be a man now to the Berglauni, but you are still a boy in many ways, Javik."

"Maybe I need to sign some paper, or something, but I swear you are free."

"Allana! Come back in. We need you to serve now," Frieda called from the common house door.

"You are foolish, Javik. I must return to my duties now, *master*, if that is what you truly are." Allana rose and returned to the common house leaving Javik to sputter helplessly.

Javik sat for a moment thinking about the problem. Tao Shan told him Allana could be won in combat, but she didn't seem to think that was the end of it. He must find Tao Shan. Javik returned to the party and found his mentor.

"Master, I must speak with you," Javik asked.

"I am no longer your master, Javik. You may address me as you would any other warrior."

"Yes, sir. I have a question for you please."

"Why so formal. This is a time to be merry in spite of the dark war clouds hanging over our land."

"It's about Allana, sir."

Tao Shan smiled at the boy knowingly. "What else would be on your mind now that you are officially a man? But, what is there to discuss? She's now your property."

"I know, I just told her she was free, but she said I couldn't do that, and she would not be free until she bought her freedom."

"You are her master, you set that price. Make it whatever you wish."

"But I would give her freedom."

"You may do that, but it appears Allana would not feel truly free unless she bought her freedom."

"How much should I set for the price?"

"A slave of her quality would bring over a hundred gold pieces at the great block in the capitol. She knows she's worth that much, at least."

"It would take her years to earn that much money teaching at your school. What can I do? I love her, and I want her to be a free woman so we can marry."

"Do you now understand why the female piece in my game has so much power?"

The rules of the master's game came back to him. He and the other boys thought it foolish that a piece representing a woman should have so much power, but he realized that all of the things he wanted most in life were wrapped up in Allana.

"Yes, Mas   Tao Shan. I see why it is so. The inventor of your game was truly a wise man, but I cannot wait for Allana to buy her freedom."

The old mentor was not surprised by Javik's haste to free Allana. He'd noticed the smitten look on the boy's face after his first encounter with the wild girl. Now that Allana was transformed into a beautiful woman, he could understand Javik's desire for her.

"I'm sorry, Javik, but perhaps you can convince Allana she can purchase her freedom for some small sum. It's the only way to accomplish what you desire, I'm afraid."

Javik could not enjoy the evening. Allana seemed to be avoiding him, and every man in the village was eyeing her with undisguised lust. He left the common house and found a quiet place to nurse his broken ego.

* * * * *

As the festivities died, and the men left the party or dozed slumped over the tables, the chores of the women slackened. Frieda sat at a table and rested her weary feet. Allana finished dumping the used mugs and bowls into the large tub of steaming water and approached her.

"Lady, may I be excused to find Javik?" Allana asked.

Frieda waved one hand at her and said, "Go to him, child. I'm sure he's slumbering somewhere out there."

Allana checked the sleeping bodies, but Javik was not among them. She found Karl leaning against a wall and roused him to some semblance of consciousness.

"Karl, have you seen Javik?"

Karl tried to sit up, but fell back to his original position. "I shink he's ou'side shome'ers," he managed with his qush thickened tongue.

"Go back to sleep. I'll find him myself." She shook her head in disgust over the way men let themselves be made fools with qush.

She stepped out into the moonlight and saw Javik sulking under an oak tree. She walked toward him, but he didn't seem to notice her.

"Javik, I've been thinking about what you said."

He looked up at her with dull eyes.

"Javik! You're drunk?"

"Not drunk enough. What do you want?"

"I've thought it over, and you may set any price for my freedom you wish." She sat down beside him.

Her words seemed to revive the boy. He was suddenly back in the land of the living. "That's wonderful. Do you have any coins?" He pointed to the small purse hanging from her waist.

"I have some coppers Tao Shan gave me." She opened the purse and produced a small copper coin. Javik took it and held it up between them.

"With this coin you purchase your freedom from slavery forever." He threw it away before enfolding Allana in his arms and kissing her passionately.

He broke off the kiss and held her close to his body without speaking. He had no words to spoil this moment.

Allana spoke, "You do love me, don't you, Javik?"

Javik looked at the girl he fell in love with the first time he saw her. Even with her wild, tangled hair and buckskin clothes, she'd captured his heart. He wanted her no matter what the circumstances—slave or free. If she was now ready to accept her freedom, that was all that mattered.

"I love you with all my heart, and I know you love me. I found your cave, you know," he said.

Allana started and recoiled a bit.

"Then you found my drawing also."

"Yes, it's a good likeness. When I saw it, I thought you must love me."

"I drew your picture because I thought you were handsome, Javik. I didn't know you then, but since I've been with you, I've come to love you more than my own life. You have to know that's true."

"I do." Javik folded her in his arms and kissed her tenderly.

Their lips parted, and Allana whispered, "When can we marry, darling?"

Javik's expression suddenly turned serious. "There's one big factor to consider before we marry. Browdat says we will have war soon."

"I've heard the talk. Will you have to go?"

"I'm a warrior now. If war comes, I must go."

She held him tightly again. "Let's hope it's not soon."

"Perhaps we should wait to see if war comes? I wouldn't want you to marry me and then have you become a widow at such a young age."

"Don't talk like that. You've been trained well, and you defeated a mighty Sentii war leader. I know you'll come home safely from any war, but I'll worry about you all the time you're gone."

"I am confident in my ability as a warrior, but anything can happen in war. Would you mind terribly if we waited a while before marrying?"

Allana thought for a moment before answering. "I think that might be wise. I'll need some time to get used to my new status as a free woman."

They sat huddled together without speaking for a long time before Frieda emerged from the common house and called to Allana. "Allana, we need your help in here."

"Come inside and tell your mother and Frieda the good news." Allana said as she rose to go.

"Give me a while to gather my thoughts, and I'll be in to announce our engagement. Now get back to your chores." He slapped her on the behind and fell back against the tree. Life was good again.

The End

Title: *Josh Martin – Space Commander*
- Author: M. L. Hollinger
- Publisher: TotalRecall Publications, Inc.
- : Paperback, ISBN: 978-1-59095-282-5
- : eBook, ISBN: 978-1-59095-283-2
- : Audiobook, ISBN: 978-1-59095-284-9

A bored teen-aged boy escorting his little brother at Disney World finds love and adventure on Space Mountain.

While waiting in line at Space Mountain, Buzz Lightyear presents Josh with a pin and suggests he'll enjoy the ride a lot more now. Josh and George board the sled, but Josh doesn't notice the cast member pushing a button on the sled. As they start the ride, Josh is suddenly propelled into another dimension where he's the Commander of a space ship. The ship is a battle cruiser, and receives an order to rescue a princess who has been kidnapped by pirates. With the help of the ships Executive officer and his staff Josh develop the perfect plan to accomplish the rescue. What could go wrong?

Title: *The Adventures of Regen the Bremen*
- Author: M. L. Hollinger
- Publisher: TotalRecall Publications, Inc.
- Hardcover, ISBN: 978-1-59095-110-1
- Paper Back, ISBN: 978-1-59095-111-8
- eBook, ISBN: 978-1-59095-112-5
- Audiobook, ISBN: 978-1-59095-253-5

Regen is a Bremen. By nature he loves only his pet skeen, sensual women, money, and adventure in that order.

Regen is an earthy, pragmatic, drug smuggler who cares little for anything but money, beautiful women, and his own highly unusual pet. The animal is a skeen, and they are usually shot on sight for the pests they are. Most people marvel that Regen managed to tame such a nasty creature. On top of everything else, he named the skeen HITLER after a 20th Century Earth dictator with a personality as evil as any skeen's. Regen is a Bremen. Bremen are known for their tough exterior, sexual prowess, and their tendency to leap before they look. I hope you enjoy following this arrogant, self-confident, egotistical and narcissistic bastard through a series of adventures in disparate sectors of the galaxy.

Title: *Josh and the Cargan*
- Author: M. L. Hollinger
- Publisher: TotalRecall Publications, Inc.
- : Hardcover, ISBN: 978-1-59095-124-8
- : Paperback, ISBN: 978-1-59095-125-5
- : eBook, ISBN: 978-1-59095-126-2
- : Audiobook, ISBN: 978-1-59095-254-2

Science tells us the speed of light is absolute, but is it? If physical objects can't go faster than 186,000 miles per second, maybe something else can.

Josh Smith is your average teenage boy. His hormones are raging and he can't wait to have sex with a girl. He also wants to be a rock star, and has an amateur band of his own. One evening after band practice he learns his rich, eccentric great grandfather, Charles Evans Bastin, is dead.

When the will is read, Josh inherits one of Charley's ugly sculptures while his father inherits the rest of the fortune. Back home, Josh accidentally discovers his sculpture is a CARGAN, a device used for interplanetary travel as a ghostly presence called an ENTITY. He travels to the planet destination of his cargan and finds it's a very exotic place indeed.

Title: *Love and War*
- Author: M. L. Hollinger
- Publisher: TotalRecall Publications, Inc.
- : Hardcover, ISBN: 978-1-59095-285-6
- : Paperback, ISBN: 978-1-59095-286-3
- : eBook, ISBN: 978-1-59095-287-0
- : Audiobook, ISBN: 978-1-59095-288-7

Allana goes in pursuit of a crown, and Javik is trapped into an unwanted marriage before the fates conspire to free him from all obligations except finding the woman he loves.

Javik goes off the war. He gains glory and gold in the war but returns home to find Allana gone. He's dismayed when Dana tells him she doesn't want him to follow her. He's also promised Tao Shan another year of training. He begins the training, and Tao Shan gives him a bonus by letting him in on the secret of a magic powder (gunpowder) and the weapon called a hand cannon.

The second book in the Javik series.

Title: *Queen of Gorgos*
- Author: M. L. Hollinger
- Publisher: TotalRecall Publications, Inc.
- : Hardcover, ISBN: 978-1-59095-289-4
- : Paperback, ISBN: 978-1-59095-290-0
- : eBook, ISBN: 978-1-59095-291-7
- : Audiobook, ISBN: 978-1-59095-292-4

Allana is held by the Turrek bandit King, Vargon.

Javik leaves to find her and learns of her predicament. With the help of her man Barinosh, Javik and his friends manage to free Allana and they set off to regain her throne. After many adventures Allana is crowned queen, marries Javik and they reign together.

Allana has begun her quest to regain the throne of Gorgos by establishing a high class brothel in another land with the help of a former madam who has been disfigured by a rejected lover. Allana gains a great deal of wealth and some allies, but she must cross the territory of a ferocious bandit king, Vargon, to reach Gorgos. She bribes Vargon with her body in order to secure his promise of safe passage, but he captures her in spite of his promise and forces her to marry him.

The third book in the Javik series.

Author M. L. Hollinger

received an Aeronautical Engineering degree from Purdue University in 1957 and went into the Air Force right after college. He worked on several space program projects including; Titan III Space Booster, Space Shuttle, Star Wars and several other special studies for the Air Force. He attended the Air Command and Staff College and the Air War College. He served in Viet Nam from 1971-1972. His decorations include The Bronze Star Medal, Meritorious Service Medal, Air Force Commendation Medal, The Vietnamese Honor Medal First Class, The Vietnamese Gallantry Cross and five unit excellence awards. He retired from the Air Force in 1980 with the rank of Lieutenant Colonel and came back to Indiana where he joined the Indiana Corporation for Science and Technology. He is now fully retired.